**KIRK MOVED FORWARD ON HIS BELLY FOR A METER, CAME UP, FIRED A COUPLE OF SHOTS TOWARD WHERE THE INCOMING ROUNDS HAD ORIGINATED, THEN DROPPED AND ADVANCED AGAIN.**

He had almost reached the front line when a group of five Victors broke from the trees and came straight toward him. Two of them fired indiscriminately, trying only to keep Freeholders from sighting in on them. The other three appeared to have a single-minded focus on Kirk. They weren't carrying guns. Two had big nets and the third a coil of rope and a short, stout club.

They were slavers, and they were intent on capture, not murder.

Kirk levered a round into the chamber and squeezed the trigger. The weapon clicked. He squeezed again, more urgently. *Click.*

# STAR TREK®

THE ORIGINAL SERIES

# SERPENTS IN THE GARDEN

Jeff Mariotte

Based upon *Star Trek*
created by Gene Roddenberry

POCKET BOOKS
New York • London • Toronto • Sydney • New Delhi

Pocket Books
A Division of Simon & Schuster, Inc.
1230 Avenue of the Americas
New York, NY 10020



This book is published by Pocket Books, a division of Simon & Schuster, Inc., under exclusive license from CBS Studios Inc.



First Pocket Books paperback edition May 2014

POCKET and colophon are registered trademarks of Simon & Schuster, Inc.

For information about special discounts for bulk purchases, please contact Simon & Schuster Special Sales at 1-866-506-1949 or business@simonandschuster.com.

The Simon & Schuster Speakers Bureau can bring authors to your live event. For more information or to book an event, contact the Simon & Schuster Speakers Bureau at 1-866-248-3049 or visit our website at www.simonspeakers.com.

Cover art and design by Alan Dingman

Manufactured in the United States of America

10 9 8 7 6 5 4 3 2 1

ISBN 978-1-4767-4965-5
ISBN 978-1-4767-4967-9 (ebook)

*For Marcy Rockwell,*
*with love and thanks*

# Historian's Note

The events in this narrative take place in 2273, only months prior to Earth being threatened by the massive machine life-form known as V'Ger (*Star Trek: The Motion Picture*).

# SERPENTS IN THE GARDEN

# One

"We've got a Klingon situation," Rear Admiral James T. Kirk said.

"A Klingon situation?" Lieutenant Rowland echoed. "Where, sir?"

"I'm glad you asked." Kirk tapped a display on his desk, and a viewscreen on the wall illuminated. He walked over to it. Rowland, no doubt, saw only dots and swirling lines, but the admiral knew what he was looking at. He had been studying it for a week. And Kirk saw trouble.

"These lines," he said, pointing, "indicate the movement of Klingon vessels through this region. All within the past few months."

"That's a lot of lines," Rowland said. Lieutenant Giancarlo Rowland was bright, but young and more than a little green. He was Kirk's flag aide, and since the admiral was desk-bound, that meant Rowland's duties were largely administrative and occasionally ceremonial. Kirk expected that Rowland would distinguish himself in starship duty one of these days, and become a captain before too long. He was young and bright and green, but he was also ambitious, and getting himself linked to an admiral was a wise move, politically speaking.

"Exactly. Which means a lot of Klingon traffic."

"Do we know why, sir?" Rowland asked. A soft southern accent revealed his east Texas roots. "I mean, why they're there?"

"Not yet," Kirk said. "Frankly, there's not much there. It's a sparsely populated little corner of the galaxy. There is one inhabited planet in the vicinity—but again, sparsely populated. I've actually been there. It's a Class-M planet, very Earthlike in many respects, but the entire global population can't be more than a few hundred thousand, if that."

"Capable of warp travel?"

"No."

"Well, maybe I'm just bein' dense, sir, but I don't see what they could possibly have that Klingons would want."

The admiral peered at the chart. He had been asking himself the same question for days. He'd been studying every reported Klingon sighting, mapping them, and trying to figure out what their big-picture plan might be. It was easy to simply assume that the Klingons were up to no good, for no other reason than that they were Klingons.

That was dangerous thinking, though. Klingons didn't think like humans did. They planned, schemed, and they had reasons for the things they did. If the

Klingons were suddenly active in this one particular sector, there was some motivation behind it.

"I don't know, either," he said at last. "But we need to find out."

"We?"

Kirk pointed toward Rowland, then back at himself. "We. You and me."

"How, sir?"

"I guess we need to go on a little trip."

"A *little trip*?" Rowland asked.

Kirk returned to his desk and backed out of the chart until it showed a vast swath of the galaxy, with Earth in the lower left corner. The sector under discussion was visible in the upper right.

"That's . . ."

"It's not next door," Kirk said.

"Boy, I'll say."

"Is that a problem, Lieutenant?"

"No, sir!" Rowland said quickly. He stood there, staring at the chart.

"Is there something wrong?" Kirk asked after a minute.

"No, sir. It's just . . . well, I've never been that far out there."

"Most people haven't, Giancarlo. It's a rare privilege. I think you'll like it."

"I'm sure you're right."

"I usually am," Kirk said with a grin.

"One more question, sir?"

"Yes?"

"The planet?"

"You wouldn't have heard of it," Kirk said. "It's called Neural."

"Neural?"

"That's right."

Realization dawned in the lieutenant's eyes. "You've been there twice," he said. "You commanded your first planetary survey there."

"That's right," Kirk said again.

"You were a lieutenant. And, what? My age."

"About that," Kirk said. *Two years younger.* "You've been studying my career."

"I know everything there is to know, sir. About your career, that is."

"Everything?"

"I mean, everything in Starfleet's records. I'm sure there's plenty more that's not in those."

"All the best parts," Kirk said. "Just the boring stuff goes in the official record." He tapped his temple. "The good stuff's in here."

"I have no doubt, sir."

"We'll need a ship," Kirk said.

"A ship, sir?"

"To get to Neural. They can't walk here, but we can't walk there, either."

"But we can't—we need to take this to the Federation Council, have them raise a protest with the Organians. If the Klingon Empire is in violation of the Treaty—"

Kirk cut him off with a wave of his hand. "No Federation, no Starfleet. Nothing on the record. Civilian transportation. A charter, since there aren't any commercial flights passing anywhere near there."

"Why not, sir?"

"It's a long story," Kirk said. "I'll tell you sometime. Let's just say I have some unfinished business on Neural. If that is in any way responsible for what's happening there now, with the Klingons, then I need to set things straight if I can. Not Starfleet. Me." He wondered briefly if this was a fool's errand. Second chances were possible, Kirk believed that with all his heart, but they were as rare as snowmen in July. The admiral shook his head to clear it. "When I left Neural, I informed Starfleet of the Klingon presence there. The Federation Council raised the issue with the Klingons, and the two sides agreed that Neural fell under the hands-off policy dictated by the Treaty of Organia. If they've broken that agreement, I want to know about it."

"So a civilian charter . . ."

"Right. Something small and fast, preferably. Something that can get in and out of orbit before the Klingons know it's there."

"Yes, sir."

"Pack an extra toothbrush," Kirk suggested. "I don't know if they've invented those yet, and we'll be staying awhile."

"How long, sir?"

"I have no idea." Kirk sat behind his desk. It was a

beautiful thing, carved mahogany with brass fittings, in a vaguely nautical design. It was big and it weighed a ton, and it felt like an anchor chained to his leg. He loved Earth, but like so many things, that love was felt more fervently from a distance. A desk in Starfleet's headquarters had never been one of his career goals. His title, chief of Starfleet Operations, sounded impressive. But to Kirk the title was little more than a cruel joke, since by definition, the chief of Starfleet Operations never operated among the stars.

Kirk hadn't realized, until he'd decided he had to go back to Neural, how much he missed it. And now that he did realize it, it was all he could think about.

Over the next few days, James Kirk had much to do. Chief of Starfleet Operations was a mouthful of a title, but it wasn't a meaningless one. Starfleet had hundreds of ships and thousands of people assigned to missions all over the galaxy. *And one day, hopefully,* Kirk thought, *outside it.* Plenty of people served under him, and although Kirk delegated as much as he could, he was still a busy executive. Before he could leave, the admiral had to make sure the people who reported to him would be able to pick up the slack. Kirk tried to look ahead, to project every major decision he might have to make, and he left instructions as to how he would act. It wouldn't do to compound his mistakes on Neural by letting something important slip by here.

Rowland was also busy. Leading a Starfleet starship on a multi-year interstellar mission involved a lot of preparation, but when one stepped on board that last time, one knew the ship was fully outfitted, provisioned, and prepared for any eventuality. But a long voyage on a civilian craft was a different matter. While one could hope that the ship was ready for anything, the reality might not match those hopes. Controls and regulations for civilian space travel were strict, but people had been skirting transportation laws since the first hot-rodder had figured out how to remove his car's muffler, if not before.

Kirk's last official act was to notify key people about where he was going. Although the trip had to be made without official authorization—the phrase "plausible deniability" had entered bureaucratic lexicon during the mid–twentieth century and had not left it since—a rear admiral couldn't simply abandon his duties and disappear.

Admiral Elaine Kucera was looking down at a data slate on her desk when Kirk entered, but she was expecting him, so he stood in the doorway until she crooked a finger. "Jim," she said, pointing toward a guest chair.

He sat. Waited. Finally, Kucera raised her chin and fixed him with gray eyes that he had always found fascinating and just the slightest bit disconcerting. "I've considered your request, Jim."

"And?"

"I don't like it. Not one little bit. It's risky. It's impulsive. It sounds like something you thought through in about fifteen seconds, while doing two other things."

Kirk didn't like the sound of that. She wouldn't dismiss his proposal without giving him a chance to argue his position, would she? "I can assure you, Admiral—"

Kucera held her hand up. "I said it sounds like that. I understand that it's not. Jim, we've known each other a long time."

"Almost—"

She stopped him, again. "I know how long."

Suddenly, Kirk was a plebe again, with Cadet Elaine Kucera inspecting his rack.

"My point is, as outrageous as this seems, on the face of it, I'm inclined to go along with it."

He felt himself relaxing. "Thank you."

"Wouldn't you like to know why?"

What he wanted was to pocket the win and leave. "Why?"

She breathed out a long sigh. "Do you remember what Gary called you? Back at the Academy?"

"Gary Mitchell? He called me a great many things. Most of them aren't repeatable in polite company."

"He once said you were a 'stack of books with legs.'" A smile broke, unbidden, on Kucera's face. "Still cracks me up to think about it. It was so *right*, so accurate. I knew you'd have a great Starfleet career, even then. But I thought it would be in a lab someplace, or one of our think tanks. You didn't strike me as the impulsive type. You were going to be the thinker, the guy who stayed behind and charted courses, or developed policy positions for others to carry out. That's what I thought."

"Are you disappointed?" Kirk asked with a smile.

"Not one little bit. I've never been so happy to be wrong."

"Then—"

"My point is that you confounded my expectations. You know your stuff. But you're not an egghead. You became a captain and then you accomplished real things. Great things. Important ones. Not as theory, but as fact. I don't know if you understand just how rare you are, Rear Admiral James Tiberius Kirk. Starfleet's packed with smart people, and talented and accomplished officers. But we don't have many who combine those traits in exactly the way you do."

Kirk wasn't sure how to respond. He was afraid she was working toward denying his request, after all. He had never wanted to be indispensable, because once you were tagged with that, you lost any freedom of movement you might once have had. "Admiral—"

Those gray eyes bored into him. "It's just us here, Jim. I'm still Elaine."

"All right, Elaine. Are we—"

"I'm saying you can go, Jim. I'm saying I'd hate to

lose you and I think your plan's a hare-brained one, but that doesn't matter. Because it's you, and if anybody can pull it off, you can. Also, because I know if I didn't let you do it, you'd make me miserable. So yes, fine. You can go, and I'll keep your secret."

"Thank you, Elaine," Kirk said.

She placed her palms flat against the desk. "Don't thank me," she said. "Tell me what your backup plan is. I know you have one . . ."

Four days later, during the hour before sunrise, Kirk met Rowland on the beach near Golden Gate Park. Dense fog made the ocean all but invisible, except where the gentle surf pushed water up across the sand. Even the sound seemed muffled, like the steady, calm, throbbing heartbeat of the planet. Kirk had always liked the park, especially this end of it, with its wild tangles of trees and underbrush. He was glad the city had maintained it; although it had suffered during the Eugenics Wars, since then it had been restored to its original glory, and it remained a landmark for tourists and locals alike.

On this early morning, the beach was empty. Kirk and Rowland waited quietly, dressed in civilian clothing thanks to the journey's unofficial nature. Each held a duffel containing changes of clothing and other personal items, as well as Starfleet-issued phasers and communicators. When Rowland suggested the park meeting point, Kirk had been surprised. "I thought we'd be picked up at a spaceport," he had said. "They have transporter technology?"

"The *Captain Cook* is a decommissioned Starfleet vessel," Rowland explained. "They have transporters. I thought that was a priority."

"It'll certainly make it easier to get to Neural," Kirk replied. "They'll only have to enter its orbit long enough to beam us down."

"Givin' the Klingons considerably less time to spot the ship," Rowland said. "That was my thinkin'."

"Good job, Mister Rowland." Kirk studied his aide as they waited. The kid was resourceful; anticipating his commanding officer's needs would serve him well in his Starfleet career.

Rowland was tall and lanky, with a long neck and huge hands. His hair was a dirty blond, with a hairline that was already receding. He had quick, green eyes that seemed to miss nothing, a jaw that could have been carved from granite, and a nose that was almost flat at the top but then angled out toward the end. He had a pretty girlfriend named Shonna, whom Kirk had met, a civilian who worked in the city. Rowland wanted to marry her but was torn about the timing. Should he do it before he was assigned a berth on a starship, an assignment that could take him away for five years? Or wait until after, when he might have worked his way up through the ranks and be assured of a planetside post? Kirk had told him, "You won't regret marrying her, even if you have to go away. But you might regret not doing it when you had the chance."

Since offering that small slice of wisdom, Kirk had informed Rowland that they were leaving on a secret mission of unknown duration. Rowland couldn't tell Shonna where he was going, or when he'd be back, and they hadn't had time to marry.

"What are we waiting for?" Kirk asked after a while.

"Them," Rowland said, tilting his head toward the park.

Kirk peered through the mist and saw two people walking their way, also in civilian clothes and carrying duffel bags of their own. "Who's that?"

"Security personnel. Apryl Burch and Titus Hay."

"Security? Why?"

"Sir, you're a Starfleet admiral. You can get away with almost anything you want. But that doesn't include goin' to a strange, potentially dangerous planet without a security detachment. Command was very clear about that."

"I told them no," Kirk said.

"They told *me* that under no circumstances could you make this trip without 'em. They wanted to send six, but I talked them down to two."

"And you didn't tell me?"

"Orders. You'd have raised a fuss and tried to get around it somehow. I happen to agree with Command."

"You—" Kirk let the sentence go unfinished. They hadn't even left the city and his young protégé had outmaneuvered him. "All right," he said. "You win this one, Mister Rowland." With a grin, he added, "Don't let it go to your head."

"Not a chance, sir."

The first wan light of sunrise paled the fog ever so slightly, and Kirk was able to make out the newcomers. Titus Hay was big and dark, a hulking man with massive shoulders and a shock of black curls on his head. Apryl Burch was smaller but sturdy, her red hair cropped short in a no-nonsense style. Hay walked with an easy, rolling gait, while Burch's movements were more controlled, her head pivoting from right to left, as if she were scanning the perimeter with every step. *Looking for threats already?* Couldn't be too careful, Kirk supposed, but this was safe ground.

Rowland made the introductions. Kirk had barely finished shaking hands all around when Rowland's communicator chirped. He answered twice in the affirmative, and the next thing Kirk knew, a familiar sensation gripped him, a sudden queasiness in the pit of his stomach, and they were all gone, leaving only the fog.

# Two

When they materialized on the transporter pads of the *Captain Cook*, Hay looked relaxed, Burch ready for action. Kirk surmised that was just their natures; Hay was big enough to take things easy, knowing he could handle whatever arose. Burch probably could, too, but only because she was always on the alert, ready to head off trouble when she saw it coming. Rowland looked even greener in comparison. The admiral took a deep breath of re-circulated air.

A man in an unmarked tan jumpsuit looked at them from a control bank, a wide grin on his handsome face. He looked vaguely familiar, but Kirk couldn't place him. "Admiral Kirk," he said, stepping forward and extending his hand. "It's truly an honor. I'm J. D. Grumm."

Kirk shook his hand. "Grumm?"

"That's right, Admiral. I was two years behind you in the Academy."

"You're not in Starfleet."

"No, sir. I had some, I guess you'd say, issues with authority. Now I'm my own boss, and I like it that way."

"So the *Captain Cook* is—"

"She's all mine, sir. She's not big but she's quick and agile. I think you'll like her."

"I'm sure I will. And since you're not Starfleet, you can knock off the 'sir.' Call me Jim."

"Yes, sir. I mean, thanks, Jim." He turned to Rowland. "You must be the lieutenant."

"Lieutenant Rowland, that's right. Giancarlo is fine."

"Giancarlo it is, then."

After Rowland introduced Burch and Hay, Grumm gave them a tour of the little starship. On the bridge were the helmsman, LaMotte, and Makin, the navigator. The rest of the crew was comprised of Sieler, the chief engineer, and his assistant, Genz. All were human, LaMotte and Sieler were men and the other two women. "Everybody knows how to do every job," Grumm explained. "We can stagger shifts and take turns spelling each other. It's a small crew, but a tight one."

"What sorts of runs do you usually make?" Kirk asked him at the tour's end, back on the bridge. "I assume this one is a little out of the ordinary."

"A little of this, a little of that," Grumm answered. Kirk assumed that was a synonym for smuggling, and he started to wonder if trusting Rowland had been a mistake. "Deliveries to and from places off the usual routes. Ferry service sometimes, like now. Small cargo loads. We're not too picky, Jim; we'll take just about any job that keeps us out in space."

"You don't like Earth?"

"Earth is fine. It's just a little . . . I don't know. Confining."

"It's a big planet."

"Not as big as the whole galaxy."

"Point taken." Kirk understood the impulse. At the beginning of his five-year mission he had expected to be sick of interplanetary travel by its finish, and he thought he'd be ready for a planetside post until retirement. But it hadn't happened that way. When the *Enterprise* had been taken away from him, Kirk felt like he'd been kicked in the kidneys. Flag rank brought with it various perks and privileges, but none of them compared to the freedom of roaming amid the stars, where every day brought new wonders. Although Grumm had offered to have Genz take him to his quarters, Kirk had elected to stay on the bridge. LaMotte engaged warp drive and Kirk watched the rush of stars outside blurring into streaks. He felt the vibration of the powerful engines and the strain of the ship's artificial gravity system striving to hold everyone in place against the force of acceleration, and he knew he was wearing a stupid grin, but he didn't care.

It had been much, much too long.

"You're entitled to know what you're getting into," Kirk told Hay and Burch. "Rowland has already heard my confession, so if there's someplace you'd rather be . . ."

"I'll stay, sir," Rowland responded. "If you don't mind."

"That's fine." Kirk had changed into his usual light-gray and white uniform; the trip was unofficial, but on board a starship he felt more comfortable in it than in his civilian clothes. He had noted, when the others filed into his quarters, that they had all made the same decision. The room was small, but it included a table around which the four of them had gathered. Kirk knew that this was as good as it got on the little ship. Hay slouched in his chair, his gigantic shoulders slumping away from his thick neck, while Burch perched on the edge of hers like a sparrow ready to take flight.

"This will be my third trip to Neural," he continued. "The first time I was a lieutenant, commanding a planetary survey mission. One of the survey crew took a tumble off the side of a cliff and landed right in front of a hunting party. The inhabitants of Neural were on a Bronze Age level, technologically, so naturally we were supposed to stay out of sight. But the people—they called themselves the Hill People—took him in and fixed him up. Because I was in charge of the survey, I showed myself so I could keep tabs on him. I stayed with a man named Tyree while my crewman healed. Tyree became my friend."

"Wasn't that a violation of the Prime Directive?" Burch asked.

"It was," Kirk replied. "But it was too late. I couldn't know how they would treat my crewman, and I wasn't about to let them carry him to their camp without me. I tried to keep our technology from them, and mostly succeeded.

"The next time, it was a different story. While an *Enterprise* landing party was studying the plant life for its medicinal properties, we detected Klingon activity. This was shortly after the Treaty of Organia, so we wanted to make sure they weren't in violation. But we discovered that a second group of people, the Villagers, had flintlock rifles. This was an impossible technological leap in such a short time."

"Klingons gave 'em to the locals?" Hay asked.

"That was our suspicion, yes. We later confirmed it. But before we did, Commander Spock, my first officer, was wounded. We transported him to the *Enterprise* for medical care, while Doctor Leonard McCoy, the ship's chief medical officer, and I stayed on the planet to secure the proof. I was injured by the poisonous bite of an indigenous animal called a *mugato,* and McCoy couldn't do anything for me. He turned to the Hill People for help. They—Tyree's wife, Nona, who was a medicine woman, a *Kahn-ut-tu* as they're called—cured me. But she had seen McCoy's phaser in action. Nona was more ambitious than loyal. She beaned me with a boulder, stole my phaser, and tried to give it to the Villagers. They killed her. We got the phaser back, but we were too late to save Nona. So people there have hints about technology, far beyond their natural development, and they know there are other races that can travel between planets. I can't be sure how many are aware of the Klingons, or how much those who do know understand. The Prime Directive has been trampled."

"Won't going back make the situation worse, sir?" Burch asked.

"It might," Kirk admitted. "We'll take reasonable precautions against further contamination. But there are more pressing concerns. The Klingon activity in the vicinity has increased to alarming levels. It's not just Neural—it's that if the Klingons are not checked, Neural could be a stepping-stone to control over the entire sector. I made the mistake of leaving the planet without finding out why the Klingons were there. I left it to the civilian authorities to investigate. Once the Federation Council reached an agreement with the Klingon Empire, I never checked up on Neural to make sure it had been honored."

He took a deep breath. This had always bothered him. "I gave Tyree and his people flintlocks, to put them on an even playing field with the Villagers. I believed there needed to be a balance of power. But I never made it back to find out if that stasis held or if one side advanced more. My error, and I regret it. I want to find out if it was an irredeemable error—if my lack of follow-up in some way caused this Klingon expansion. If so, I want to discover if there's a way to stop it, to reset the status quo."

"Makes sense to me," Hay said. He had such an easygoing, casual manner that Kirk couldn't imagine anything that wouldn't meet with his ready approval. Burch looked less convinced.

"Lieutenant Rowland told you that this was an off-the-books operation." Kirk got nods in return, and went on. "I assure you, it's not my intent to needlessly violate any Federation laws. It's to find out whether the Klingons are violating the treaty, and if so, to figure out a way to deal with it that won't touch off a war. Are you comfortable with that?"

Hay and Rowland nodded again. Burch sucked in her cheeks, pursed her lips, then said, "Aye, aye, sir. People have sometimes called me a stickler for the rules—actually, they call me a lot worse than that—so thank you for explaining."

"You're welcome, Mister Burch," Kirk said. "I'm glad to have you on board."

"You can count on me, sir."

Somehow, he was sure that was true.

The *Captain Cook* could accommodate up to fourteen people, according to the specs. Kirk thought it would be unpleasantly crowded with that many; with five crewmembers and four passengers, the little galley was strained to the breaking point, as were the heads and other public areas. The trip was largely uneventful, but even so Kirk felt like an uninvited in-law, sitting on the bridge watching Grumm give commands while the crew carried them out. Grumm was pleasant, even deferential, but the *Captain Cook* was his ship and Kirk was just a paying customer. The admiral didn't take issue with the orders he gave; it was watching someone else give them that was hard.

He spent the time reading, telling the others what he remembered about Neural, taking a refresher course in Neuralese and drilling his small team in the language, getting to know J. D. Grumm and his crew, and exercising. But those activities offered only temporary relief. By the time they finally reached planetary orbit, he was ready to burst.

They were already wearing an approximation of local clothing—vests, trousers, and boots fashioned from animal skins, the design based on Starfleet records Kirk had accessed before leaving Earth. He had brought along coordinates that would enable the ship to beam them down fairly close to the Hill People's camp. He didn't see any way to complete his mission without their assistance. They would take their communicators, phasers, and a universal translator, in case there were unexpected language issues, but the landing party would try to keep them hidden from the locals.

Once they had achieved orbit, everything happened fast. They reported to the transporter room, which was just a corner of engineering. Grumm met them there, wearing the same cocky grin he had when they'd arrived. "It's been a pleasure having you on board, Jim," he said. "Sorry we didn't get better acquainted in the Academy, but I'm glad we were able to make up for it."

"So am I," Kirk said. "Thanks for the hospitality."

"The longer we stay in orbit, the better chance we have of being spotted by Klingons," Grumm reminded them. "We'll put you down at the coordinates you provided."

"That'll work," Kirk said.

"As we discussed, we'll be back in two weeks, Neural time."

"Right."

"If you're ready for pickup then, just say so. If we don't hear from you, we'll come back in another week. We don't hear from you that time, we'll alert Starfleet that you're on the planet and in trouble."

This was the most uncertain part. He liked Grumm, but the man's priorities were his own. *What if he forgot about the deadlines? What if he never came back into communicator range?* If Kirk couldn't reach Grumm at the end of the third week and the captain didn't relay an emergency message, Admiral Kucera would have to wait another week or two to realize the landing party was in trouble.

Grumm must have read it in his face. "Don't worry, Jim," he said. "We'll be here. You have my word. I'm not going to let you rot down there."

"I appreciate it, J. D." He shook the captain's hand and stepped up onto the pad. The others found their places.

"Ready?"

"Ready," came four voices in unison.

Grumm stepped back to the control panel. "Energizing," he said. "Be safe . . ."

His words trailed off as the beams kicked in. Next stop . . .

# Three

*Neural.*

At first glance, it was just as he remembered it. The initial impression was of an Earthlike world, with familiar-looking vegetation, blue skies dotted with puffy white clouds, hills that might have been sandstone in the near distance, and mountains farther out. Yellow sunshine blanketed everything with a pleasant warmth. The air had a clean crispness to it that Kirk thought must have been what Earth's air was like before the Industrial Revolution. He filled his lungs with it. On the second inhalation, he coughed a little at some unexpected, bitter aftertaste.

"Nice place," Hay said.

"Are we in the right spot?" Rowland asked.

Kirk looked around, got his bearings. "I think the campground of the Hill People is right over that ridge," he said, indicating a rocky outcrop. "Fifteen minutes, maybe."

"Should we get started?" Burch asked.

"I don't see why not." The admiral led the way up the slope. As he did, he noticed that the sky in that direction didn't quite have the crystalline blue clarity he had expected. *Was he remembering wrong? Idealizing the place beyond what it had really been?* Maybe. He had visited many planets during his days as captain of the *Enterprise*. It shouldn't have been surprising for some of them to run together, blurring in his memory.

The landscape looked familiar, and after a minute Kirk found a foot trail he had used before, the one Hill People had been using as long as anyone could remember. It led to a gap in the ridge through which the landing party could pass, and the camp would be set among the trees just on the other side. Finding the path made him feel better; Kirk picked up the pace, suddenly eager to see Tyree.

When they reached the gap, he stopped cold.

"Sir?" Rowland asked. "Somethin' wrong?"

"The camp," Kirk said.

"What about it?"

Kirk waved a hand at the scene below them. What had been a couple of dozen primitive tents, clustered around some caves and a few fire pits, had turned into a walled encampment. It wasn't quite a city, but it had become a good-sized town. Most of the trees around it had been felled, their trunks used to build the fortified walls that snaked across the hillsides. The structures within those walls were more solid than they had been, built from stout branches and hard-packed earth. And there were at least a hundred of them, more than Kirk could count at a glance. Even from this distance, he could make out Hill People on the wall, their distinctive light hair and clothing identifying them even from this distance.

"It's a *town,*" he said. "It's easily five times the size it used to be. Those walls—they weren't there before. This was a forest, but now it's a denuded wasteland." His gaze drifted up, past the town toward the distant valley, where the Village lay. The air above the valley was thick with a sinister cloud of dark smoke blocking the horizon. It was most likely the source of the aftertaste, even at this distance. "There was a simple village in that valley, but now it looks like it's become an industrial city."

"How long since you were here?" Burch asked.

"Nowhere near long enough for all this to happen."

"Not at a natural pace," Rowland said. "But those flintlocks weren't natural either, right?"

"No," Kirk agreed. "They weren't." He looked at the black smoke again, a blot against the sky. "Klingons," he whispered, as if that single word explained it all.

He pointed toward a small stand of trees nearby, on this side of the ridge. "Let's bury our phasers and communicators there. It's far enough off the trail that nobody's likely to come across them, and those trees will help us remember the spot."

"Bury them?" Burch echoed. "Sir, that's not a good idea."

"Prime Directive, Mister Burch. However it might already have been violated, we don't want to make it worse. Nona getting her hands on my phaser got her killed. I don't want to walk into that town with technology that's centuries ahead of what they've got."

"What if we need—"

Kirk cut off her protest. "We won't need the communicators for a week, maybe three. We've all studied the language, so we shouldn't need the UT. And we won't need phasers to defend ourselves against the Hill People."

Burch looked at her phaser like it was part of her arm and parting with it would require major surgery. "As long as your friend is still alive."

"That's a chance we'll have to take." Kirk started toward the trees.

"Are any of these trees or plants dangerous?" Burch asked.

"Most are as harmless as those on Earth," Kirk said. "And many of them are beneficial—Doctor McCoy said there were plants here with enormous medicinal potential. The animals are mostly harmless, except the *mugatos*. And there's a sort of rabbit with three ears and double rows of needle-sharp teeth. You don't want one of those grabbing your ankle."

"But you want us to bury our phasers, sir?"

"The people of Neural have survived for hundreds of years, if not thousands. We can do it for a few weeks."

"I got no problem with it," Hay said. "Sounds like a challenge."

"I didn't think you would," Kirk told him. "It will be a challenge, but I'm certain we can meet it." He took a bag from his pocket and unfolded it. "This will keep the dirt out. Mister Hay, drop your things in here and start digging, please."

"You got it," Hay said. He tossed his phaser and communicator into the bag, as casually as if they were dirty laundry, and squatted down to dig with a fallen stick. "I mean, you got it, sir."

It didn't take long once Hay got to digging and Burch finally relinquished her gear. When it was done—twigs and leaves laid on top to make it blend in with the surroundings—they returned to the gap and started down toward the walled town.

The landing party was walking toward a tumble of boulders, around which were clustered some of the few remaining good-sized trees, when suddenly they could smell wood smoke from the town's fires and the pungent, slightly greasy order of roasting game. Without warning, a dozen men and women emerged from behind the boulders and pointed guns at them. Some of the weapons were flintlock rifles, probably the same ones the *Enterprise* had provided.

But some weren't.

The flintlocks resembled those from Earth's past to a remarkable degree. Kirk had noted that on his last visit, but he had explained it to himself with the supposition that it was a fairly primitive firearm, not hard to make, and its form was dictated by its function to the extent that any design that worked for humanoids—and the people of Neural were physically indistinguishable from humans—would be much the same anywhere.

The other guns, however, were definitely not from Earth's past. They had common features and looked to have evolved from the flintlocks, but skipping some steps along the way. They were all rifles, lever-action guns with wooden stocks. But those early rifles on Earth had ended in fairly straight butts, and these were curved to fit more snugly against the shoulder. The levers and barrels were made from some dark brown metal, not the brass and blued steel of Earth. Gun sights along the top of the weapons were large and primitive, designed to help the untrained marksman take aim. They were wicked-looking weapons, but there would be no confusing them with any found on Kirk's home planet.

Most of those carrying the guns were recognizable as Hill People, sharing that tribe's most prominent features: thick platinum hair, clear, tanned flesh, strong bodies. The men had decorative gems implanted in their foreheads, and the women had similar designs on their cheeks and around the eyes. But there were others in the group, men and women alike, with different aspects, darker hair, physiques that were shorter and broader through the chest and shoulders, heavier brows. All were clothed in a manner similar to what the Starfleet personnel wore, so their dress hadn't changed. Kirk didn't recognize any of them.

"These are not Victors," one of the gunmen said.

"Nor Freeholders," another replied. "Should we kill them?"

"We are . . . visitors here," Kirk said, holding out his empty palms to display his lack of weapons. "You are Hill People. We seek my friend, Tyree. My name is Kirk. You might have heard him speak of me."

At the mention of Tyree, the people exchanged puzzled glances. The weapons were not lowered, but the mood changed from one of confrontation to something else, slightly less tense.

"You know Tyree?" one of the women asked. She had rich, dark hair, and her powerful physicality reminded Kirk of Nona. Unlike Nona, who had favored a garish wardrobe, these women dressed like the men, in plain-colored garb that was more functional than revealing.

"Yes. We're old friends. I haven't seen him since . . . since Nona died."

"He knows of Nona," another one said.

"I do not trust him. Any of them," still another

offered. This from a man, one of the shorter, darker ones. His eyes were small, his expression suspicious.

Kirk focused on the woman. She was near the front of the pack, and he sensed leadership in her carriage and attitude. "I knew Nona and Tyree, and some others. Yutan and Endel, are they still among you?"

Those names brought more looks and murmurs from the group. "He knows names, that's all," the small man said. "Tyree's name is spoken in every corner of the world, so that means nothing. They are not from here."

"Which tribe are you from?" the woman asked. "Name it, so we may know where your sympathies lie."

"I told you, we're visitors. From far away. You wouldn't know the place. Just take us to Tyree. He can explain."

Another of the Hill People moved to the front of the group. He was the tallest one there, almost as big as Titus Hay. "I think we kill them," he said. "And take their corpses to Tyree."

"I remember the Hill People as peaceful," Kirk said. "Have you changed so much in such a short time?"

"Kill them," the shorter man said. He shouldered his rifle and aimed it at Kirk's chest.

"No!" the woman cried. She made a lowering gesture with her hand, and the gun barrels were shifted toward the ground. "No killing. We take them to Tyree, as he asks. They are not Victor slavers, and they are unarmed. They pose no threat to Freehold."

Kirk wanted to ask about "Victors" and "Freehold," but to display his ignorance might have counteracted the progress he'd made. "We are no threat," he said. "We are friends to all the Hill People."

The woman stood there, her gun pointed at the ground, sizing Kirk up. He didn't see trust in her eyes, or fear. But he didn't see welcome, either.

"Take us to Tyree, but keep your weapons ready," Kirk said. "If he does not welcome us with open arms, then you can kill us."

"Sir!" Burch said sharply.

He didn't respond, just held the woman's gaze.

She made up her mind. Her stance softened and she took her finger off the trigger, held her weapon loosely in her hands. "Very well. We will take you to Tyree." At grumbling from behind her, she snapped, "And if he does not know you, you will all die."

"Deal," Kirk said. *Possibly a bad one, but a deal just the same.* Tyree had been his friend, but the last time they'd been together, Tyree's wife had just died, and Kirk had been part of the events leading to her death, however inadvertent. It was possible that his opinion of Kirk had soured over time.

He turned to his companions. "We'll be fine," he said. "Just cooperate with them and we'll get this all straightened out."

Burch shot him an unhappy glare. Rowland didn't look any more enthusiastic than the security officer did. Hay's expression never seemed to change; he wore his relaxed half-smile, as permanent as a tattoo.

The Hill People led them down toward the walled town that had swelled to envelop the old campsite Kirk remembered. The cliffs housing the cave that had been such a central part of their camp were outside the walls, but otherwise, the walled compound contained all the land where the tents and lean-tos had been pitched, and considerably more besides. It had aspects in common with forts from frontier America, Kirk realized. The logs used to build the wall had been hewn into points at the top. Lookouts stood on platforms high up on the walls, watching over the landscape. Kirk saw a couple of them nod to the group as it approached. A double gate big enough to allow access by people or wagons, if they had them, was centered in the wall they approached, and at a signal from one of the lookouts, he heard the efforts of those on the inside to draw back the bar that held the gate fast.

As they waited for the gates to open, one of their captors called up to a lookout. "Alert Tyree," he said. "These strangers asked for him."

"They look strange indeed," the lookout replied. She held one of the lever-action rifles. Other lookouts had flintlocks, or bows and arrows. "I will tell him." She disappeared from the wall. Kirk heard a mumbled conversation from inside, and after a few moments, a new lookout appeared.

"The settlement is much bigger than last time I was here," Kirk said to the woman who seemed to be in charge. "And the wall is new. Is your conflict with—"

She poked him, hard, with the barrel of her rifle. "Silence! Save your talking for Tyree."

Kirk decided not to press her. This new version of the Hill People's home was considerably less friendly than the last. A nagging concern grew in the pit of his stomach. The enlarged, walled town, the distrustful attitudes, all hinted at a people at war. When he had left Neural, the Hill People and the Villagers had been on unfriendly terms, which had been a surprise, since on his first visit they'd lived in peace. Kirk had hoped that by arming the Hill People, he might have spurred a new peace initiative, even if it was born from the threat of mutually assured destruction.

Instead, it appeared that hostilities had worsened.

What role he had played remained to be determined. The fact that he might have played any weighed heavily on his conscience. As Kirk walked through the gate, arms raised in surrender, he looked for familiar faces and longed for a way to set things right, to atone for any harm he might have done these once-gentle people.

What greeted the landing party were hard-set jaws and cold eyes. People were missing limbs.

Some sat on chairs outside their homes, malnourished. There were others he didn't see but only sensed from the flutter of a curtain or the bolting of a door as he and his fellow captives were paraded down the street. He saw suspicion, fear, and hatred directed toward them. Any atonement would be too little; it would never bring back the dead or heal the brutalized. Actions had consequences. Although Kirk tried to spread the seeds of peace, he knew that some of his efforts had not succeeded, and in many cases he never knew the results.

This time, his failure appeared to have been spectacular.

# Four

"James!" Tyree cried as they entered a large building just off an open plaza at the town's center. The mud walls were at least two feet thick, with a few slits to let in light and air. Guards stood sentry outside the only visible door. "It is you!"

"It is," Kirk said. He glanced at the woman whose gun was pointed at his kidney. She gave the briefest of nods, and Kirk approached his friend. Tyree had aged more than Kirk in the intervening years—new, deep crevices ran from beside his nose to the corners of his mouth, and his eyes were tired and sad—but his smile seemed to erase the years. He sprang from a seat that, despite its plainness, had the aspect of a throne and rushed to meet Kirk in the center of the big room. He opened his arms wide and Kirk stepped into them, embracing his old friend. "It's good to see you, Tyree."

"And you as well." He stepped back, clapped Kirk twice on the upper arms. "Welcome to Freehold. What do you think?"

"It's . . . different. Freehold, you call it?"

"We are too big now to be a campsite without a name. We number too many."

"Some of them aren't Hill People," Kirk observed.

"True. We have joined with other tribes, other races."

"Why?"

"To defend ourselves."

"Against the Villagers?"

"Their village has also changed its name, James. They call it Victory, now. As if they had already won the war."

"There's still a war?"

"It never ends," Tyree replied. "The Victors do not simply attack, overwhelm our defenses, and crush us, although I believe they could. Instead they let us continue to breed, to grow, and they take us a few at a time to serve their needs. Freehold is the last bastion of the free people, and we will continue the fight until all are free once more."

"Freedom's a noble goal," Kirk said. "But the cost appears to be high, too. You're living behind walls. I remember the Hill People as a carefree people."

"Carefree?" Tyree echoed. "Perhaps once, but no longer." He flashed a quick grin, but it was an icy one. "We can talk of such matters later, though. Who are your friends?"

Kirk made introductions, and Tyree, in turn, introduced them to the various people gathered in the big room. "Go," Tyree said when that was done. "Tell the rest of Freehold. James Kirk and his friends are Freehold's friends. They are to be accorded every courtesy."

"Thank you for the hospitality, Tyree," Kirk said. "We appreciate it a great deal."

Tyree put a hand on Kirk's shoulder. "You are my brother, James." When he lowered his hand, through, sadness had come back to his eyes. "Seeing you reminds me of Nona."

"I know," Kirk said. "I am sorry."

"You have nothing to regret," Tyree said. "I understand what happened—that it was her actions, not yours, that led to her death. Still, you were there. You kissed her—"

"I'm sorry for that, too. More than I can say."

"It was not you, it was her power. The *mahko* root and the abilities of a *Kahn-ut-tu*. You could not resist. I know you tried. This does not mean that my heart does not ache when I see you and think of her."

"We can leave," Kirk said. "We need to stay here, on Neural, for a few weeks, to . . . investigate some issues. But we don't have to stay in Freehold."

"Nonsense!" Tyree tried on a smile again. It looked genuine for an instant, but keeping it there was an effort of will. "We are brothers. You will stay in Freehold, as our guests."

"Then we accept your hospitality, happily," Kirk said. "I hope we'll have a chance to get reacquainted, Tyree. I've missed you."

"And I you, James. And I you."

* * *

"Captain, I need to make those improvements we talked about, to the Bussard collectors. I cannae make any progress on beefin' up . . ."

Captain Will Decker interrupted his chief engineer. Montgomery Scott was pacing before his desk, and Decker patiently said, "We've talked about this, Commander. Until the Corps of Engineers tests and signs off on your concept—"

"Captain Decker, if ye don't mind, you asked me—you ordered me—to get the *Enterprise* refitted and ready for space. I'm telling you, we need this to get her ready for space!"

Decker leaned back in his chair. "Sorry, Scotty. I like your idea, as I told you the four previous times you've mentioned it. I really do. But Command has its own procedures. They like to do things according to their rules. You and I know that has ever been the case with bureaucracies, and likely always will be. I'll keep pushing, though, all right? See if I can't shake something loose."

"I can do that testin' myself," Scott *humph*ed. "In half the time. SCE's got good people, but they're busy."

"Trust me," Decker said. "I understand your frustration. I'll talk to Command, all right?"

"Aye, Captain," Scott said, biting back the frustration so it didn't sound in his voice. He understood that innovations had to be tested, and he even understood why testing in a controlled environment was preferable to in-service testing. At the same time, he knew that his idea would work. It was less a whole new concept than a series of structural improvements to existing technology. Each would build upon the last, and although the difference in performance would be marked, he wasn't creating any safety issues.

More than that, he'd been tasked with getting the *Enterprise* spaceworthy on a specific timetable, and waiting for SCE to sign off on his improvements was throwing a wrench into the works. He was being told to do it now, while at the same time being deprived of the capability to make a change he considered necessary.

Decker was looking at him, as if waiting for something. Scott liked the man, but he would never feel toward him the way he did toward James T. Kirk. Will Decker came from a distinguished lineage—he was the son of Commodore Matthew Decker of the *Constellation,* who had sacrificed his life to save countless others from a doomsday device, and Matthew Decker came from a long line of Starfleet officers. Will had served honorably, and Kirk had personally selected him to take over the *Enterprise* upon Kirk's promotion.

"I appreciate anything you can do, Captain," Scott said finally.

"I'll let you know, Mister Scott. I'll do what I can."

Scotty *did* appreciate that. But Captain Decker wasn't the obstacle, and there was only so much he could do to overcome the real hurdles ahead.

The *Enterprise*'s chief engineer found Nyota Uhura and Pavel Chekov working at their usual bridge stations. Since the ship was in space dock, he assumed they were doing system checks. They took their jobs seriously, as he did, and would strive to make sure that everything was fully functional before they cast off.

"I love Starfleet," he said. "But like any bureaucracy—" He realized he had been complaining since he'd arrived. Uhura and Chekov watched with interest either real or feigned. "Sorry," he said. "You're busy, both of you."

"It's all right, Scotty," Uhura said. She sat forward in her chair, which was swiveled away from the communications station to face where he leaned against a bulkhead near the turbolift door. "We're old friends. If you can't complain to us, what good are we?"

"She's right," Chekov agreed. "You can went to us any time."

"I can what, lad?"

"*Went,*" Chekov repeated. "Blow off steam. Complain."

"Vent," Uhura translated.

Scott grinned, letting Chekov know he'd been

teasing. "That's why you're good at your job, Nyota. You can understand anybody."

"Sometimes a universal translator helps," she said.

"Once in St. Petersburg, I saw the home of the man who inwented the uniwersal translator," Chekov said. "Pyotr Illyich Uniwersal, his name was."

The three of them broke into laughter. After a minute, Scott straightened his spine. "I'll get back to it," he said. "It's frustrating, though, to spend so much time waitin' when we should be getting back into action."

"It'll happen soon enough, Scotty," Uhura said. "I'm enjoying being home for a while. I'm in no hurry to leave."

The turbolift doors opened as the engineer stepped toward them. "Well, that's good," Scott said as he stepped inside. "Because no hurry is exactly the timetable we've got at the moment."

# Five

"Freehold is not as you remember it," Tyree said. His tone indicated that he thought that was a good thing.

Kirk was trying to withhold judgment until he had more information. "Not at all," he said. He touched the black bars tattooed from Tyree's right shoulder and down his arm. More than twenty of them. "Nor are you. What do these signify?"

"Victor lives I have taken," Tyree said. "Some make necklaces of ears, or fingers. That, to me, is unclean. But most of us choose to mark the lives in some way."

"Before, you didn't want to kill. You fought with Nona about it."

"She was right," he said, bitterness lending an edge to his voice. "I was wrong. I have since learned better."

Tyree was leading him around the town. Two guards followed, a dozen paces back, providing them a modicum of privacy. Tyree hadn't needed guards the last time Kirk had been to Neural. This Eden was not the paradise it had once seemed.

Rowland, Burch, and Hay had gone to the guest quarters generously offered them, knowing that Kirk would recount what he learned. Tyree took Kirk to the wall, showing him defensive positions, the system of walkways, ladders, and stairs that enabled the quick deployment of personnel to any point, and the weapons and equipment storage lockers at the foot of the wall. It was an impressive operation, and Kirk said so. "You seem focused on defense," he said. "But I thought you believed the Villagers—sorry, the Victors—could overcome all your defenses if they wanted to."

"I do," Tyree said.

"Why put so much effort into a defense that can't ultimately succeed, against an attack that's not coming?"

"We do what we can do, James." Tyree waved to a lookout high up in a corner tower. "There has not been a concerted Victor offensive against us, but there might yet be. If we can hold them off, we will. If we can delay the end, we will do that."

"How did your population grow so much?" Kirk asked. "How many tribes have you brought together in Freehold?"

"Seven," Tyree said with what sounded like pride. "People from throughout the hills and mountains. For their protection, against being taken."

"Taken? For what purpose?"

"The able-bodied, they want as laborers. The less

able as breeders. The children, for when they grow up to be either one."

"They're taking slaves?"

"Yes. Slaves, to do the work they would not do themselves. Many of those you knew, from before, are either dead or enslaved."

"And they've expanded their village. Victory."

"Yes, James. They have brought together twenty tribes or more. Given them homes within the walls of Victory, in return for their fealty to Victory's governor, Apella. They have capabilities that we do not, and enough people to pose a serious threat."

Kirk indicated a lookout with one of the lever-action rifles. "Those rifles?" he asked. "Those aren't the flintlocks I gave you. Did you make them?"

Tyree chuckled, but without humor. "We captured them from the Victors. They can make them, but we cannot. We are a simple people, James, as you know. Would that we could remain that way."

"Amen to that," Kirk said.

"Excuse me?"

"Never mind. You're still the chief? Of everyone, including the new tribes you've brought into Freehold?"

Tyree raised his hands in a kind of shrug. "Not by choice. The people demand it. Ever since you provided those rifles. It is strange, James. I hear my name spoken by those I have never met. I hear stories from far away. Everyone knows my name, it seems, as if I were some creature of legend, not a simple man who can bleed and die like the rest."

"You've become a symbol," Kirk said. He suspected it was difficult for Tyree, who had always been humble. That had been the root of the problem between Tyree and Nona, and the underlying cause of Nona's death—she had greater ambitions for her husband than he had for himself, and she had seen his humility as a drawback. "Of the fight for freedom."

"Perhaps," Tyree said. "I would rather be a man than a symbol."

"We don't always get a choice."

They turned down one of the roads that cut through the town, heading away from the wall. There were shops along this road: a butcher, a woodcarver, a wheelwright, a weaver. The economy of Freehold still seemed to be largely agrarian and hunting, but a merchant class appeared to be establishing itself. People cast suspicious gazes at Kirk as they walked by, but seeing him with Tyree seemed to mellow that distrust. "Why have you returned, James? You said to investigate something, but you did not say what. How can we help you?"

"Your hospitality is already helping," Kirk replied. "My people need a safe base of operations. We'll want to get into Victory during the time we're here, but staying there would be too dangerous."

"Going near it is dangerous enough."

"I'm sure you're right, but I'm afraid we must."

"We will help in any way we can."

"Thank you, Tyree," Kirk said.

"They killed Nona," Tyree said. "They also killed my brother, Salree."

"I'm sorry to hear that."

"I have taken in his widow, Elanna, and her son, Nyran. He is almost a man. Elanna is not *Kahn-ut-tu*. There are few *Kahn-ut-tus* left among us. Another part of our heritage that the Victors are stealing from us."

"Is she . . . your new wife? Elanna?"

"No," Tyree answered quickly. "It is tradition for a man to take in his brother's widow. So there is always a father to help teach the children. If a woman with children dies, her sister takes in the widower and children, so there is always a mother. This is our way. It—"

He was about to continue, but a young man came tearing up the road, bumping into pedestrians and calling Tyree's name. When he saw Tyree, he made a beeline toward him. When he stopped, he was out of breath, cheeks flushed. He bent over, hands resting on his knees, and tried to breathe.

"What is it, Nok?" Tyree asked. "Take a breath, now, and tell me slowly."

"Victor slavers!" Nok said. He didn't look older than twelve, maybe thirteen. His hair was the same platinum color as Tyree's. "Coming up the Trail of the Four Sisters."

Tyree caught Kirk's gaze. "That is too near," he said. "We will have to respond." He clapped Nok on the back. "A war party," he said. "Tell Yutan and Kah'lee to gather a war party. I will join them shortly near the gate."

Nok nodded his understanding and darted off.

"I'll come, too," Kirk said. "With my people."

"You do not need to—"

"I'd like to see their capability," Kirk said. He hoped to spot some clue to a Klingon presence. And protecting Freehold was important, since they were guests there. "Give us guns, in case we need to defend ourselves."

"I have seen you fight, James. I would welcome your help."

"We'll want to stay neutral if we can, but I'd rather not be unarmed. I'll get the others and meet you at the gate."

"At the gate, then," Tyree said. With a last touch of Kirk's shoulder, he hurried away.

Kirk found the others in their temporary quarters, enjoying a brief moment of relaxation. "Come on," he said as he entered. "There's a Victory party on the march and we've got to go."

"A victory party?" Rowland asked. "What victory?"

Kirk reminded them about the name, realizing he would have to be more careful with his phrasing until everybody got used to the somewhat self-aggrandizing title the Villagers had bestowed upon themselves. "Let's go."

Ten minutes later, they had joined the gathering throng near the main gate. A couple of Freeholders stood at a weapons locker, handing out guns—flintlocks that had seen better days and some newer lever-action rifles—to those who didn't already have them. Most people brought their own weapons, some rifles, others carrying a bow and a quiver full of arrows, or a spear. Almost everyone wore a knife.

On the way, Kirk had run through a brief summary of what he'd discussed with Tyree. "We don't want to engage the Victors if we can help it," he'd added. "We're officially neutral. At the same time, there won't be peace if the Victors achieve total . . . well, victory. And inasmuch as we're guests of the Freeholders, we should try to make sure they aren't slaughtered or enslaved."

"Sounds like a reasonable goal," Hay said.

"How neutral do you want to stay, sir?" Burch asked. "We either fight on the Freeholders' side, or we don't fight and run the risk of them getting beat."

"We'll play it by ear," Kirk replied. "If there's a way to avoid fighting, we take it. If there's a way to head off conflict altogether, that's better still. But if push comes to shove, we side with our hosts."

Now, armed with the Freehold-provided guns, they moved at a quick pace down the hill from the fortified town, across a grassy plain, and toward a boulder-strewn patch of wilderness. Someone pointed out the "Four Sisters," and from this angle Kirk understood the name: four rock formations flanking the trail, they towered over the landscape, and their shapes vaguely resembled standing humanoid figures with heads bowed. Weeping, maybe, or lost in prayer. It helped if he squinted.

Just beyond the Four Sisters, the trail descended steeply, winding through a rocky maze of a canyon. There, a pair of scouts joined them from down-trail, and the group stopped to develop a plan of action. Knee-tall grass imparted a rich, lush aroma to the day, but thirty or so armed and sweating men and women overwhelmed it.

"They will come up here, out of that canyon," Tyree said. "This is where we fight them. As soon as they are all in the open, we attack."

"Do we know how many are in the raiding party?" Kirk asked.

Tyree looked to the scouts. One of them did a quick head count of the Freeholders. "Perhaps twice our number," she said. "Or a little more than."

"A direct confrontation could be tricky," Kirk said. "Unless we can send word back to Freehold for more fighters."

"There is no time," the scout said. "They are too close."

Kirk scanned the surrounding landscape. Huge

piles of boulders were everywhere, rocks on top of rocks stacked on bigger rocks. The canyon's mouth was a relatively narrow gap in the middle of it all, and until someone emerging from it reached the boulder fields, they would be out in the open.

"Can I make a suggestion, Tyree?"

"Of course, James. I trust your judgment."

Kirk had once shown Tyree how to use a flintlock; he guessed that was what it took to be a military expert in the man's eyes. "What if instead of engaging them directly, you positioned your people among these boulders?" he asked. "Everybody who has a gun points it toward the mouth of the canyon."

"And then we shoot when they appear?"

"No," Kirk said. "Every third person steps a few paces away from his or her gun. Leave the weapon so it's visible, pointing into the canyon, but then when the time comes, each warrior shows himself—or herself—to the enemy. Not enough to be in danger, but enough to let them know they're up here. That way, your force looks a third again larger than it is. With all those guns pointed at them, and uncertainty about how many people you really have, maybe they'll be discouraged."

"If not?"

"Then everybody returns to their guns—quickly—and fires from the shelter of the rocks. Only seconds will be lost, but if it works, the Victors might be turned away with no loss of life."

Tyree chewed his lower lip, thinking. Kirk could almost read his thoughts from the expression he wore. On the one hand, direct engagement with the enemy, which might be satisfying on some visceral level but might also result in a number of dead Freeholders. On the other, an ambush might, or might not, result in bloodshed.

Finally, he smiled. "Yes," he said. "We will try your plan, James." He repeated the basic instructions, louder, so everyone could hear. After some initial objections—nobody wanted to walk away from their guns, but they didn't mind if the person beside them did—the Freeholders acknowledged their orders and set about stationing themselves in the rocks.

Kirk, Rowland, Burch, and Hay joined the defenders, interspersing themselves rather than standing together. As he moved into place, Kirk studied the gun he'd been given. He was surprised by how comfortable the lever-action rifle was to hold and presumably to shoot—it was remarkably light, and the stock nestled into his shoulder. Whoever had designed the thing had done a good job.

He wedged the weapon between a couple of good-sized rocks, positioned so the muzzle pointed directly at the canyon's mouth. With that in place, Kirk moved three steps to his left, to a spot where he was protected from incoming fire by a large boulder, but he could show himself in such a way that he would be visible from below. On a whim, he grabbed a downed branch from a nearby tree. It still had some leaves on it, and he thought that if he occasionally shook it on the far side of the boulder, it might look like the movement of yet another Freeholder.

The Freeholder immediately to his left watched him with a bemused look on her face. She was muscular, several centimeters shorter than Kirk, but not petite. Her hair was a caramel color, her skin sprayed with freckles. Rose-colored gems glittered on her cheek, accentuating high cheekbones. Like Tyree, she had a series of black bars tattooed down her arm. He counted nine. "This was your idea?" she asked. Her blue eyes blinked a couple of times. "Hiding like this?"

"Yes," Kirk admitted. "So they don't know that they outnumber us."

"It is . . . clever. I like to see the eyes of my enemy when I kill him. But this too might be satisfactory."

"I'm not opposed to killing when it's necessary," Kirk said. "But I always think it should be a last resort, not a first choice."

She eyed him anew, as if she expected to see a second head or a third arm on him. Her smile had grown a little, and Kirk realized she was very, very pretty when she smiled. "You are a strange one," she said. "Your name is James?"

"That's right."

"I am Elanna."

It took him a moment to connect the dots. "Tyree's brother's wife?"

"Yes. Tyree told you?"

"He and I are old friends."

"He has spoken of you many times."

Kirk was pleasantly surprised. He had expected that most of Tyree's memories of him would be sad ones. Elanna hadn't said that Tyree had spoken well of him—he might have used Kirk's name as a curse every time he hit his thumb with a hammer. Or whatever people with limited metalworking capability used for a hammer. *A rock.*

"I'm pleased to meet you," Kirk said. He nodded his head toward the canyon below. "I wish it were under better circumstances."

"Soon the circumstances will improve. The ground will be soaked with the blood of our enemies."

*Not exactly what I had in mind,* Kirk thought. He left the words unspoken, and waited for the signal.

Soon enough, it came. Kirk heard *Hssst!* sounds travel around the defensive force, and he looked down to see the first Victors emerging from the canyon's mouth. They looked much as he remembered: mostly men, dark-haired, wearing clothes that covered a little more than the typical Hill People garb. He didn't know if it was colder in the valley, or if the people were more modest, but he had noticed the same thing on his last visit.

More of them issued from the canyon, and he saw that they had prisoners with them. The captives had ropes knotted about their wrists, each one connected to the ones in front and behind, so they made a chain of almost a dozen people. He had counted forty Victors—and they were still coming—when one of them looked up toward the rocks, pointed, and shouted an alarm.

In response, a Freeholder fired at him.

The round fell short—probably a flintlock, Kirk thought, its trigger yanked by someone in a panicked reaction to being spotted. The Victors below dropped behind whatever cover they could find and started shooting, almost indiscriminately, toward the rocks. Freeholders returned fire. Kirk held his ground, showing his head and hands occasionally, sometimes shaking the branch, and he hoped others were doing the same.

Watching the Victors, it was obvious that the arms race had continued, and the Victors still had a technological advantage. Some of their weapons held ammunition clips, so they could lever and fire until the clip was finished, and then reload by simply ejecting the empty and ramming home a new one. The few Freeholders who had more modern rifles fired as quickly as they could, but they couldn't keep up, and those armed with flintlocks, or worse, arrows and spears, had no hope of doing so.

Despite their technological disadvantage, Kirk saw that most of the Freeholders had held their positions. Better still, their protected placement meant that the Victor rounds were making a lot of noise but doing little damage. The Victors were, in large measure, out in the open, and dropping fast under the Freeholder onslaught. A couple of the Victors, ones he took to be leaders, were eyeballing the Freeholder positions, and after a few minutes, they gave orders to fall back into the canyon.

Shortly after that, all gunfire ceased. The ringing in Kirk's ears filled the sudden silence, and his nose and throat were ragged from the thick cloud of smoke hanging over the hills. Then a whoop went up throughout the Freeholder ranks. The Victors—and Kirk had to question that self-appellation more than ever—were running away, retreating through the canyon as fast as they could. They had even left their prisoners behind. And their dead.

Kirk scooped up his rifle and started toward where the Freeholders were gathering. Elanna caught up to him. "Your plan seems to have worked, James," she said. "Well done."

"Thanks," he said. "I'm just glad we didn't take many casualties."

"Tyree was right about you, I think."

Kirk didn't respond. He had not made up his mind about Tyree. The man had changed, hardened. The admiral wasn't at all sure he wanted to be the kind of man the new Tyree would admire.

# Six

That night, a celebration was held in Freehold's central plaza. The place had not existed during Kirk's last visit, but then, neither had most of the town. When people had gathered in the Hill People's camp, it had been to sit on stones around a small fire pit. Now there were permanent structures, set on roads of hard-packed earth. Tables hewn from logs too small to have been used on the settlement's walls were scattered about the plaza. A fire burned in a massive central pit, its flames roaring into the air and hurling up showers of sparks that almost seemed to merge with the stars. At secondary, smaller fires, people took mammals about the size of squirrels, skewered them with fresh vegetables from Freehold's gardens, and held them over the flames. The aroma of roasting meat mingled with the smells of sweat and alcoholic drink and the wood smoke from the bigger blaze. It made Kirk glad he was here just now and not stuck behind his desk, listening to the complaints of some Federation bureaucrat.

Hundreds of people had crammed into the space.

They laughed and sang and spoke in loud voices. Every now and then an argument broke out, but those were spirited rather than angry. Liquor flowed freely. Kirk tried a mug when it was offered to him, but the taste and texture made him think of insects dug up out of the ground—with a healthy chunk of ground remaining—then thrown into a bowl and slightly liquefied. He turned to Burch, who was sticking close to him. "I'd have to have a whole lot of this before I could take another sip," he said. "I'm not sure that works."

She nodded her head toward Hay, who was downing a big mug of something. "Titus says it's strong."

"Looks like he would know."

"It takes a lot to get Titus inebriated."

"I'd rather he stayed sober," Kirk said. "We don't know if there will be other problems. We might need him."

"I mean, *really* a lot," Burch said. "He's fine, sir."

Kirk watched Hay hand the mug to someone, who refilled it for him. The idea of drinking that much of it turned Kirk's stomach. But Hay tipped the mug to one side when no one was looking, pouring much of it out onto a sapling. Hay was paying attention to his intake, not letting it get out of hand. At the same time, he was making friends with their hosts. One of the people staying particularly close to him was Elanna, Tyree's sister.

Rowland worked his way through the crowd.

"Quite a bash," he said when he reached Kirk and Burch.

"It's good to win once in a while," Kirk said.

"That is true, James," Tyree said. He had come up from behind them, and took a seat on a wooden bench next to Burch, a glum expression clouding his face. "Many of the enemy fell. Today's victory was a sweet one." He spat off to one side. "I hate that word now. Victory. It does not mean what it once did, and when I speak it, I feel like a traitor."

"You're not, Tyree. And it was a win, a good one."

"I know. Thanks to you. But it showed us that they are on the hunt again. The Victors. They seek more slaves. They were quiet, for a time. We had begun to feel safe. *Safer,* not safe, but better than it had been. Now, they are on the prowl again, and no one is safe."

Kirk observed Tyree for a few moments as the man sat and stared, unseeing, at the crowd. His friend had once been full of life and energy, but now he seemed sapped, anger and bitterness having taken over his spirit.

"I am sorry, James," Tyree said. "This is a celebration, and I cast gloom over everything I touch." He rose suddenly from the bench. "Enjoy your evening, James, and thank you again for what you did today."

*A celebration,* Kirk thought as Tyree walked away. *It is that. But tomorrow, there'll be work to do, and it's not going to be easy.*

* * *

Nyran watched his mother talking to the big stranger. He had dark hair and a handsome face and a casual manner, with a ready smile that he could tell his mother responded to. He wasn't sure how he felt about that. His mother and the stranger were not lovers, although they might become that if the man stayed long enough. And his mother was lonely and sometimes inexpressibly sad. Tyree was good to her, but he still grieved over the loss of Nona, and sometimes Nyran saw the two of them together, the sadness in each of them overflowing and catching the other like a fish in a net, and he was torn between wanting to slap them both and wanting to burst into tears at the futility of it all, the waste that violence had visited upon his family.

He felt Joslen tugging on his arm, and he tore his gaze away from his mother. "Come *on,* Nyran," she said. "While everybody's busy, this is our chance!"

"You're right," Nyran agreed. He took her hand in his, marveling as he always did at the warmth that started with the touch of her flesh against his and spread in a heartbeat throughout his entire being. As they wended their way through the crowd, Nyran thought he felt eyes burning into him. Not Freeholders, who had known him since birth and his family before that, but people from Rocky Bluff. Joslen's town. Victor marauders had forced them to abandon their ages-old settlement and to move into the expanded Freehold for their own protection.

Not all of them liked living in close quarters with the Freeholders, even if they appreciated the relative safety that the arrangement provided. A smaller but vocal contingent didn't like the idea of mixing with the Freeholders. They could associate with them, trade with them, live side by side as long as was necessary. But they didn't like their young people pairing off with them. As well known as Nyran was among the Freeholders, Joslen was known and loved by her people.

In a few minutes, they had negotiated through the crowd and made their way around a corner. They could still hear the merriment, still smell the roasting *carzapals,* but the settlement was dark here, and they were alone. Joslen moved closer to him, snaked her arm around his waist, and he wrapped his across her shoulders. "I hate crowds," he said, glad to be able to speak without shouting and still be heard.

"So you've said," Joslen replied.

"They're just . . . I don't know. They bother me."

"You've said that, too."

"So you know everything about me, already?"

She laughed and pinched his ribs. "Of course not, silly. But more than I did a few weeks ago."

"I'm glad," Nyran said. Joslen's hair was long, the color of honey, and it spilled down her back in an almost liquid cascade. Her big eyes glittered in the silver light. She was, at that moment, the most beautiful thing he had ever seen.

"So am I," she said.

He shook his head to remember what he'd been talking about before he looked at her. "But this town . . . I have to get away from here."

"To go where? What's better than Freehold? Not Victory."

He shivered. "No! Not that. I don't know where. It's a big world, isn't it? Us—Freehold, Rocky Bluff, the other small settlements, even Victory and all the villages they've annexed—we're just a small part of it. Beyond the mountains, past the Elder Forests, there have to be other places. Towns, people. Right? It's not all just empty out there, is it?"

"Who knows, Nyran? I guess you can find out, if that's your dream. You can be the one to explore those places."

"Perhaps I will. Anything to get out of here. When I was growing up, our little campsite didn't even have a name, no walls around it. I could play anywhere. Up in the hills, down by the river. Nobody cared. It really was free. Now they say the walls are to keep the Victors out, but they also keep us in. So many of us, with people from Rocky Bluff and Highbridge and the rest all here, it's like I can barely turn around without bumping into somebody." He didn't think he was expressing himself well, and it made his cheeks burn with anger. "I need space. I need to be able to *move*, Joslen. Do you understand?"

"I think I do," she said. They walked down an empty road, the houses flanking it bathed in moonlight. "It's not easy for us either, you know. Coming to Freehold, carrying everything we could with us. Helping to build the town, but knowing we might never be able to go home. I'm glad we came to Freehold, because I met you. But I had to leave so much behind in Rocky Bluff."

"Like what?" He was glad they were off him and onto her. He needed to not talk about how hemmed-in he felt, because that only made it worse.

"Not really so much, I guess," Joslen said. "Some of my childish things. Toys, clothing. There is one thing I miss."

"What?"

"It's a pot I made when I was much younger. Mother helped me. We found the clay and worked it with water until it was good and wet, and she showed me how to spin it into a pot. She helped me form it and glaze it and cook it in an oven until it was hard. She was a *Kahn-ut-tu,* my mother. You knew that, right?"

"You told me before."

"Right. Anyway, she left special gifts in it."

"What were they?"

"Roots and herbs, mostly. But also, she sang into the pot. It might be my imagination, but I feel like if I hold it to my ear, I can still hear her voice, whispering and singing to me. She died, not long after that, but I was always able to remember her voice by listening to the pot. When we left Rocky Bluff, I forgot to grab it. But now . . ."

She didn't finish. Nyran stopped walking, took her shoulder in his hands. "Now, what?"

"It has healing powers, she told me."

"It does, or you *think* it does?"

"I'm not certain, Nyran! But I think it does, yes. And father . . . he's been so ill. What if I could use it to help him get better? I should have brought it. I was foolish."

"You were in danger, Joslen. You had to choose fast and carry everything you picked. You shouldn't punish yourself over it—wait! *Shhh!*"

He had heard something, or thought he had. The scuff of a boot on the road? Maybe it meant nothing; not everybody in Freehold was in the plaza, even if it had felt like they were. Or it could be somebody who had given up on the festivities, become tired or sick or too drunk to stay.

But there had been slavers on the hunt earlier, and though Nyran had not been allowed in the battle party—he was too young, they said, too untested, although how he would ever *be* tested if they didn't let him fight, he didn't know—he, like everyone else, was on the alert, wary of another attack.

His hand dropped to the knife on his belt.

He heard it again, closer, followed by the unmistakable murmur of soft voices. "Hello?" he said. "Who's there?"

A breathy laugh came from around the corner, then three men stepped out from behind a wood-and-mud walled house.

Not Victors.

Young men from Rocky Bluff.

They were all bigger than he—almost everybody was, everyone, at least, his age or within a few years on either side of it. He had always been the smallest of his friends, and even Joslen was a bit taller. These young men were older than he, too. One carried a short, stout club that he slapped against the palm of his free hand.

Nyran gripped his knife tighter.

"What do *you* want?" Joslen demanded.

"To know why you're spending time with this Freeholder pup," the one with the club said. He had broad shoulders and a deep chest, and his muscular arms popped with veins. Nyran thought his face dull, lacking in character and intelligence, but that might have been because the young man scared him.

"Because I like him. Which is more than I can say about you, Keran."

"*I* don't like him."

"No one asked you to."

"I still think it matters," Keran said. He glanced at his friends. "Don't you?"

"It matters a lot," one said.

"You're a Rocky Bluffs girl," the other added. "Too good for his kind."

"I'm too good for *your* kind," Joslen said. "Now leave us alone."

"Funny the pup hasn't said anything," Keran said. "Can these Hill People even speak, or are they too stupid?"

"You're not worth the effort," Nyran said. He released the grip of his knife, to demonstrate how utterly unconcerned he was. He hoped they believed it. "Come on, Joslen." He touched her shoulder, and then released it, in case he needed his hands free.

"He *does* speak," Keran said. "Or yawps, like the pup he is."

"She said to leave us alone," Nyran said. "Go on, you've had your fun."

Keran laughed. "Now he gives orders. I think you need a lesson, pup."

"Joslen, run," Nyran said. "I'll be fine. You need to go."

"I'll not leave you, Nyran."

"If you touch a hair on her head," Nyran said, "it will be the last mistake you ever make."

"We're not interested in hurting *her,*" Keran said. He smacked the club down against his palm one more time and advanced on Nyran.

"Would you like to meet her, James?"

Kirk blinked and saw Tyree standing beside him, though he'd thought his friend was gone for the night. He hadn't been consciously aware that he was staring, but he must have been for Tyree to take notice—and for him not to notice Tyree's return.

The woman in question had thrown her head back, laughing uproariously at something Kirk couldn't hear. She was tall and sturdily built; the way her booted feet were planted made her look like she could withstand hurricane-force winds without difficulty. It was those things, her attitude and spirit, that Kirk noticed first. Then he saw her sculpted jaw and the full lips, her deep brown eyes and dark brown hair drawn back into a long braid, and he guessed he had still been taking all that in when Tyree spoke.

"She's lovely," Kirk said. "But I don't think so. Thanks anyway." He had not come to Freehold to meet local women. He'd come to investigate the Klingon presence, and he didn't need any unnecessary distractions.

"Yes, she is." Tyree took Kirk's arm and drew him from his seat. "Come, James."

Kirk allowed himself to be tugged through the crowd. The woman noticed Tyree and Kirk approaching, and although her laughter faded, a broad smile illuminated her face. "Meena," Tyree said as they neared her. "This is my friend James. Meena is the daughter of my grandmother's brother's son."

"It's a pleasure to meet you, Meena," Kirk said.

"And you. We do not see many strangers here of late." She chuckled. "Or it might be more accurate to say we are all strangers here, of late. You have been here before, yes?"

"A couple of times. But it was much different then. Smaller. Not so crowded."

"Exactly. We all knew everyone else. It made misbehaving difficult, although some of us managed just the same. But now, we have taken in the people of other towns and settlements, for our safety and theirs. It is the right thing to do, and I would never change that. It has changed us, though."

"I'm not surprised," Kirk said. "I very much appreciate the welcome everyone has extended, especially considering that times are . . . challenging, at the moment."

"We have always prided ourselves on our hospitality. I hope that is never taken from us, as so much else has been."

"As do I. It's good to meet you, Meena. I'm sure I'll see you again, during my stay here, but I'll let you get back to your friends now."

She gave a brisk nod, dismissing him. He was briefly stung by the ease with which she spun away. But he was the one who hadn't wanted to be introduced, and then giving in to Tyree, had first signaled that the conversation was ending.

He returned to his seat at the celebration's edge. Burch still sat there, half-tense, as if expecting trouble at any moment. Rowland was there, too, looking worn out by the day's events. Only Hay still mingled with the locals, deep in conversation with Elanna, Kirk noted. "Mister Rowland," he said.

"Sir?"

"Please remind Mister Hay that we have a busy day ahead of us. I think it's time we all turned in."

"Sounds good to me, sir," Rowland said. "I'm more'n ready." He ventured back into the crowd while Kirk stifled a yawn, suddenly aware of just how tired he was.

That borrowed bed would feel very, very good.

# Seven

"What can you tell us about Victory, Tyree?" Kirk asked. They were on their way toward what had been a village, but was more of a city now, from the sound of it, and judging by the thick cloud of smoke overhanging it. "Why do they need a constantly replenished pool of laborers?"

"I wish I could say," Tyree replied. "They tear apart the world beneath their feet, that which gives life to all things. Not to plant seeds or cultivate crops. A few of the Hill People have escaped and told stories that can scarcely be believed. Stories of slaves forced to rip the heart from the earth."

"A mine, Admiral?" Rowland suggested. "That'd explain the smoke, too, if they have smelters to process ore."

"That's what I'm thinking," Kirk said. "Backbreaking, dangerous labor, especially at a low-tech level. They'd need a constant supply of workers."

"I wish I could tell you more, James," Tyree said. "We are simple people. We eat what the world provides us as game in the forests and crops in the fields.

I do not understand why the Victors would choose to abuse it so."

"There are lots of reasons for mining," Kirk said. "I would have to know what they're extracting to make an educated guess as to why." The question couldn't be answered here, but it had to be answered. To do that, he had to get close to Victory. Toward that end, they were trekking down the rocky hillside, following the path that had connected Hill People and Villagers for generations untold, according to Tyree, until conflict had made trade unthinkable. The sun was rising as they hiked, but had not yet warmed the morning air, which was scented with an aroma that reminded Kirk of cinnamon.

At a bend in the trail, Tyree held up a hand, stopping the small group. "We should leave the trail here," he said. "From this point forward, there is much likelihood that we will run across Victor scouts or slavers." He pointed off to the north. "There are ancient game trails through the foothills. We will take those and be safer."

"That's fine, Tyree," Kirk said. In addition to his old friend, three other Freeholders had come along. Their names were Enjara, Kenomo, and Bardee. Tyree had told him they were all skilled marksmen, in addition to being practiced hunters who knew the landscape well. Kirk was happy to let the locals choose the best path.

They cut cross-country, wading through high

grasses, sometimes sidestepping around red bushes laced with thorns that Tyree warned were poisonous. The trees they passed were in full leaf, and in a few minutes they were descending a steep hillside beneath a canopy so dense that the morning's sunlight had not yet penetrated. The air within the forested canyon smelled slightly musky. The trees and the brush around their feet rustled with the sounds of seldom-seen inhabitants: a flock of birds burst from a tree once; at one point Kirk spotted what looked like a rodent's tail vanishing into the crevice between two boulders; and Burch reported sighting a snake twined about some branches overhead. Insects buzzed around them in swarms, like gnats, but they didn't bite and rarely landed, so Kirk soon learned to ignore them. He noted that deep within the shadowed canyon, Tyree and his friends appeared tense, which he put down to their concern about Victor scouts rather than worries about the birds and the bees.

Farther down-canyon, the musky odor intensified, and the tension of the Freeholders increased accordingly. The scent triggered flashes of memory in Kirk, though he couldn't yet piece them together into a cohesive picture. He was trying to do just that when the beast broke from the trees and rushed them, head down. A high-pitched roar tore from its throat.

*Mugato.*

Kirk remembered it all now, the memories

rushing through his mind like floodwaters from a bursting dam.

The creature was pink-fleshed and covered in a thick mat of white fur. Vaguely apelike, it had a thick bone horn on top of its head and spikes jutting from its spine. When it charged, a wave of stink preceded it, like a miasmic cloud of effluvium from which there was no escape. Its bite was venomous, a painful lesson Kirk had learned on his last trip to Neural, and nearly always fatal. Only the intercession of Nona and her timely application of *mahko* root had saved Kirk's life.

His hand dropped to his side, but his phaser was buried in the hills. All he had was the lever-action rifle the Freeholders had provided.

The Freeholder nearest the attacking creature raised his flintlock, but the *mugato* batted it aside before he could get off a shot. Tyree fired once, his shot going wild and crashing through overhead branches. With another roar, the beast knocked the man it had disarmed to the ground and fell atop him, snarling and snapping as it tried to close its jaws on the man's throat. Its tail whipped back and forth, discouraging anyone from interfering.

The Freeholders crowded around, one swinging his flintlock like a club. The *mugato* swatted it away. "I can't get a clean shot," Hay complained. "They're too close! I might hit one of them." Burch and Rowland angled for shots, too, but with similar results.

Kirk had the same concern, but the Freeholder had only seconds to live. Once the creature buried its teeth, the venom would be transmitted. They were already too far from the settlement to get him back in time, even if there were a *Kahn-ut-tu* with a handy supply of *mahko* root there.

He couldn't wait for an opportunity; he had to make one. Kirk threw himself into the midst of the Freeholders, knocking Tyree and another one aside. The second man fell to the ground, swore at Kirk, and whipped a knife from his belt as he came up, seemingly intent on punishing Kirk for the assault. The admiral ignored him and pressed his rifle's barrel against the *mugato*'s skull. The creature yanked its head away at the last instant, but the shot grazed its head, and the noise and flash must have had an impact. The *mugato* staggered, releasing its hold on the downed man. Kirk fired again even as the *mugato* grabbed his gun barrel and wrenched the weapon away. His second shot tore through the thing's upper arm.

With a final horrific growl, the thing threw Kirk's gun at him and raced back into the woods. Hay and Burch, their way clear now, fired several shots at its retreating form, until Kirk waved them down.

"What in the hell was that?" Rowland asked.

"That was a *mugato,* Mister Rowland," Kirk answered. "The local predator I mentioned, a real top-of-the-food-chain type. Enjara's lucky he wasn't bitten—the *mugato*'s bite is almost always fatal. It's gone now, though. Tyree, is your man all right?"

Tyree was kneeling beside the fallen man. "He is not bitten," he reported. "Only stunned. I think he will be fine."

"Sorry I had to crash into you like that."

"You and your friends saved Enjara's life," Tyree said. "Thank you for your actions."

Kirk extended a hand to the man on the ground and helped him to his feet. "My thanks," Enjara said. "That *mugato* nearly had me."

"Glad we could help," Kirk said.

"But at what cost?" Bardee asked. He wore a necklace made of dried human ears strung together, one of the grisly souvenirs Tyree had mentioned. "We drove off the *mugato*, but the noise of our fire sticks will surely have alerted any Victor patrols in the area."

"We'll just have to be wary," Kirk said. As they started once more down the canyon, he thought again about his phaser, with which he had easily dispatched a *mugato*. It was a far quieter weapon than these, and more efficient.

*The Prime Directive is a sound policy,* he thought, *but sometimes it's a giant pain in my neck.*

Sticking to the seldom-traveled game trails, they managed to get within a few miles of the city—near enough that the industrial stench from the smelters overpowered the natural smells of the forest. Kirk was reminded of what historians said London, in Victorian times, looked like when smoke from chimneys in what was then Earth's largest city bonded with moist air coming off the Thames to create a choking fog that left every surface it touched covered with a black, sooty film. Victory was a long way from that, but if it continued on its present course, it might yet achieve it. It even had a river that, like the Thames, bisected the town, sparkling now in the midday sun.

Nearing the juncture where the hills gave way to the flat valley beyond, Kirk noticed an uneven quality to some boulders they passed, as if something had split them and then set them back slightly off level. He halted the party and eyeballed the landscape in both directions from there. Sure enough, there was a visible seam running in a fairly straight line.

"What is it, Admiral?" Rowland asked.

"It looks like a fault line," Kirk replied. He pointed out the differentiation to the Freeholders. "Do you know anything about this?"

The Freeholders conferred briefly. "It has not always been here," Tyree said. "Only for a few years. In fact . . ." He pondered for a moment longer. "In fact, it came here not long after you left, the last time. A few months, perhaps. Some said it was caused by a giant snake slithering out from underground. Others believed we had done something to make the world angry."

"When it appeared, was there a . . . a violent shaking of the ground?"

Another brief conference ensued. "We cannot be sure, exactly," Tyree reported. "But near that time, yes. It even toppled trees near our home. This was before we built walls around Freehold, but some of those fallen trees were the ones we used first, when the time came to raise the walls."

"It was an earthquake," Kirk said.

"A what?" Tyree asked.

"Beneath the surface of your planet, the continents rest on giant masses of rock and earth. We call them plates, tectonic plates." He demonstrated with his hands. "They are in constant, very slow, motion. They pull away from some and move toward others, and sometimes they collide. When they do, mountain ranges can be formed by the upthrusting of material from below. And sometimes as they shift around, earthquakes occur. The earth shakes and rifts like this can be formed. It's entirely natural."

"Tyree!" This was Enjara, who was out in front. He lowered himself to a crouch and motioned for the others to do the same.

"What is it?" Tyree asked.

Enjara pointed across the valley. The wild grass here grew nearly as tall as a man, but through occasional gaps Kirk could make out figures walking toward the hills. "Slavers," Enjara said.

"I see them," Tyree said.

"I make twelve, no, fourteen of them," Kirk whispered.

"To our eight," Kenomo said. "We should fight them."

"That's not why we came," Kirk countered. "We came to see what the Victors are up to. If we engage with a small party, they'll just send reinforcements out. That's a no-win game."

"A what?"

"Never mind," Kirk said. "Point is, fighting them won't achieve our goal, and it might get us killed. Let them go."

"Our homes are that way, James," Tyree reminded him.

"I know. But what's better, stopping one small group from possibly getting near Freehold? Or figuring out how to stop the Victors once and for all?"

"When you say it like that," Tyree admitted, "the answer seems clear."

"Let's get a look at their operation," Kirk said. "On the way home, if we see those slavers, you can decide whether you still want to engage with them. Fair?"

"Fair," Tyree said. He checked again. The slaver party was out of sight. "Come," he said. "But stay low. We might encounter more Victors at any time."

# Eight

Another hour or so of cautious movement, following the general course of the fault line all the way, brought them near a vast pit surrounded by a tall wire fence with coiled razor wire topping it. Guard towers stood at periodic intervals along the fence line. What looked like banks of spotlights were mounted on the towers, and although they were dark, they indicated some form of electrical power. Between the fence and the grassy plain at the edge of which they had stopped were forty yards of bare earth, scraped clean of even a single wayward weed. Kirk doubted that Victor technology had made the fence or the lights, but he couldn't be certain. In the near distance, on the other side of the pit, brick chimneys spat smoke into the air. This close, he could hear a steady rumble from the building beneath the chimneys, in addition to voices wafting from inside the pit.

"Looks like this is as close as we get," Kirk announced.

"But we can't see inside," Burch said.

"No, but look across the way." He pointed to the far

wall of the pit, terraced by pathways. The raw earth inside the pit ranged in color from brown and rusty red through oranges and yellows. On Earth, Kirk would have thought those colors signified iron-rich soil, perhaps threaded with copper. But as Earthlike as Neural was in many respects, when it came to the geophysical makeup of the planet, he could make no such assumptions. "That's definitely a pit-mining operation."

"Which confirms our theory that that thing's a smelter," Rowland said, graciously omitting the fact that it had been his theory to begin with.

Kirk eyed what he could see of the city beyond the pit and the smokestacks. It looked like any city from Earth's early industrial age—low-rise buildings and streets paved with stone, more chimneys issuing streamers of smoke into the air. "Victory is no garden spot," he said. "But it's significantly more advanced, technologically, than it was the last time I was here. They've got electricity, for one thing."

"Which confirms our other theory," Rowland said.

"I don't know if I'd say 'confirms,' Mister Rowland. But it does point in that direction."

The unspoken word hung between them.

*Klingons.*

If the Klingons had returned, taken up where they left off in providing technology and know-how to the Victors, then such a city could have developed in a few short years.

Still, Kirk was left without hard evidence. He scanned in every direction for some sign of a Klingon presence. He saw only Neuralese people—Victor overseers and slave labor that looked to be predominantly Hill People, but all of them locals. The guards held lever-action rifles and wore knives at their belts, but not Klingon disruptors or *bat'leths*.

"Do you see any Klingons?" he asked Rowland quietly.

"No, sir. We could try to get in closer."

"The guards in those towers would spot us the second we got out onto that bare patch," Kirk pointed out. "If they haven't already."

"I haven't seen any signs that they have," Rowland replied.

"Neither have I. But we should fall back before they do. Getting caught here isn't on my agenda for the day."

"We haven't accomplished much, sir."

"Being captured or killed won't change that. We wanted a closer look, and we got one. Eventually we're going to have to get inside the city, but we'll need more prep time for that. In the meantime, we've ascertained that they are indeed engaged in a large-scale mining and smelting operation, and using forced labor to do it. That fits in with the theory that Klingons are behind this. It's a small step," he admitted. "But it's progress."

"Yes, sir."

"Come on," Kirk said. "Let's get out of here." He didn't add, *while we're still in one piece.*

But he thought it just the same.

Apella led the way into his security office, resisting the impulse to rub his hands together with glee. But only *just.*

Krell had put his faith in Apella from the very beginning. There had been times over the years when he'd worried that the Klingon warrior had considered that faith misguided. The terrible period when the Klingons had left the planet and the Hill People had gained new weaponry, from some as yet unknown source, had been one of the darkest patches of Apella's life—never knowing if he would survive from one day to the next, not knowing if his benefactors would ever return, or if his village would fall to the Hill People's wrath.

But the Klingons did come back before long, and they brought the power to quell resistance once and for all. Oh, the Hill People's settlement yet stood, under its foolishly audacious name. But Apella's village had a new name, as well, one that was more suited to its new status: *Victory.* Apella had chosen it himself, after being told of a statement that the wife of Tyree, the Hill People's chieftain, had made. She had approached some Villagers, offering what she said was a weapon that would guarantee Apella's victory. The woman had died, and after that the Hill

People had somehow acquired flintlocks of their own, and the Klingons had left.

But when the Klingons had returned, the Villagers had expanded their advantage. Apella had used the woman's word for his city's new name as a taunt, his own private joke. The name Freehold was a desperate fable, something its residents clung to, knowing all along that whenever the Victors decided enough was enough, they could march in, knock down Freehold's walls, and take whatever and whomever they desired.

For now, let the Freeholders raise up a new crop of laborers. The Victors would take them when they were strong enough to be useful.

"What is it you wish to show me?" Krell demanded as they entered the office. His accent was so thick that he was almost unintelligible, a condition made more pronounced when his patience was waning. "My time is valuable."

"I believe you will be pleased by this, honored Krell," Apella said. Again, he tamped down the urge to gloat, even though he doubted that Klingons had a problem with gloating. They probably valued it as a noble act.

Funny, how he could work so closely with them for so long, yet know so little about their culture.

"I had better be," Krell said.

In the security office, a single Victor sat in a straight-backed wooden chair before a viewscreen.

The office contained two desks, a rack of weapons, and some equipment Vlettor knew how to use but Apella didn't. The image on the screen was fuzzy. Klingon technology, when powered by Victor energy sources, often functioned at less than full efficiency.

"Show Krell what you saw, Vlettor," Apella instructed.

"Yes, Governor Apella," Vlettor said. Krell had promised Apella that title, and now every Victor called him that, as did every prisoner and laborer, at least once they had felt the sting of the lash. Vlettor's hands flew across the control panel too fast for Apella to follow. Klingons had trained him well.

In a few moments, the screen went dark, then blinked back to life showing what appeared to be a distant view of a grassy field. But as Vlettor twitched a control stick, the grass fell away, as if seen through the eyes of someone moving quickly through it. When the image settled again, it showed eight people hunkered at the edge of the field. All were armed. Apella recognized only one of them, the tall, lean man with pale blond locks who was the acknowledged leader of Freehold: Tyree. In days gone by, they had been friendly rivals, sometimes cooperating on hunts. Some of the others had the features common to Freeholders, the tanned skin and long, light hair. But despite having donned local garb, something about the other four hinted to Apella that they were strangers here.

"We had visitors today," Apella said. "These people stared at the pit for long minutes, but did not dare to approach."

"Let me see," the Klingon said gruffly. "Stand aside."

He shouldered Apella out of the way and stood before the viewscreen, his legs apart, hands clasped behind his back. After a moment, he stiffened, the muscles of his neck going taut. Krell's hands tightened almost to the point that Apella wondered if he was hurting himself. "What is it, Krell?" he asked.

The Klingon whirled around. He didn't look cheerful at the best of times—Apella was accustomed to that, and he had taken to wearing an approximation of Krell's typical sour grimace when he wanted to intimidate those around him. But now Krell looked positively furious, and a momentary fear for his life made Apella's knees start to buckle. He caught himself on a nearby console. "What?"

Krell stabbed a finger at one of the figures on the viewscreen. "*Kirk,*" he said. "That one. I recognize him. He is the enemy of every Klingon."

"And he is here? On Neural?"

"If this image was captured today, then he is here. Close by."

"I will find him," Apella said. "I will put the Klingon's hated enemy to work in the mines. No day will pass without my lash flaying the flesh from his bones."

Krell's expression softened. "If you can," he said, "you will truly be a friend to the Klingon Empire." He moved past Apella, toward the door. "I must report this," he said. "Qo'noS must know that Kirk is here."

Then he was gone. Apella turned to Vlettor. "Tell no one of this," he said, trying his best to adopt the tone of haughty arrogance Krell typically used. "If you see that one again—any of those—report it to me immediately. But only to me. Is that understood? Only to *me,* on pain of torture and a long, slow death."

Apella left the security office and strode out to a deck from which he could look down into the pit. He liked this view—the Freeholders and other captives laboring away, working with shovels and picks and simple steel bars, or loading carts with ore and hauling them up the sloping ramps that snaked around the pit's sides. His own people standing watch, alert for signs of sluggishness or resistance and ready to punish either. One of the guards raised his gaze and met Apella's eyes briefly. He gave him a casual nod, all the acknowledgment the man needed or deserved.

They looked up to him. Every Victor did. And in their own way, the laborers did as well. They knew who their ruler was, at any rate. Apella was the governor of Victory, and Victory held sway over all the people of the flatlands.

But it wasn't enough. Krell had promised him

domination over all of Neural. The Klingon had hinted that there were distant lands, far out of sight, where people dwelled who had never heard of Victory, much less Apella.

The fact that he ruled meant that he was supposed to rule. Krell had explained that about himself, and about the Klingon presence on Neural, and Apella had extrapolated it to himself and his situation. He deserved power. He had earned it, taken it, amassed it by force of will and personality and by throwing in his lot with the strongest of the strong. Now, he wanted more. He wanted it all. Not for his own aggrandizement, of course, but for what he could do for his people and for all the people of Neural. Theirs was a poor world, backward compared to the advanced civilization of the Klingons. They needed the wealth that Klingons could help bring. They needed the technological advantages the aliens offered, and when they had those things they would be equal partners in the Klingon Empire.

Apella's destiny was to help Neural achieve its destiny. He *knew*, with every bit of confidence imaginable, that he would be the vehicle, the catalyst, that could drive Neural from its stunted, primitive state into the magnificent future it was meant to have.

If he could capture this man Kirk, if he could prove himself a "friend to the Klingon Empire," that might be enough. With the might of the empire at his back, all of Neural would bow before him, and he would have the power he needed to drag his world toward its rightful tomorrow.

This man Kirk had been close by, and not that long ago. Apella needed his best trackers, and he needed them now. He relinquished his beloved view, and went to gather them together.

# Nine

"I've had all I can stand," Scott said. "And then some! I'm supposed to get this tub worthy of the name *Enterprise*, but I'm blocked every way I turn."

"What is it now, Scotty?" Uhura asked. He had found her and Chekov in the mess, comparing notes over a late lunch.

"It's Command! I need a wide spectrum capacitor lock—a wee thing, really, but I can't guarantee performance above warp six without it. But because the overhaul I'm proposin' is considered experimental, they don't want to provide the part until the Corps had a chance to do their tests."

"There must be something you can do," Chekov offered. "Some way to cut through the static."

"There had better be," Scott replied. "Or I'll just retire and let the button-pushers figure out how to run a starship. I'm thinkin' I'll pay a visit to Admiral Kirk. If anybody knows how to work the system, it'll be him."

"Good idea," Uhura said. "You're right, he's always known how to get things done."

"Tell him hello for me," Chekov said. "Do you think he's enjoying desk duty?"

Scott raised an eyebrow. "Have you met the man?"

Chekov chuckled, and Uhura joined in. "I didn't say I *expected* him to. That doesn't mean I cannot hope to be surprised."

After a quick meal, Scott went into Starfleet Command's headquarters. He always felt a little uncomfortable there, amid the busy bustle of bureaucrats. Most of them didn't speak his language, even if they had served among the stars. And he didn't speak theirs. He understood many of the words, and the topics of conversation tended to revolve around sending starships into space, which was a subject he could discuss at great length. But his concerns were the actual, physical requirements of space travel—how did one balance the conflicting needs of cargo, personnel requirements, and engine power? What kind of gearing mechanism was required to make the doors iris open smoothly in zero gravity *and* in full artificial gravity? The concerns of those at Command were logistics, strategies, and politics, and sometimes the deeper philosophical questions pertaining to the whys and wheres. Scott was all about the hows.

But one didn't reach his position in Starfleet without learning how to work the system. He pasted on a smile and entered the headquarters building. He nodded to those he saw—those who acknowledged his presence, at any rate—spoke a few friendly, noncommittal words when he had to, and made his way to the admiral's office.

The door was open, but the lights were off. Scott walked in, expecting to find Kirk's flag aide, Rowland, even if the admiral himself was off at one of the endless meetings he sometimes complained about. The lights blinked on when he entered, but Rowland's desk was vacant. Same with Kirk's.

On his way out of the office, Scott was almost mowed down by a female ensign carrying an armload of data slates. His sudden appearance startled her, and her arms flew into the air, scattering the slates everywhere.

"Och, I'm sorry, lass," he said, dropping to his knees to help gather them up.

"You should really watch where you're going, sir," she said.

"I'm not the one who was barrelin' down the hall like I'd been shot from a torpedo tube."

"I didn't expect anyone to be coming out of an office I know is empty," she argued. "And—" She stared at him for a long moment, slates beginning to slip once more from her grasp. "You're Montgomery Scott!"

"That I am."

She let the last of the slates crash to the floor and stuck out her hand. "It's an honor to meet you, sir," she said. "I'm Belinda Fairweather."

Scott racked his memory to determine whether the name was supposed to mean anything to him, other than sounding like someone who might live next door to Rebecca of Sunnybrook Farm. He couldn't come up with anything. "It's my pleasure, Ensign Fairweather."

"Admiral Kirk talks about you *all the time*."

"Speaking of the admiral, d'you know when he'll be back?"

Her eyes were green and wide, her hair was brown and long but piled and pinned atop her head, and when he asked his question, her mouth made an O shape until she bit down on her lower lip. "I can't say."

"Well, where is he?"

"I can't say."

"Who can say?"

"I can't say that either. I'm sorry, Commander Scott. So sorry. I've probably said too much already."

Scott scooped up a couple of handfuls of her slates and thrust them at her, then regained his feet. "Well, somebody's got to know something and be able to talk about it. He's a rear admiral in Starfleet; he can't just vanish into thin air."

"Well, he sort of can."

"I'm not following you, Ensign Fairweather."

"I've said too much."

"If you won't tell me where he is, I'll find somebody who can. Good day, Ensign."

She clutched the slates, losing her grasp on half of

them again—a fact that might have disturbed Scott more had she not annoyed him so—and grabbed his arm with her free hand. "Commander," she said. "I—"

"Let me guess. You've said too much already."

"Yes, I have. But what I was going to say was, I know he's a friend of yours. I can't tell you where he is or when he'll be back—I don't know those things myself. But if you'd like, I can pass the word up to Admiral Kucera that you're looking for him, that you'd like to know. I don't know that it'll do any good, but I can try."

"Are you saying he's on some kind of secret mission?"

"I'm saying I don't know where he is."

"Who *does*?"

"I can't say, sir."

Scott started to snap at her, then caught himself, his right index finger pointing across the short distance between them. "You—you are good, I'll give you that, Ensign. All right, yes. Send the word up. Tell 'em I want to know and—"

"As soon as possible."

"Ensign Fairweather?"

"Yes, Commander?"

"I'm glad I ran into you today. Not literally. But otherwise."

"As am I, Commander Scott," she said.

He left her with her slates, wondering what the

admiral could possibly be up to, and why anyone would need to carry so many data slates around.

A light rain fell during the early afternoon, cooling them as they hiked back toward Freehold and washing away the industrial stink Kirk had been afraid would cling to him. By the time they reached the walled settlement, the sun had reappeared and dried them off. The trail was muddy in spots, coating their boots until they kicked or stomped it loose. Enjara exulted in the rain, declaring it a gift that would help feed every mouth in Freehold.

Upon their return, Kirk found out firsthand what he meant. A group of Freeholders was preparing to go out to Providence Valley, an area of cultivated fields far beyond the walls, to harvest fruits and vegetables ready for the picking. Tyree encouraged Kirk to go along, and Kirk agreed. Recognizing that his people might be tired from the long hike down into the valley and back, he offered them the chance to stay behind.

"Not a chance, Admiral," Rowland said. "I wouldn't miss it. There's nothin' like an apple fresh from the tree."

"I'm not sure there'll be any apples," Kirk said. They'd had an assortment of the local produce at the feast the night before, and more on the trail today, and while he was willing to proclaim it "interesting," so far none of it had been comparable, in Kirk's mind, to what he was familiar with at home. "But if you liked the *regalu* we had last night," he continued, naming a red, leafy vegetable that had tasted something like a cross between beets and cauliflower dowsed in vinegar, "then you're probably in luck."

"The *regalu* was okay," Hay said. "I liked the *confolli* better, though. That was tasty stuff."

"It sure was," Burch seconded. Kirk nodded. *Confolli* was a spiny fruit, not quite as prickly as cactus, but with a sweet, juicy pulp underneath the forbidding skin. Eating it was an exercise in patience, because to rush it might mean a spine through the tongue or cheek. But taking the time to separate the skin from the inside was worth the effort.

"We'll all go, sir," Burch said.

"Fine," Kirk said. "We can rest later, after the harvest. Fair warning, though—they'll probably put us to work."

"No problem," Hay said. "I've picked produce before. That way you get first crack at the good stuff."

Soon they were leaving the walls behind again, this time heading deeper into the hills, in a direction Kirk had never been. Everyone carried a large basket, which they would be expected to fill. There were about twenty of them, and they stretched out in single file, following a trail that wound through wooded sections and climbed narrow hillside paths.

The high valley was lush and green, with a slow-moving river drifting through it in a series of sweeping curves. Cultivated fields and orchards were laid out in neat rows, crisscrossed by irrigation ditches fed by the river. Tall trees fringed the edges of the fields and marched toward hills on the valley's far side. Massive flocks of birds moved about, their iridescent feathers sparkling in the sunlight.

"It's beautiful," Kirk said, pausing at the peak of the trail leading down the hill and into the valley. He hadn't been speaking to anyone in particular, but a female voice answered him.

"Yes, it is. I love Freehold, but I love this place more."

Kirk looked at the speaker. Meena, the woman he had met at the previous night's celebration, stood behind him with her basket resting against a cocked hip and a flintlock across her back, its strap cutting between her breasts. His adjective described her as well as the valley, he realized. Her beauty was more subtle than that of Tyree's sister, Elanna, or Tyree's late wife, Nona, but was perhaps more penetrating for that understatement. Kirk had to look at her a couple of times to see it, but once he had, he couldn't look away. "You're fortunate," he said, "that you get to come here. Do the Victors know about it?"

"They do," she said. "They have raided it a few times, but in the end, they have taken no steps to destroy it. I believe they ignore it because they know it feeds us and makes us strong, which suits their ends when they put us to work."

The people in line behind them were catching up, so Kirk and Meena started down the final slope, side by side, their baskets occasionally colliding. When they reached the fields, they remained close together, Meena showing Kirk how to use a knife to cut the *confolli* fruits from the barbed thickets of the waist-high bushes they grew on, and occasionally sharing other harvesting tricks. Within an hour, his basket had started to grow heavy.

And he liked it, he realized. He liked Meena, who kept him laughing with her stories of Freehold life, and he liked working under the sun, sweating from honest labor, with dirt under his fingernails and a pleasant soreness developing in his neck and shoulders. It was the furthest task possible from captaining a starship, but he couldn't deny the visceral pleasure he drew from it. He wasn't the only one, either; despite constant anxiety over the Victors, he heard more jokes than complaints, and he saw smiling faces and healthy, hardworking people.

Kirk had been angling so hard for a way to get back into space, he hadn't stopped to wonder if that was really what he wanted. At this moment, he wasn't sure. Maybe what he wanted was a break from the responsibility of carrying all those lives on his shoulders, of making every hard decision. Maybe his shoulders were better suited, at this stage of his life, for picking fruit and carrying baskets. Laughing in the sun wasn't a bad way to spend a day, or a year, or a lifetime.

* * *

Nyran filled his baskets with *fuferan* pods, working diligently to select only the ripe ones. He hated the bitter, stringy insides, no matter how they were prepared, but they were one of his mother's favorite vegetables, and she would be upset if he brought home anything less than the best.

As he worked, though, he made his way toward the field's distant edge. At one point he set his basket down, wincing, his ribs still aching from the beating he'd taken the night before. He touched his left cheekbone, bruised and raw. Joslen had raged against her townsfolk, had pummeled them with fists and feet, and Nyran had fought back as hard as he could. But they were three, all bigger and stronger than he, and just intoxicated enough that even his best shots didn't seem to hurt them. He hoped that today, they were at least feeling residual pain from the brawl, because his pains were more than residual, they were all-encompassing. And they were more than just physical—they hurt from the inside out.

He thought about a day, years before, when his mother had taken him aside to tell him a story. "Selanee was the first hero," his mother had said. He had seen only thirteen summers at the time, had not even earned his forehead gem yet, though he had it now. He would always remember that year, because it was the year his father had died, murdered by Villagers.

He'd heard the story of Selanee many times throughout his childhood, but she had never before told it in just this way.

"Our people lived in great danger, in those days. Everyone lived in the valleys, close to the rivers, because that was where the fields were rich and fertile and where there was always game to be hunted. But there were terrible beasts in the valleys, as well. They roamed about freely, and whenever they found people, they attacked. No one was safe.

"Selanee was born the third son of a third daughter. The night he was born, a ferocious storm was sweeping through the valley where the people lived. It rained for three days and three nights, and the river rose until it was beginning to overflow its banks. The people knew that if it did, their fields would be flooded and their homes would be lost. On that third night, Selanee was born. As soon as he came into the world, he gave a loud wail, and as if at his signal, the rain stopped. The river receded and the homes were saved.

"That was the first time people realized what a hero he would become. I have told you other stories, of young Selanee and the *magong*, of Selanee fighting off the fish-men, yes?"

"Yes, mother," Nyran had replied. "But I like hearing them."

They sat out of the day's sunshine, in the shade offered by their lean-to. The life of the settlement went on around them: people skinned and tanned the hides of animals that hunters had brought them, others prepared meals of fresh vegetables and fruit. From the nearby stream came the joyful sounds of those bathing and washing the skins they wore.

But in his mother's eyes, in the slump of her shoulders, and in the desultory tone of voice with which she spoke, Nyran knew that sadness weighed heavily upon her.

"The year Selanee reached sixteen summers," she went on—just the age he was now, he realized, though at the time it had seemed impossibly far away, "the valley suffered one catastrophe after another. First the rains did not come in spring or summer, causing the crops to wither and die. *Mugatos* and other beasts raided often, killing many. Fire came and burned the homes of the people, killing more.

"In the middle of it all, Selanee vanished. He went up into the hills and explored, and then he came back to the valley and bade all the people follow him. The people did. Selanee led them high into the hills, climbing and climbing and climbing, until they found places to settle where it was safe and cool and the streams flowed freely and there were lush valleys in which to plant crops. Selanee kept climbing, until he grew wings, and then he took flight and watched over the people always, for the rest of time. And thus were born the Hill People.

"Selanee's bravery will always be remembered,"

she said. Then Nyran noticed that her voice caught in her throat, and her eyes glistened. "Just as . . . just as your father's courage will always be remembered. Selanee showed us what is best in us, and your . . . your father showed us again. And you, Nyran, you have the stuff of heroes in you, too."

"Me?" Nyran asked. He was just a boy, a mere slip of one, and he did not feel like a hero. Instead of answering, his mother fell to her knees beside him and locked him in an embrace that he thought would surely snap his bones.

And Nyran thought, *One day, I will live up to my father's example. And Selanee's.*

*One day, I will be a hero.*

He was still waiting for that day to come.

He had been no hero with Joslen. He'd been humiliated in front of her. He couldn't live that down.

Unless . . .

Glancing around him, Nyran saw that working toward the far side had put space between him and the rest, as he'd hoped. They moved down one row and up the next, but he stopped at the end of his last one, moved to the next row's end, and picked the *fuferan* pods there, then to the next one, each row increasing his distance from the others.

Finally, nobody was looking his way. Nyran had been waiting for this chance, planning for it. He'd brought a skin pouch from home and had tucked some fruits into it as he worked his way through the fields, for rations. Knowing he would be in for serious punishment for deserting his basket and his harvest, he darted for the shelter of the trees. Soon he could see the fields no longer, which meant those working there couldn't see him. The forest was dense and gloomy, the canopy overhead cutting off the sunlight except in a few spots where it broke through and illuminated individual branches, spreading ferns, and mushrooms of various descriptions growing up the sides of trees.

He could be at Joslen's town by nightfall. Sooner, with a little luck. He could locate her house, find her special pot, and be home tomorrow. He would take whatever punishment came his way if he could just save face with her by delivering her most precious item. He would do whatever it took.

He was young, and he was in love, and that was enough.

# Ten

Kirk's basket was growing heavy with spiny *confolli* fruits. Everybody had the same size basket, even the children. Carrying his basket back to Freehold would be wearying. He guessed there was some trick to basket wrangling that he didn't know. He knew people sometimes carried baskets on their heads, but that was something they didn't teach at Starfleet Academy, or back home in Iowa.

He was still pondering the question when the gunfire started.

The first volley came all at once. In the valley, with the river's constant murmur and a soft breeze rustling the trees and the voices of the Freeholders calling out to one another, it seemed muffled, distant popping sounds. But the rounds flew into the field, whining like angry insects. A man a couple of rows from Kirk was hit, blood spraying from the side of his head in a fine, red mist.

"Get down!" Kirk shouted to Meena, who was working beside him. She was slow to respond, but before he could push her down she had dropped and scooped up her flintlock. She rose up on one knee and aimed at the trees. Kirk cocked his lever-action rifle and did the same. While he waited for the attackers to show themselves, he scanned the fields. Most of the Freeholders had taken up arms, but several were visibly wounded, and he saw people tending to those who had fallen.

Another volley came from the trees, and then the firing became sporadic. Freeholders fired back at unseen targets. Kirk held his fire, not willing to waste the ammunition. He hadn't come to take up arms for one side or the other, but fired upon, he was obligated to defend himself.

"Damned slavers," Meena said. Kirk risked a quick glance at her. She was sighting down the long barrel of her flintlock, one eye closed, but she had not fired. "Nothing is sacred to them. Even here, to this spot so rich with beauty and life, they bring violence and death." Sleeves covered her shoulders and most of her arms, but Kirk wondered how many tattooed bars were there.

Kirk returned his gaze to the trees. He was starting to see bursts of motion there, people darting through the shadowed depths and the lighter spaces in between. When one froze, half in shadow, and fired toward the field, Kirk aimed at the muzzle flash and squeezed the trigger. He thought he heard a cry, but in the general cacophony it was hard to be sure.

The other Starfleet personnel were on guard duty

at the edge of the fields, between the harvesters and the trees, along with a dedicated force of Freeholders. The first volley of shots had cut into their numbers, but now workers in the rows of crops moved toward them, heads down, baskets left behind and weapons in hand. Others stayed where they were, partly hidden by trees and bushes, firing when they had targets or simply laying down a barrage to allow the others to move unimpeded.

Kirk located Rowland and Burch, but not Hay. He didn't know if the big man had taken refuge in the fields or was simply crouched down on the front lines. He whispered to Meena to stay put—without a clue as to whether she would obey—and started toward the field's edge at a low run. A shot rang out from the trees and the round whipped past him, close enough for him to feel the breeze. He threw himself down as two more pocked the air where he had just been.

Kirk moved forward on his belly for a meter, came up, fired a couple of shots toward where the incoming rounds had originated, then dropped and advanced again.

He had almost reached the front line when a group of five Victors broke from the trees and came straight toward him. Two of them fired indiscriminately, trying only to keep Freeholders from sighting in on them. The other three appeared to have a single-minded focus on Kirk. They weren't carrying guns. Two had big nets and the third a coil of rope and a short, stout club.

They were slavers, and they were intent on capture, not murder.

Kirk levered a round into the chamber and squeezed the trigger. The weapon clicked. He squeezed again, more urgently. *Click.*

The Victor slavers were closer. The outer pair fired, and fired again. The three in the middle closed on Kirk, their faces eager, bright with the thrill of the hunt.

Kirk spun the weapon around in his hands. He had played some baseball, in younger days. What he had lacked in fielding ability, he'd made up for by being a power hitter.

He held the rifle by the barrel and swung for the fences.

The rifle's stock caught the nearest man in the jaw. The blow snapped his head to the right, spraying teeth and blood from his open mouth. He fell forward, carried by his own momentum, and almost landed on Kirk. The admiral sidestepped and the man flailed past.

Kirk brought the gun back around, low, out of time to raise it. The man with the club and the rope was almost on him, but Kirk shoved the rifle into the man's way. Its length tangled with his legs and he went down in a heap, yanking the gun from Kirk's grip as he did. He threw out one arm in a desperate attempt to steady himself, and Kirk grabbed the club from that hand. As the man tumbled down, Kirk stepped forward and swung the club in a short, tight arc. It struck the back of the man's head with a sickening crunch, and the man went still.

Turning to the third one, Kirk saw that he was spinning his net over his head, getting it ready to toss. He looked skilled with it, practiced. Its diameter increased with every spin. If it reached Kirk, he would be entangled, helpless to defend himself.

He still held the club, though. And it would travel faster than a net.

He rocketed it toward the man with the net. It crashed into his upper chest. He staggered, falling back three steps, losing control of his net. It draped partly over him as he tried to regain his composure. He clawed at it, but before he could free himself, Kirk covered the distance between them. With a running leap, he landed on the man, driving him to the ground. A few well-placed blows rendered his foe unconscious. Kirk snatched up the club again and looked for the next attacker.

But there were none. Any remaining in the trees had retreated, already out of sight. The dead and the wounded littered the space between the tree line and the cultivated fields, still forms with splayed-out limbs, or twitching, quaking, bleeding ones crying out for aid or stoically enduring obvious agony. Kirk realized that there were fallen within the fields, too;

Freeholders had been killed and injured, though not in the numbers that the Victors had.

Then his gaze landed upon Apryl Burch, crouched beside a body, and her expression told him the worst had happened.

Kirk started toward her, scanning the survivors and spotting Rowland, also making his way in that direction.

The big man had taken three rounds, two in the chest and one in the throat. His Freeholder clothing was soaked in blood, as was the dirt where he lay. Burch's eyes were dry, though her face showed that her lack of tears was an act of will, not a dearth of emotion. Elanna had seen Hay and come running, pushing past her fellow townspeople and throwing herself over Hay's lifeless body. Her wailing reached to the sky, and the tears slicked her face and pelted the ground like rain.

Kirk glanced up, once. Somewhere up there, out of sight, out of orbit, was the *Captain Cook*. Had he a way to reach the ship, he could arrange to have Hay's body beamed off-planet, stored until appropriate arrangements could be made. He had hoped this mission would be quick and easy, that it would not necessitate the hardest part of an officer's job: notifying next of kin that a loved one had paid the ultimate price.

It had turned deadly.

"Oh, no," Rowland muttered as he approached. "Is he—?"

"Yes," Kirk replied. "I'm afraid so."

Rowland looked on in stunned silence. His skin had gone ashen. Kirk realized this was probably the first time he had lost a comrade.

"We'll bury him," Kirk said quietly, so the Freeholders around couldn't hear. Most, save Elanna, were busy with their own wounded and dead. "With all appropriate formalities. When the opportunity arises, we'll beam him out. One way or another, we'll get him home."

"Aye, sir." Rowland swallowed. Kirk could see him fight to hold back tears, blinking his eyes, stiffening his posture. "Thank you, sir."

*For what?* Kirk berated himself. *For asking you and Hay and Burch to put yourselves in harm's way? For failing to prevent the civil war I saw brewing the last time I was here?* He didn't know what he could have done—the ensuing years had not offered an answer—but if there had been anything, any possible solution, he should have stayed until he found it.

That had been impossible, of course. He was just one man, not a god, not some kind of super-being. Free people made their own choices, and sometimes those choices included hating one another. He could try to offer an example, he could step in on those limited occasions when he might actually do good. But he could not blame himself for every failure, every missed opportunity. That was an invitation to madness.

He couldn't tell Rowland all that, though. Now Burch stood beside them, a trembling hand gripping Rowland's arm. "We'll do what's right," Kirk said softly. "We'll take care of him."

There were only the four of them on the hill, as the sun's last rays touched the peaks of the nearest mountains. Kirk had explained to Tyree that this was the way of his people, that they needed solitude for their mourning ritual. Tyree had bid the other Freeholders give them their privacy, and he had posted guards around the hill's base to ensure it. They had taken turns with borrowed shovels, digging a hole deep enough to protect Hay from predation, but not so deep as to be a final resting place.

Titus Hay was in the grave and covered with soil. Kirk stood at the head of the mound, his head bowed. "I wish I had known Titus Hay better," he said. "I would have been proud to have him as part of my crew, on any ship at any time. He was brave and stalwart and true, that much I can say with certainty. He formed friendships fast, strong ones, lasting ones. He was always ready with a joke or a story or a pleasant word, but during the time I knew him, I saw him to be a listener, too, genuinely interested in whoever was speaking at the time. He was curious and kind and smart, and any world would be a better place with him in it. The people of this one may never be able to appreciate the treasure they had here, for a few days. All we can do is try to see that his sacrifice was not in vain. He gave himself to try to secure peace for them."

"Amen," Rowland said.

"This is not good-bye, Mister Hay," Kirk added. "Only a temporary resting place. We will be back for you."

The admiral said no more. The three officers stood together, heads lowered, as the last sunlight winked from the sky.

". . . they were not there for us," someone was saying. He rose up on the balls of his feet, finding Kirk, Rowland, and Burch standing at the crowd's edge, up against a wall in the town's great hall, and thrusting an accusatory finger at them. "They came for *them*!"

"Bad enough we have to worry about our own lives," another Freeholder added. This one was a sturdy woman with flaming red hair. "Without *them* making it worse."

"My friends," Tyree said, raising his hands in a conciliatory gesture. The people had gathered in the big hall just off Freehold's central plaza, where Tyree had been holding court when they arrived. "We have had trouble with the Victors for years now. Never have we blamed it on outsiders. No matter how many different settlements emptied out, how many towns we absorbed into Freehold, we never said this tribe, or that one, were the cause of our woes. We will not blame these three—who came to help us, who lost one of their own today in our defense."

"You call us friends, Tyree," the first speaker said. He was tall and leaner than most Freeholders, and his long, platinum hair had been pulled back and tied behind his head. "But you call *them* friends, as well. Perhaps both cannot be—"

The door flew open and the man's diatribe halted mid-sentence. He stared toward the doorway. Kirk followed his gaze and saw Elanna there, standing straight and strong, though her eyes and nose were red from grief. Beside her stood a girl in her teens, her shoulders hunched, sorrow and fear marking a face that still glistened with tears.

"Elanna?" Tyree said.

"Joslen would speak."

"Very well. Joslen?"

"Nyran," the girl said, her voice tremulous. "Has anyone seen him?"

"Of course," someone answered. "Just this morning—"

"Since the raid," she interrupted. "At Providence."

"You haven't seen him since?" Kirk asked.

"I did not know he had gone," Joslen said. "I was looking everywhere for him, searching the town. Elanna said he was there, but she could not remember if he had returned with the rest of the group."

"All the wounded, the dead. The confusion," Elanna said. "And Hay, who had become my friend."

"I do not hold you at fault," Joslen said. "Or anyone. I merely wish to know if he has been seen, since then."

No one came forward.

"Then I must go there," Joslen said. "To the Valley."

"Not tonight," Tyree said. "It is not safe."

"If not safe for her," Elanna said. "Is it safe for my son? Out there, perhaps hurt? Alone?"

"The night belongs to the *mugatos,*" Tyree reminded her. "And to the Victors, with their weapons. Come morning, we will—"

"Come morning it may be too late!"

"There is nothing else for it," Tyree said. "To send out a party now would be to risk the deaths of all. And we do not know if he is even there. Until we have searched every home in Freehold—"

"My son was there this afternoon," Elanna said, tears tracking down her cheeks. "I helped bring home the injured and lost sight of him. A mother's gravest duty is the safety of her children, and I failed in mine."

"But to go out there now would be to risk leaving Nyran without a father *or* a mother. The boy's no fool. If he's there, he'll seek shelter until the dawn."

"If he's hurt—"

"We can but hope for the best," Tyree said. Nobody pointed out that if Nyran was hurt, and out there alone, he was likely already dead.

Finally, Elanna and Joslen gave in, after the townsfolk agreed to launch a major expedition at first light. In the meantime, they would turn Freehold upside down looking for him.

Kirk wished, and not for the first time, that he had the *Enterprise* at his back. But instead, he was stuck here on the surface, without backup, armed only with the ancient weapons of the day. A part of Kirk raged against the restrictions Starfleet had placed on him, while another part whispered to him that his interference, all those years ago, was responsible.

He would join the search party, offer what help he could. It was less than he would have liked, but it was the best he could do.

# Eleven

"Do you know him well?" Kirk asked. "The missing boy."

"Nyran? As well as any, I suppose," Meena said. They were walking the streets of Freehold, after the meeting had broken up. It was dark, with the only stray illumination coming from un-shuttered windows here and there, and the silvery glow of a half moon. "We are—we were, a small settlement. Everybody knows everyone. I am younger than his mother but quite a bit older than him. I watched him grow up."

"Does this sound like him? Disappearing?"

"As Elanna said, if he were hurt—"

"If he'd been hurt, we would have seen him. We scoured every row of those fields, after the attack. We knew there were wounded and dead. We looked everywhere. He wasn't there," Kirk said.

"You did not say so, during the meeting."

"I'm an outsider here. You heard—some of them were ready to blame us for the attack."

"You speak the truth. If Nyran had been there, we would have found him."

"We know he was with us."

"Yes . . ."

"So he left on his own. Before the attack."

"So it would seem. I had not thought of it before, but yes, it must have been that way."

"In the morning, we'll accompany the search party," Kirk said. "But we'll have to be prepared to expand the search area. If he had something in mind, some specific destination, he'll have had plenty of time to get there."

Meena turned to face him and put her hands on his forearms. The contact sent a thrill through Kirk; more so than he had expected. He didn't want any kind of romantic entanglement during this mission. But he was surprised by the almost electric tingle he felt, beginning in his arms and coursing through his body. "These are not even your people, James. And yet, you are so willing to help them, even at the risk of your own safety and that of your friends. You lost one today. Many people would have walked away from us after that, would have decided the cost is too great, that our problems are not yours. But not you. You are still here, still ready to help, even when you know it could be dangerous."

Kirk paused, enjoying the contact. He couldn't tell her about Starfleet, about the oath he had taken when he joined, or the more private one he'd made to himself. He had, over the course of his career, put himself and his crew in harm's way, over and over again. That was part of Starfleet's mission. They traveled through space to extend the protective arm of the Federation wherever they could. They sought to stand up for the defenseless and to stop those who would oppress them. The concepts were old ones, although they had often been set aside: freedom, justice, equality. With Starfleet, he had been able to bring those concepts to dozens of worlds.

He would do the same here. True, his interests here on Neural were personal. He genuinely liked the Freeholders, and his concern for them was as authentic and as vital as they themselves were.

"It's my fight now," he said, unwilling to try to put the rest into words she could understand.

"There is one other possibility," Meena said after a moment's hesitation.

"What is it?"

"Did you see Nyran's face?"

Kirk hadn't. He had been watching for signs of ambush and then had been struck by the beauty of the valley. "Not really."

She indicated the town around them with a turn of her head, and gave a sad sigh. "We pretend we all get along. The original Freeholders, and those who've joined us from other settlements throughout the hill country and beyond. The truth, I'm afraid, is not so pretty. There are rivalries, old feuds reignited by forced proximity, feelings of prejudice and distrust. Nyran has taken up with Joslen, a girl from the settlement called Rocky Bluff—you saw her there tonight, with Elanna. Some of her people resent Nyran for it, and it appears he took a bad beating sometime in the last few days."

"What are you saying, Meena? Do you think they came for him in the valley? Took him away somewhere?"

"I do not see how they could have, without being seen. But I think the possibility should be explored, if he is not found quickly."

"Something else to keep in mind, then," he said. "We should get some rest. It's going to be an early morning, and a long day."

Nyran had spent the afternoon alternately jogging and hiking briskly, following trails already being overgrown by brush and wild grasses. They led out of Providence Valley, up a steep slope, and through a mountain pass. On the far side was a narrower valley, and beyond that the mountains rose higher still. They were thickly forested, but at a certain altitude the trees gave way to bare earth, then snow. The peaks were rounded and white, appearing soft from here. He suspected that was illusion—that would be hard country for anyone, particularly for a young man on his own, with no experience there.

But somewhere up there—before the snow, he fervently hoped—was Rocky Bluff.

Over the course of numerous conversations,

Joslen had described the journey she and her people had taken to get to Freehold. Nyran had a good memory for details and had tried to recall everything she had told him, then had found a map that substantiated her description, for the most part, and had brought it along. Between her memories and his map, he was convinced he could find the place.

He wondered what Rocky Bluff would be like. Her tales had only told part of the story, and he knew the reality would not match the impressions he carried in his mind. Nyran thought he would like the place, because it had given him Joslen, and if it wasn't love he felt toward her, he didn't know what else to call it. He thought her the most incredible creature he had ever encountered. Her smile enchanted him; her soft brown eyes, when they looked into his, transfixed him. He liked the lilt of her voice; the full-throated way she laughed with her head thrown back, as if her laughter could reach the very stars overhead; the way she whispered, her lips so close to his ear he could feel her breath on him, when they held each other tight on a dark evening. When he was with her the time raced past, and when they were apart minutes seemed to slow, to stretch into hours or days, until they were together again. She was the last thing on his mind at night and the first he thought of when he woke each morning.

Rocky Bluff had become a magical landscape, as if no normal settlement could have produced someone who was so clearly at least half goddess. Her mother must have been all goddess, he had decided, because her father was decidedly human, frail and sickly. Still, he felt he owed the man his thanks, for the part he had played in bringing Joslen into being.

Night fell early in the mountain valley. Though sunlight still glimmered around the snowy peaks, where he was, the mountains blocked it. The shadows kept the air cool, and despite his quick pace, Nyran's cheeks were chapped by a cold wind. He hadn't brought heavy clothing or provisions, just what he could stuff into a leather pouch strapped across his chest. He had not wanted anyone to guess his intentions, and if he'd been carrying anything unusual, he'd have given away the game. If he was wrong and had to spend the night outside, Nyran knew he would regret the lack.

His way was slowed by the steepness of the hillside and the rocks and trees that lay in his path. Once, trade between Rocky Bluff and the community that had come to be known as Freehold had been commonplace. That had been before the slavers had started preying upon them all, before the communities took a defensive crouch that kept their people isolated and estranged from the others. The years since that change had been few, but the effects were quickly felt. The route from one settlement to the next became seldom traveled, and people who had once been friendly turned suspicious. The old paths had fallen into disrepair, a condition exacerbated by the harsh mountain climate.

Undaunted, Nyran climbed. He was alternately sweating from the effort and gripped by sudden chills as cool winds dried his sweat. Nyran began to worry about losing the trail in the encroaching darkness. If he lost his way in these mountains, he might never find Rocky Bluff, and he might never see home—or Joslen—again.

Nyran came to a place where three paths converged. Joslen had described it from the other direction, as a spot where the narrower route from Rocky Bluff came together with others to join the wider pathway toward the valley. He had thought he remembered which fork was the correct one, but now that he saw it he realized the picture in his mind's eye didn't match the reality. He unrolled the map he had borrowed, but it was hard to make out in the dim light. The path on the left, he thought. But he couldn't be absolutely certain. He would have to follow it for a while, see if it took him to the next landmark he expected to see: a huge tree, split down the middle by lightning. If he didn't find that soon, he'd have to return here and try another fork.

He was beginning to question the wisdom of this venture. He couldn't turn back now, though. He'd never make it back to Freehold before full night. As it was, he probably wouldn't make Rocky Bluff in time, either, but at least he was closer to that than to home.

He swallowed back his anxiety and started up the left-hand path. Hunger gnawed at him; he had expected to be able to find edible fruits along the way. In his pouch he had a couple of *confolli* that he had picked, but that was all. Since he'd discovered how quickly dark was falling, he hadn't wanted to spend time searching for other food. Nyran knew he needed to maintain his strength, though, and eating something might help calm his nerves. He reached into the pouch, brought out a small, firm *confolli,* and set about carefully peeling it as he walked.

He had taken just a single bite when he heard a sound in the trees.

The wind was picking up, so there was a constant rush through the leaves and branches. But this sound wasn't like that. It was a footfall, deliberate and stealthy. Nyran dropped the fruit and drew from his belt the only weapon he had, his curved-bladed knife. He froze and listened. The sound didn't repeat, so he continued on his way, at a faster clip this time.

Moments later, he heard something different, a chuffing sound that could only have been made by an exhalation of breath. It came from the other side of the path, and slightly ahead of him. Two of them, then? But who, or what? Slavers? They would have attacked by now.

No, this was more likely beasts of the forest. Four-legged hunters like *eldas,* with their powerful jaws and legs that allowed them to spring a dozen paces or more to bring down their prey, or—

Another footfall, this one louder and closer. He spun around and saw a *mugato* coming toward him, clawed arms outstretched. The thing paused, threw its head back and released a roar, then charged. Mated pairs often hunted in teams, he knew. With one behind and at least one other ahead, he was hemmed in. He couldn't fight two *mugatos,* not with just a knife.

Which meant he had to abandon the path.

One *mugato* was rushing toward him from behind, and he saw the other break from the trees on his left. So Nyran broke right, darting into the cover of the forest. Here, though, he was deprived of the moonlight that had been his only illumination. His shoulder slammed into a tree trunk and he nearly lost his footing. Regaining it awkwardly, his left leg became ensnared by some ground vine. Wrenching it free sent him sprawling onto the forest floor. The knife flew from his hand. He found it and scrambled to his feet again, threw his arms out to probe for obstacles, and moved as fast as he dared.

Now the *mugatos* were running on slightly different tracks, from the sounds of it. They communicated through growls and grunts and whistling noises. They were trying to catch him in a kind of pinch, one following a route that would take it ahead of him while the other flushed him from behind. It was the same tactic they had used on the path, he realized. Maybe it was the only trick they knew, short of catching their prey by surprise or simply wearing it down.

Knowing that gave him one advantage. If they did the same thing each time, then he had to vary his response to it. Last time he had gone to his right, so this time he angled left, crossing the path of the one who had moved ahead of him. That one would have to backtrack to catch him.

Still, it was only a momentary victory. The *mugato* could see in the dark, and they knew the forests like few other creatures did. There were rumors that they grew impatient quickly, or simply lost track of what they were about—jokes were made all the time, comparing people with short attention spans to *mugatos*. But Nyran didn't know if those jokes were grounded in truth or in some popular misconception. Few people who had been individually tested by the beasts were still around to tell about their experiences.

From the sounds they made, it took the *mugatos* several moments to adjust to his change of strategy. There was a brief flurry of confusion, signaled by high-pitched grunts and angry thrashing about, but then they were after him again.

He shifted to the left again, not giving them time to flank him. This direction would reconnect to the path, he believed, and the path might give his longer legs an advantage, as long as both *mugatos* were behind him. The *mugato* had short legs, though they could build up speed by dropping down and using the knuckles of their arms as well as their feet. With a head start, Nyran thought he could outpace them.

But a crashing in the brush nearby told Nyran he hadn't gained as much ground as he'd hoped. He altered course again, trying to veer away from the *mugato* that had surprised him, and he barreled into another tree.

It probably saved his life.

He hit it headlong and the impact stunned him. He bounced and fell flat on his back. The rest of his *confolli* bounced out of his pouch, but he barely noticed. The *mugato,* just reaching him, leapt but soared over Nyran instead of crashing into him. Nyran sensed the beast—smelled its rank odor, heard its rapid panting and its grunt of shock as it hit the forest floor empty-handed, followed by a curious huffing as it wondered where its prey had gone—more than he saw it. He had managed to hang on to the knife, and as his vision cleared, he discovered that the *mugato* was right in front of him, facing away, slowly turning in a circle to seek him out.

He had only one chance. He lashed out with the blade, catching the thing in the upper back. It screamed—a truly horrific sound that made his teeth hurt—and lurched away.

The other *mugato* was coming fast. The one he'd stabbed was wailing, hunched over, slapping at its back with one clawed hand as if to swat whatever was hurting it.

Nyran sheathed the knife and ran. He would not get a better chance.

The *mugato* before him flailed out an arm that almost knocked Nyran off his feet again, but he stumbled and kept going.

When he reached the path, he raced flat-out, taking long strides, coming down lightly on the balls of his feet, pumping his arms. He breathed through his open mouth, and before long, the uphill slope had him panting. Still, he ran, devoting every ounce of strength to the effort. His lungs ached from the cool night air. He figured expending this energy, punishing his body in this way, wouldn't kill him. But if he didn't do it, the *mugato* very likely would.

It really wasn't much of a tradeoff.

When he was certain they were no longer following him, Nyran allowed himself to slow to a walk. The muscles of his legs were complaining; they might give out at any moment. He couldn't push them much longer, though, and he already knew they would ache miserably by morning.

Nyran was still breathing hard, his heart galloping in his chest, when he saw Rocky Bluff.

Just over a rise, the settlement was spread out below the ridgeline on the other side. It was small, with fewer than three dozen permanent structures interspersed among massive boulders. Beyond the settlement's edge the ground fell away sharply, in a nearly vertical cliff. Joslen had told him they had built here for defensive purposes—if they could guard the ridgeline above, they wouldn't have to worry about anyone attacking from below.

In the pale light of the moon, Nyran got his bearings, again working from Joslen's description. A large building in the approximate center was the roundhouse or public house. Off to that one's left was a slightly smaller, squared-off structure that spanned a trickling creek; that had to be what Joslen had called the bathhouse. From that central point, pathways stretched out like the spokes of a wheel, and the homes were arrayed along those spokes, most of them with small garden plots where the residents had teased vegetables and herbs from the rocky soil. Every building was made from the native stone, making the whole place look like something that had sprung from the earth itself rather than being constructed by the hands of the people.

Joslen had said her home was so close to the cliff's edge that the time the earth shook, stones from its outer wall had gone over the side, and she had feared that the whole building would follow. She had slept outdoors for weeks after that, afraid to go back inside, in case it happened again. Finally, winter weather had forced her inside.

She also had described the home next to hers,

where she said the family kept growing and kept having to build on new sections to accommodate their members. It only took a minute to identify that house: a larger central structure with wings built onto it on almost every side, and additional chunks tacked onto those. Given those landmarks, he knew which house had to be Joslen's.

In the silence and the faint silvery glow, the place was eerie, its homes abandoned, doors open like the gaping mouths of the dead. He half-expected to see movement; children playing, someone cooking over one of the fire pits, people carrying game strung over their shoulders. Despite appearances, this was a place built by people, built for people, never meant to stand vacant. The homes hinted at lives lived, at lovers and parents, at feuds and shouting matches, games played, stories told, babies birthed, elders breathing their last.

Only none of that was happening now. Rocky Bluff was as empty as a broken promise, and the only sound was a faint whistle as a night breeze scoured the abandoned pathways.

Reaching Joslen's home, he stifled the impulse to announce himself at the door—that would be foolish; the place was empty, and if there *were* anyone around he didn't want to call attention to himself. He went inside, into the blackness where not even moonlight filtered, and sat down, back against a wall, to wait for the dawn.

# Twelve

Apella preferred dealing with Krell at the mine office. There, he was in control, he had power. Power granted him by Krell, but power just the same. The Klingon couldn't help but see how deferential others were toward him. And when necessary, Apella could put on a display of his power, could have a laborer whipped or beaten, for instance. That reminded everyone of Apella's strength, and he knew the Klingon derived pleasure from the demonstration.

But the Klingon refused to go along with his request this time. That's what they always were with Krell: requests—Apella liked to think of them as *demands,* but he was realistic enough to know the truth. Krell had to pay a visit to the spaceport the Klingons had built nearby, to handle what little starship traffic there was. All of their visitors were Klingons, and while most of the traffic was freighters coming in to load ore from the mine, there was also a steady trickle of bureaucrats and other officials arriving for what business Apella did not know. When he asked, Krell told him it was none of his concern, and he said those words with such a fierce finality that Apella let the matter drop.

This time, Krell told Apella that if he wanted to talk, they could talk while he walked to the port. "I am a busy man," Krell added. Apella knew if this opportunity wasn't seized it might be some time before another one arose.

Krell was taller than Apella, and he walked with a brisk, long-legged stride. Apella had a hard time matching his pace, and he often found himself scampering a few paces to keep up.

". . . tried to capture the one you wanted, the one called Kirk," Apella was saying. Krell forged ahead down a crowded pathway, eyes front, not slowing for anything. Victors knew enough to get out of the Klingons' way, even if most of them still didn't know whom the Klingons really were or understand the significance of the spaceport. His fellow Victors, Apella feared, were mostly simple people, incapable of higher reasoning.

"Tried?" Krell echoed.

"Yes. A valiant attempt. Unsuccessful, in the end, I'm sorry to report. We lost many warriors in the attempt, but they killed one of those who were with him, as well as some Freeholders."

"Still, you *failed*."

Krell's scornful tone stung, but Apella was getting close to his point. "Yes, honored one. This time. We will try again, with more warriors."

Krell made a dismissive noise. It might have meant something, in his language—Apella had never learned more than a handful of those harsh, guttural words—but if it did, Apella was glad he didn't understand. Then Krell said, "If you knew how Klingons reward failure . . ."

That, Apella understood. He was just as glad that Krell had not gone into greater detail on that score. "If we had better weapons, though . . . more advanced . . . we would have no trouble with them. With the sorts of weapons you keep for yourselves, we could storm Freehold itself. We could take the town, increase our labor pool, and speed up production."

"You are the worst kind of fool, Apella!" Krell snapped. "You have ideas, but you lack the ability to know if they are good ones or bad. Laborers are resources, just like the ore itself. They must be used wisely. You would run them all ragged, but we need that mine to remain operational, to supply the empire for decades."

"Yes, of course, Krell. I merely thought—"

"Perhaps you should do less thinking and more overseeing. Make the workers you have work harder, but tend to the breeding stock so you will never run out."

Apella recognized that the conversation was veering away from his intended target. "But the weapons," he said, desperate to swing back around to the topic at hand. "With better weapons, we could—"

"More foolishness!" Krell interrupted. "You will have put Kirk on guard. I have reported his presence to Qo'noS. They will respond, in due time. Better that you had not meddled at all."

"I meant only to show you how we could handle such matters."

Krell laughed. "And you *did*. You showed me *exactly* how well you could do."

"Success is never certain," Apella argued. "Only failure is certain. If a man does not try, he is certain to fail."

"But apparently if *you* try, the result is the same."

They had arrived at the spaceport. Klingon guards, wearing the kind of weapons that Apella wanted—what Krell called "disruptors"—stood watch at the gate. When they saw Krell approach, they drew back the gate and stepped aside. "He is with you?" one of the guards asked Krell, gesturing toward Apella. "The colonist?"

Krell turned toward Apella with a dismissive, almost contemptuous look on his face. "Are we finished?"

"The weapons?"

"If I feel you have a need for them, I will provide them. But I would rather you focus on the mine and leave such matters to me."

"But, Krell—"

Rage clouded the Klingon's face, and he raised his hand. Apella saw the blow coming but didn't know how to dodge it, or even if he dared. That might only infuriate Krell all the more. The back of Krell's hand swung toward him, and the Klingon stopped it mere inches from Apella's cheek. There the sting was only emotional, and worse than a physical blow. "Enough," Krell said. "Back to your mines."

He turned on his heel and the guards clanged the gate shut behind him, then glared at Apella like he was a dog standing outside a butcher shop. As he walked away, he heard the guards speaking Klingon behind him, and laughing.

He had tried to be a partner to Krell, to make the city of Victory a partner to the Klingon Empire. He had never imagined that Krell thought of Neural as a colony, or of him as a subject. But the way Krell had swung at him . . . he could easily have struck him.

He was not a partner, he was simply a means to an end. Everything the Klingons did was in service only to themselves, not to Neural. And Apella himself would never, he was coming to believe, attain the power and prestige due him. Even if every Victor dropped to the ground and genuflected when he passed by, all it would take was another demonstration like that, from some Klingon or other, to reveal the truth. He was a figurehead, more puppet than partner.

And it was too late to do anything about it. After their initial overture, he had invited the Klingons in. He had made his choice in ignorance, but it was made, and there could be no turning back. He would just have to take what power was offered, with the knowledge that it might be snatched away at any moment.

He didn't like it, but when he got closer to the mine office, away from the glares of the Klingons, people recognized him and greeted him with respect, and in a few cases, with something like fear.

That, Apella did like. He would suffer almost any indignity to maintain that status. He worked his face into a scowl and headed for his desk.

Scott knew he was in trouble, but he didn't know how much trouble until he entered Admiral Kucera's office. The admiral sat behind a desk you could almost have landed a shuttle on, with her mouth set in a grim line and her eyes alert but not friendly. Captain Willard Decker sat in another chair, and although he was usually quick to smile, he was not smiling now. There were two other officers in the room, but Scott didn't know them and no one introduced them. Large windows gave an expansive view of the bay and the Golden Gate Bridge arching across it. The water glinted in the sunlight, throwing light daggers at the sky.

"Commander Scott," the admiral said. "Have a seat, please. Thank you for joining us."

*I had a choice?* he thought. Instead, he said, "Of course, Admiral." He took the only empty chair and nodded to Decker and the other two as he sat.

"Scotty," Decker said. "We appreciate you taking time out from your important work. How's she coming?"

"I could use more cooperation and less red tape," Scott said. "But that's always true, isn't it?"

"We'll try to make that happen," the admiral said. Her voice had a husky edge to it, a rasp that made Scott think she had not always piloted a desk. She sounded like she had lived hard. He didn't know much about her background, but Decker seemed to respect her, and that counted for something. "But I understand you've been a bit distracted, lately. By another matter."

"If ye mean me tryin' to find out what's happened to Admiral Kirk, then you're right, Admiral. And I'll nae quit doing that until I get some answers. Somebody's got to know."

"You're wading into some difficult waters, Scotty," Decker said. "We're here for your own good, whether you know it or not."

"Forgive me if I'm not especially cheered by that. From your faces, it looks like I'm here for an inquisition."

The admiral allowed herself a smile, but it didn't reach her eyes. She had a firm jaw and those eyes were a steely gray, and Scott took her for someone not to be trifled with. "Not at all," she said. "We understand your concerns, and we would like to allay them. But there are . . . complicating factors."

The phrase sent a chill through him. "Is he all right? Admiral Kirk?"

Kucera hesitated, and he could see by the tilt of her head and the furrow of her brow that she was considering her answer. Before she spoke, she shifted her gaze to the two officers who had not yet been introduced. "Gentlemen, could you give Commander Scott and me the room?"

The three men left the room without comment. When the door closed behind them, Admiral Kucera met Scott's gaze again. "You and Admiral Kirk are very close," she said.

"Every single person on his crew feels that way about him. He's a remarkable man."

"He is indeed," Admiral Kucera said. "And those of us in Command appreciate that."

"So where is he? Why can't you tell me that?"

"Just what do you think we're doing here, Commander Scott?"

"I'm still tryin' to figure that out, Admiral."

"My aide, Ensign Fairweather, says you buttonholed her the other day asking about Admiral Kirk. I've heard from others, as well. The truth is, while we'd prefer that nobody be talking about him just now, thanks to you, he's become a topic of conversation. Commander, Kirk is on a very secret mission. Secret, I might add, at his own request, though I agreed with his reasoning and agreed to help maintain the secrecy."

"So you'll not be tellin' me where he is, because it's a secret?"

Admiral Kucera sighed. "He went to a planet called Neural. You may remember it, although according to our records you did not visit the surface."

"Aye," Scott said. "I remember it, all right. The captain confused me when he called in, ready to return to the ship."

"Confused you, how?"

Scott didn't know how much more he should say. He remembered the words exactly. Kirk had asked how long it would take to supply a hundred flintlocks. Scott had thought he'd misheard—whatever the captain said, it could not have been "flintlocks," because that made no sense. He'd asked for clarification, and Kirk had said, "A hundred . . . serpents. Serpents for the Garden of Eden. We're very tired, Mister Scott. Beam us up home."

As it turned out, the captain *had* said flintlocks, and after he'd returned to the *Enterprise*, he made his orders clear. Doctor McCoy had insisted that providing guns was a terrible idea. But Kirk had made a promise to a friend, and he said that without the guns, his friend's people would be slaughtered. He was the captain, so Scott had manufactured flintlocks according to historical Earth specifications, and the captain took them down to the planet.

Which made him complicit, if providing those weapons had caused a problem of some kind. He had no clue as to what that problem might be, but if James Kirk had returned to Neural in secret, it likely wasn't to sightsee.

"Never mind," he said at last. "Can you tell me anything about his mission?"

The admiral steepled her fingers under her chin. "I shouldn't, no. If Kirk chose not to tell you, he must have had a reason."

"Then why are you telling me at all?"

"Because I'm concerned, Commander Scott. We've had no communication from him. He took civilian transport there and presumably made some sort of arrangement for the journey back. That part, I didn't like, although I understood his decision. Since he's been gone, however, it's been weighing on me. I don't think he took enough people with him, and I don't like the idea that Starfleet can't reach him. I want someone to go to Neural, to back him up or pick him up—preferably the latter. Since you have made it very clear that you're not going to stop rattling cages until you know where he is, I thought that perhaps you'd like to be part of that mission."

"Admiral Kučera," Scott said, a smile spreading slowly across his face, "try and stop me."

Uhura and Chekov were on the *Enterprise* bridge, but they looked up when Scott entered from the turbolift. "That's a wery big smile," Chekov observed.

"I suppose it must be."

"Is something funny?"

"I wouldn't say that."

"It is an unusually broad smile, Scotty," Uhura pointed out. "Even for you. Is there news about the admiral?"

Scott nodded. "Aye. You two need to pack your bags," he said. "We'll be taking a wee trip."

# Thirteen

The search party gathered at the gate shortly before the sunrise. Kirk, Rowland, and Burch were there, as was Meena, who told the others their belief that Nyran had intentionally left the fields, rather than being a victim of the attack. The overall plan didn't change—the party would begin their search in Providence Valley, at the field where Nyran had last been seen, and would look for tracks or any other clues as to where he might have gone, whether of his own free will, or taken by force.

The trek into the valley was considerably more subdued than the last. Conversation was hushed; nobody laughed or sang. Their mission was a serious one, with a potentially grim outcome, and while the Freeholders claimed optimism, none engaged in small talk.

By the time they arrived, the sun had cleared the hills and the valley gleamed with brilliant clarity. Kirk looked at the green fields, the meandering river, once more struck by how lovely the view was, a pastoral scene like something out of Earth's long-ago. He knew that although ancient times on Earth had been dangerous times, with the exception of a few major wars that killed millions, the chances that anyone on Earth would die from an act of violence had fallen, century by century. The planet was largely at peace now, and violent death rarer than ever.

Neural, though, had far to go to reach that state, if it ever would. With its population pushed toward ever more bloodshed by the interference of Klingons and Federation alike, Kirk worried that the idyllic scenery would be replaced by ever gorier battlefields.

Arriving in the valley, the twenty members of the search party fanned out, looking for any sign of the boy. Blood still darkened the earth where some had fallen. Plump fruit weighed heavily on limbs, left there by the harvesters when the Victors had attacked.

Nyran was not there. Searchers checked every row, looked under bushes, even walked down to the slow-moving river and waded across. The flow was not strong enough here to carry a body far, but they searched in both directions for a time.

Finally, a shout of discovery went up. Kirk ran to the edge of the field, farthest from Freehold and from where the Victors had attacked, where a woman was calling out and waving. Several others reached her at the same time.

"What is it?" someone asked.

"Tracks," she said, pointing out distinct footprints in the soft dirt. "Look, they lead off toward the hills."

"They could be anybody's," Burch suggested.

"Nobody else went that way. We were all focused on the harvest, until the attack. And then we went the other way, toward the slavers."

"She's right," Kirk said. "These tracks weren't made by somebody running. Walking fast, possibly—trying to get away without being seen." He pointed toward a stand of trees a dozen yards away. "He only had to reach those, and then he'd have been almost impossible to see from here."

"Why would he have done that?" Turan asked. He was one of the Hill People Kirk had known on his first trip, an older man with stooped shoulders, his platinum locks going gray. He was still strong, with unflagging energy that Kirk admired.

"Nyran has always had his own mind," Elanna said. "Even as an infant, he had ideas I could not comprehend. Whatever he did, he had his reasons."

"Let's see where he went from there," Kirk said. "Maybe we can figure out what those reasons were."

The trees offered no clues as to Nyran's goal or his destination, but the searchers found his signs: footprints and snapped twigs and crushed grass, a thread caught on a thorn in one spot, a tumble of rocks in another, their long-buried undersides turned toward the sky by a mislaid foot. Nyran's trail led out of the valley, across another, and up the thickly forested slope of a tall mountain.

The search party was drawn out in a line, those in front studying the ground for any further trace of the boy, those behind alert for the various dangers the forests of Neural held, while also watching for anything missed by those ahead. Kirk was near the front, Rowland midway back, Burch bringing up the rear. The admiral glanced back and saw her, wary as ever, constantly scanning the trees in every direction.

But when the *mugatos* attacked, they took everyone by surprise.

There were two of them, one slightly more massive, with arms like tree trunks and powerful legs and a roar that echoed up and down the mountainside. That one came first, charging at the front of the search party. Guns were raised, but the beast attacked too quickly, and the couple of shots fired went well wide of their target. During the chaos of the attack, when everyone was focused on the *mugato* at the front, the other struck from behind, approaching with such unexpected quiet that even the ever-wary Burch was caught off guard.

As if recognizing the greatest threat, the creature went for her first.

Kirk's attention was on the larger of the two. He swung the rifle by its barrel, and its stock crashed into the thing's jaw. Blood and teeth and spittle streamed from its mouth, and the *mugato* turned toward him with a startled growl. As it advanced on Kirk, Rowland and Meena both opened fire. Their shots were loud and filled the air with acrid smoke, and the beast took a couple of steps back, blood blooming on its white fur like red roses in springtime. Behind him, Kirk heard screams and shouts and more gunfire, but he didn't dare look back. The *mugato* shook off the impact of the two rounds and charged again.

This time Kirk had his rifle at the ready. He fired, levered another round into the chamber, and fired again. The bullets slammed home, but still the creature came, arms out, clawed hands raking empty air. It came near enough that Kirk could smell its hot, foul breath, the rank muskiness of its body. He squeezed the trigger again, but the weapon only clicked, empty.

He braced for the assault, knowing nothing could break the *mugato*'s momentum now. Its last couple of steps were an awkward half-shuffle, and then it was falling onto Kirk, as inevitable as the toppling of a redwood tree sawed off at its base.

Kirk was immersed in fur and stink and hot, acidic saliva dripping onto him and burning his flesh where it landed. He felt the beast breathe its last and slump atop him, dead weight, the only life left in it coming from the insects infesting its fur. Kirk tried to shove it aside, but it was too heavy and he couldn't get any leverage. He couldn't see anything but dirty white fur, but he heard voices, slightly muffled, and then he felt the weight lifting. He was able to get his arms underneath the thing and help push it away, enough that he could roll out from underneath.

He found his feet, but he was drenched in the *mugato*'s blood and spit, and he felt like he was on fire everyplace the thing's fluids had touched his skin. He took a few deep breaths, sucking in fresh air to clear away the stench of the creature. The beast had a fresh, gaping wound on its back, not something that had been done to it today, but it hadn't been there long; the damaged flesh around the cut was still red and raw.

Remembering the second one, Kirk spun around. That *mugato* was dead as well, lying on its back, arms and legs splayed out to the sides. Freeholders were gathered around it, blocking his view. But Elanna saw him looking, and so did Tyree, and they parted, making way for Kirk.

That was when he saw Rowland, on his knees. Rowland looked up, locked gazes with Kirk. There were tears in his eyes. He shook his head, made a shooing motion, trying to steer Kirk away.

But Kirk was the commanding officer on this mission. He had a responsibility to his crew, small as it was. And he couldn't see Burch anywhere.

He managed to keep himself from running the short distance, but his stride was quick and determined. Breaking through those gathered around the *mugato*, he saw her, facedown on the ground behind the creature. It had got its claws into her. "Admiral," Rowland said, choking back a sob. "Don't look."

"I'm sorry, James," Tyree said, putting a hand on Kirk's back.

"A *Kahn-ut-tu* . . ." Kirk began.

"Could not help her now," Tyree finished. "It is not just the venom."

He was right, and Kirk had known it before he even raised the possibility—a desperate hope, not a realistic one. Her head was torn almost from her body, and massive claws had ripped her back open to the spine. No medicine on this world could heal those wounds; even a starship's doctor would be hard-pressed, with a fully equipped sickbay.

"It took us all by surprise," Elanna said. She looked stricken, her eyes still wide with terror, tears streaking her dirty cheeks. "We were watching the one you fought and this one came at us from behind." She nodded toward a young man Kirk knew, one of Tyree's closest friends. He sat on the ground as another Freeholder packed a bleeding chest wound with leaves. "Burch saved Yutan—the *mugato* would have killed him, had she not come between them. But no one could reach them in time to save her."

Rowland rose uneasily to his feet and approached Kirk. "I shoulda been able to do somethin'," he said. "I let her down."

"You were shooting the *mugato* up front," Kirk said. "I saw you."

"I know. But when I realized you had it under control, I ran back to help Burch. Only . . . well, I was too damn late."

"Under control?" Kirk might have laughed, had

the circumstances been different. "The thing landed right on top of me."

"You always come out ahead, Admiral Kirk. I don't know how you do it, but you do."

"I always have," Kirk said. "And I probably always will, until the day I don't."

"I'm glad this wasn't that day, then."

Kirk looked at the sun, high in the sky. "The day's a long way from over."

Nyran slept only fitfully. He woke once to the sound of feet, or paws, stepping carefully on the ground outside. He heard huffing breaths and soft snorting sounds. Not the *mugatos* that had chased him earlier, but maybe *anayla* or *scorids*; both man-eaters. Nyran sat in the darkened house, watching the doorway and hoping whatever animal passed by outside couldn't smell his fear.

The night lasted forever. Finally, he dozed off as the sun was rising, and by the time he awoke again full daylight had come, washing the little settlement with brilliant gold. He was hungry, but couldn't find anything to eat in the house, and he had lost his own provisions during the chase.

The house had two rooms, the big front one in which he had slept, and a smaller one off it, through a doorway hung with animal skins. There were two sleeping mats in that second room, one larger than the other. Nyran guessed the smaller one had belonged to Joslen. Around the smaller mat, he found a couple of dolls made from sticks and scraps of fabric; playthings Joslen was too old for but had probably been too sentimental to abandon. She had left behind other things, too, as she'd told him. Clothing was folded neatly and stacked beside the mat, almost as if she might return at any moment. On top of the stack was a shard of mirrored glass, its edges wrapped in hide so they wouldn't cut.

What he didn't find was her pot. She had said it was a ruddy red color on the bottom, sky blue around the rim, and about the height of both her hands put together. It did not seem like something that would be hard to spot, but he turned in a circle, scanning the whole room, and didn't see it.

Back in the big room, he walked slowly, eyeing every surface. Finally, he saw it, mixed in with the cooking pots on a rough-hewn shelf. He rushed to it and picked it up. He hadn't been convinced by Joslen's story about it—it was, after all, just a thing of clay. But when he lifted it he felt something, almost a vibration, an intimation of power he could not deny.

It was no wonder she wanted the thing; the only surprise was that she had left without it in the first place. She had told him there wasn't much notice—the town's elders had made the decision to go, and they left that same day. The panic must have been palpable, urgency preventing her from thinking straight.

He put it in the leather pouch that had started the trip with his pilfered fruits. He needed to get out of Rocky Bluff. He needed to find something to eat and then get back to Joslen, before he broke the pot or did something else foolish. Coming here had been foolish enough, or so he had thought at the time. Now that he actually had the pot, he felt accomplished, even proud. Maybe he had done something right, something she would appreciate.

All he had to do was live long enough to show her.

He was almost back to where he had encountered the *mugatos* when Nyran heard shouts, roars, and the familiar crack of rifles. His first instinct was to drop to the ground, to try to become invisible until the sounds had faded. But he thought better of that. The animal sounds he heard could hardly be anything but *mugatos*. But the other sounds meant the *mugatos* were battling with people. He needed to get close enough to find out if those people were Freeholders, Victors, or somebody else. If they were Freeholders, and they had weapons, the battle would likely be brief, and he could show himself to them. If they were Victors, he would stay out of sight until they were gone.

He made his way down the slope, veering off the path and taking to the woods, where he could keep trees between himself and whoever was down below. The sounds of battle grew in intensity as he neared;

Nyran could hear individual voices crying out, but he could not yet understand the words.

Then, even before he could see anyone, the fight was over. Voices were still raised, but now in wails of sorrow rather than the heat of combat. Nyran could almost see them. He eased his way nearer, moving quickly and quietly from one tree to the next. Soon he could make out figures, and then details. They *were* Freeholders!

When he heard his mother's voice, he broke into a run.

Kirk and Rowland were using hands, rifle stocks, and knives to carve a shallow depression in the ground. Freeholders were gathering rocks from the forest floor. They didn't have a shovel with them, and Burch's body was too damaged to be moved. They would leave her here, covered with stones to keep her safe, until the *Captain Cook* was back within transporter range.

Two graves, now.

Only Giancarlo Rowland and himself left. Rowland had said they needed to bring the other two along for security, to ensure Kirk's safety. Hay and Burch had given their lives in defense of people they didn't know, and the concept Kirk could only sum up as personal liberty.

An honorable sacrifice. But he wished those sacrifices had not been made. Liberty was the birthright of beings everywhere. Too many times, however, someone had to die for that right to be protected.

If he and Rowland were to die, as well, would their efforts here have amounted to anything? Would Starfleet just close the books on this mission, write it off as another one of Jim Kirk's wild ideas? He had violated regulations the last time he'd been to Neural, and he had involved himself in a nascent war. This time he had cleared the mission with Command, but that clearance was given reluctantly, and only after Kirk had made it clear that he would make the trip with or without permission.

There was another alternative. He didn't have to die here soon, but he could still die here. There were worse places in the galaxy. Here, he had friends, clean air, fresh water, and natural beauty all around. Kirk thought, given time, he could find love, if not with Meena, then with someone else. Over the course of his Starfleet career, he had visited many places, and a small handful of planets he had given momentary thought to settling down on. Always, though, the pull of exploration had been stronger. He had accepted a five-year mission and he'd had to complete it, even as he filed those few planets in the back of his mind for later consideration.

Neural had always been near the top of his list. Although he had worried about the growing hostilities between the Hill People and the Villagers, he had liked the friends he'd made. The prospect of a simpler life, in tune with nature, marked by hard work and honest pleasures, was an appealing one.

He stepped away from the digging for a moment to catch his breath. The struggle with the *mugato* had taken a toll. The weight of the thing had knocked the wind out of him. Burch's death had compounded the damage, making it emotional as well as physical.

"You okay, Admiral?" Rowland asked.

"Yes, fine. I just need a second."

As he stood back, eyeballing the depression to determine whether it was deep enough, he heard the sound of footsteps coming through the trees. There were people gathering stones, but these sounded different: a little farther away, and more deliberate. Another *mugato,* or some other creature? He bent over, trying to appear casual, and picked up his rifle. The stock had been splintered, but it would still fire.

Then a young man broke from the trees, calling, "Mother! Mother, it's me!" Elanna shrieked, threw out her arms, and ran to him. They met and embraced, and although he was a teenager, as willfully independent as that age ever is, in that moment, wrapped in his mother's arms, he looked to Kirk like the boy he had once been, frightened, relieved, and feeling safe.

# Fourteen

The other Freeholders gathered around Elanna and Nyran. With everyone jabbering at once, Kirk couldn't make out all that was said, but he heard the boy apologizing profusely for having worried his mother and the rest of the townsfolk, and for causing them to send a search party out looking for him. Elanna seemed to forgive him immediately, which was no surprise. Kirk was not in such a forgiving mood. The boy's thoughtless escapade had cost a good officer her life. Kirk wouldn't harbor a grudge, but at the moment he was none too happy with Nyran.

Heading back across the two valleys toward Freehold, though, Kirk's thoughts wandered in a different direction. He took Rowland aside and caught Tyree's attention. The three of them brought up the rear of the pack. "I've been thinking," Kirk said. "About that mine."

"What about it?" Rowland asked.

"I can't help thinking it's the key to all this."

"All what?" Tyree inquired.

"The weapons the Victors have, always slightly more advanced than what you've got. Their increased aggression. Taking more slaves, consolidating whole populations within their growing city."

"How does the mine connect to that?" Rowland asked. "I mean, I understand they're takin' laborers to work in it. But the weapons?"

Kirk had wrestled with how much he should reveal to Tyree since he had arrived here. But the man understood that he was from somewhere else, somewhere beyond the sky. Letting him know that there were other races out there, some not so friendly, might be a violation of the Prime Directive, but that directive had largely been torn to shreds and tossed to the winds. If Klingons threatened Tyree's people—even indirectly, through their puppets in the city called Victory—he had a right to know.

And Kirk couldn't get the final confirmation he needed without Tyree's help.

"The Victors have, I believe, teamed up with a race of beings called Klingons. They're an aggressive, violent people, intent on spreading their empire as far and fast as they can, and they don't care who gets in their way. The actions of the Victors, these past few years, are in line with how the Klingons do things. I think there's something here on Neural that they want—some kind of mineral, presumably. They're using local labor to extract it. Their home has always been resource-poor. That's part of what drives the perpetual effort to expand their empire, in addition to their tendency to want to conquer whatever they see."

"What could it be?" Tyree asked. "This mineral you say these people want?"

"I don't know," Kirk said. He almost heard Bones's voice in his head as he continued. "I'm not a geologist, I'm a . . ." He paused, realizing that he'd been about to finish the sentence with, "I'm a starship captain."

He wasn't, though. Not anymore. But on the bridge of a starship was where he belonged. He knew that, suddenly and with absolute clarity. He couldn't stay on Neural, any more than he could remain parked behind a desk at Starfleet headquarters. He belonged in the captain's chair.

"Never mind," he finished. "There's only one way to find out for sure if I'm right."

"What's that, Admiral?" Rowland asked.

"I've got to get inside Victory," Kirk said. "There's no way to be sure from the outside."

"I'll go with you," Rowland offered.

"As will I," Tyree said.

"Not you, Tyree. Too many people there know you, and you're too important to your people to risk it. But nobody there knows me. The number of people in the galaxy who even know I'm on this planet, besides you and your fellow Freeholders, I can count on one hand."

"But, James—" Tyree began.

Rowland cut him off. "Don't bother, Tyree. When Admiral Kirk makes up his mind about somethin', he's stubborn as a mule. Well, I guess you don't know what a mule is. But it's just about the most stubborn animal we've got, back home."

"I have observed that, about our friend," Tyree said. "Very well, James. You and Rowland, then. But I will keep an eye on you, as much as I can from outside."

"Fair enough," Kirk said. "Sounds like a plan."

"Do not do it, James. The danger is too great."

He was sitting with Meena on a bench in Freehold's central plaza. An intermittent breeze carried gray smoke rich with the smell of roasting meat from a nearby fire pit. With Nyran's safe return, the mood of the town had lightened somewhat. Freeholders had lost loved ones over the past few days, and those losses weighed heavily, but Kirk had seen that they accepted the inevitability of mortality. They grieved, they mourned the loss, but they refused to let it define them or cripple them with sadness. They turned to one another, survivor to survivor, and the sturdy fabric of their society bolstered their spirits. There was also talk of revenge, which concerned Kirk, because it would only perpetuate the cycle.

"There's danger everywhere, Meena," Kirk reminded her. "I've lost two of my people already. If

I can't get the answers I need, the danger will never cease, for any of us."

"I do not understand how risking your own life will lessen the threat to the rest of us."

"I . . . wish I could tell you more. Wish I could tell you everything. About me, where I come from. What I'm doing here. But I can't."

She had been looking at him, but now she turned away. He studied the curve of her neck and shoulder as she gazed toward the fire. "Why not?"

"There are . . . rules . . . that govern how much I can say." Tyree already knew more than he should, but he had held that information close. Kirk didn't dare make matters worse by telling anyone else.

"Whose rules?"

"I can't tell you that, either. They are wise rules, and as difficult as it sometimes is, it's better for everyone involved if I obey them."

She turned to face him again, and he saw uncharacteristic anger flash in her eyes. "Better for you."

"Not always better for me, no. I didn't come here to change Freehold, Meena. I came to fix my past mistakes, if I could. To help protect you and your people from a danger that you can't even know about. But your people, your society . . . those things have to be allowed to grow, to evolve, with as little interference from outside as possible."

"And that is where you come from? Outside?"

"That's as good a word for it as any."

"I would like to know this outside," Meena said. She put a hand on Kirk's leg, just above the knee. It felt good there. Right. He liked its warmth, and the firm, confident pressure of her squeeze. "I would like to know you."

"I would like that, too. Very much. But I can't stay here, Meena. It's a beautiful place, and you're a beautiful woman. I like being with you. I like the Hill People. But I can't stay much longer."

"How long?" She didn't move the hand, didn't let up on the pressure. He didn't entirely want her to.

Kirk calculated the days until the *Captain Cook* returned, at the end of the two-week window. The days were shorter on Neural, so it wasn't a direct comparison. "I don't know. Tomorrow, I'll go to Victory. What I find there might affect how long I stay. If I find the answers I need right away, then I'll be here for another week, perhaps."

"And if you do not?"

Then Grumm would make another flyby in another week. At some point, however, the *Captain Cook* would have to leave the vicinity, and Kirk would either be on it or he'd be stranded. "Then I'll stay a while longer," he said at last. "But not much longer. I have . . . other obligations."

"A family?" Meena asked. "A woman?"

"There have been women," Kirk replied. "But no, there's no one I have to get back to. Not like that."

"What, then?"

"Again, things I can't tell you about. Duty. A job that needs doing."

"You are an honorable man."

"I try."

"No." Now she took her hand off his knee and pressed it to his cheek. Her palm was rough, a working woman's hand, but her touch was gentle. "You are. And I think . . . I think even if you cannot stay for long, for one night, at least, I would like to be with an honorable man."

"As long as you understand—"

"I understand perfectly well, James. I am honorable, too, in my way. If I do not offend—"

"Not at all."

She rose from the bench, took Kirk's hand, and tugged him to his feet. "Then come with me. My home is not far. We will be honorable together."

"All right," Kirk said, letting her take the lead. "Together is good."

When they neared the gate into Freehold, Joslen darted out and ran straight into Nyran's arms. She squeezed him so tightly he was afraid she might rupture something, and she pelted him with kisses. He knew his mother was watching, and he blushed, but at the same time, he enjoyed her welcome so much, he thought going away more often might be a good idea.

Later, they sat on the floor of the home she shared

with her father. It was a tiny place, even compared to what she'd had in Rocky Bluff. Joslen slept in the front room, surrounded by the few belongings they had brought with them, plus the pots and cooking utensils they had acquired here. Her father's room was in back, and he had not left it since he'd become gravely ill. It was left to Joslen to feed him, breaking his food into tiny bites and helping him chew it. The girl was nurse, caretaker, and servant to a man who was conscious only for moments, sometimes with days in between. He had been a big man, stout and strong, but illness had wasted him away. The stench of it wafted into the front room, and Nyran sat near the door, to get as much fresh air as he could. Joslen was accustomed to it, she told him, and hardly noticed it.

Nyran pulled the pot from his pouch and held it toward her. "Is this it, Joslen? The one you wanted?"

Her face answered before words did. "Yes! Yes, that's it! You really did it? You really went all the way there by yourself?"

"I had to."

"But it's so far. And dangerous."

"I did have to stab a *mugato*."

Joslen's mouth dropped open, forming a perfect O. "You *didn't*!"

"There were two of them—the same two the search party killed today. I saw my knife wound on the back of one of them."

"And you fought them alone?" She plopped down beside him, took the pot from his hands, and kissed him full on the mouth, a long, lingering kiss. He would, he thought, be tasting it for days. "You are my hero, Nyran."

Pride filled him almost to bursting. To change the subject, he asked, "Can you cure him? With the pot?"

"I do not know. My mother said it had healing properties." She looked inside. "The roots and herbs are still here, but I am not sure how to use them. I will ask it, though."

"Ask it?"

"It speaks to me. I told you that! In my mother's voice. This is how I remember how she sounded." She looked inside.

"Right," Nyran said. "You did tell me." He hadn't heard the thing speak the whole time he'd carried it, but then, he hadn't known Joslen's mother, nor had he asked it any questions. "Is it magic, then?"

"She said no. She was *Kahn-ut-tu,* and she said everything she did came from nature, not magic. Sometimes, she said, it looks like magic, but only to those who do not understand."

Nyran didn't see the difference. There was nothing to be gained from arguing with her, though. And so much to lose.

"You should go, Nyran," she said.

"Go?"

"I have to try to heal my father. It might take a

long time. It might be unpleasant. I would rather be alone. Do you understand?"

He didn't, not really. "I suppose . . ."

"I love you," she said. "You were so brave, to do this. To get this for me. I do not deserve such courage expended on my behalf, but I appreciate it."

"You do," Nyran said. "Of course you deserve it."

"No. I am a simple girl, and you are a great hero."

"Not so great."

"Great, to me. And soon enough, to everyone. I have no doubt of this." She kissed him again. "Go, now. I will come to you when it's done."

Nyran left the little house, the imprint of her kisses still felt upon his lips. He had her scent on him, too, so much sweeter than the sick odor of the rooms. He didn't know if he was in love, but thought he might be.

He was thrilled by her praise, by the evident pride she took in him. He was proud of himself, for making the trip, finding the right pot, surviving the elements.

As he walked home through dark roads, though, another thought came to him, carrying its own weight of conflicting emotions. He had come back to Freehold because Joslen was here, and because the point of his journey had been to fetch her pot.

But as much as he liked Joslen, he had discovered something else. As he had always known, there was a big, wide world outside Freehold's walls. That world held the promise of adventure, of new vistas around every bend, of discovery and danger and excitement. Having seen it—having tested his own courage, and found it adequate to the task—could he be happy, remaining here inside walls thrown up against an omnipresent threat?

He didn't believe he could. He had tasted the world and found it suited him. He would rather see it with Joslen than without her, if he could, but someday—someday *soon*—he would have to go back out into it.

That time, Nyran doubted that he would return.

# Fifteen

Kirk and Rowland left Freehold before first light. They carried lever-action rifles and followed the path they had taken before. Once the sun lit their way, Kirk recognized landmarks: an igloo-shaped boulder the size of a house; a tree with three trunks emerging from the same root ball; markings made by water running down the side of a cliff, over what must have been eons, that had etched a scene that looked to him like a forest growing upside-down, rooted in the sky, with a canopy that pressed against the earth. These assured him they were on the right path.

Twice, they had to leave the trail and hide amidst the trees, while parties of Victors passed by.

"What do you expect to find there, sir?" Rowland asked at one point. "In Victory?"

"I'm trying to keep an open mind," Kirk said. "I was there briefly, on my last visit to Neural. Bones—Doctor McCoy—and I went in with Tyree, at night. McCoy and I found a forge, and some gun barrels, none of it of local manufacture. It was obvious then that the Villagers, as they were called, had help from some more advanced civilization. Then one of the Villagers walked in, with a Klingon. We knocked them out and got away fast. I'm not sure I'd recognize either of them if I saw them now, or that they would recognize me.

"So this time, I don't know what we'll find, but if it's evidence of a Klingon presence, I want to be able to take it back to the Federation, or at least to detail it as thoroughly as possible, to prove they're violating the treaty. Neural won't be able to evolve at its natural pace as long as the people here are being used by Klingons."

"You don't like them at all, do you? Klingons, sir."

"Never had any use for them," Kirk said. "There are probably some good ones—every group has good and bad, right? But I'm not sure I've ever met one I'd trust for an instant."

"I've never met one at all."

Kirk regarded the lanky young man. They were picking their way down a dry creek bed, which cut an easier path along a steep slope than the alternative, littered with loose stones and sharp drop-offs. "You haven't missed much, Giancarlo. If you don't meet any on this trip, I'm sure that'll be fine with Shonna, too."

"Yes, sir."

"You miss her?"

"Of course."

"Let's get this done, then. Sooner we finish, the sooner you'll be home."

"Do you really think we'll make it home, Admiral?"

"Of course. Don't you?"

"I don't know. I mean, Hay and Burch were trained security officers, and look what happened to them."

"I regret that more than I can say. But it doesn't have any bearing on our chances."

"Maybe not," Rowland said. He stepped around a large rock in the streambed, which had rolled a little when he'd tested it with his foot.

Rowland, descending a few feet ahead of Kirk, tried another stone. It too rolled down the slope when the weight of his foot released it from his moorings. "Do you know what the 'angle of repose' is, Admiral Kirk?"

"I've heard the phrase," Kirk replied. "Climbers and mountaineers use it sometimes. But I'm not sure I know the dictionary definition."

"It's an engineering term. That's what I studied at the Academy, sir, geophysical and astrophysical. It describes the angle at which soil settles instead of slippin', or the maximum angle at which an object can rest on an incline without slidin' down." Rowland crouched down and held a rounded stone against the creek bed. "See this rock? Well, it's too steep here." He released the stone, and it tumbled down the bed. He moved forward a couple of feet, to a spot where the angle lessened, and picked up the same stone. "But look here." When he released it this time, it stayed put. "Here, it's at its angle of repose. It won't go down on its own. That's a rough example, and the angle isn't precise—it could be that another couple of degrees wouldn't make a difference. But that's the gist of it."

"It's interesting, but what does it have to do with our present circumstances?"

"I was just wonderin'," Rowland said. "Have we passed that angle? I don't mean this hill, I mean on our mission here. Are we already unmoored, and just gonna go crashin' down a slope that necessarily ends in our deaths? Or are we still stable on the slope?"

"I guess we can't know that," Kirk said. "Until we start sliding, or we don't."

"That's what bothers me, sir. Not knowin'."

Kirk reminded himself that Rowland had not seen any real action before this assignment, and this was clearly not the kind of thing he'd expected when he signed on as an admiral's flag aide. "At best," he said, "we can only engage in somewhat informed speculation about anything that hasn't happened yet, in any area of life. This one is no more certain—or uncertain—than any other. I understand that the stakes seem particularly high, especially given what happened to Burch and Hay. But I assure you, I've been in plenty of equally dangerous situations, and worse. And I'm still here to tell about it."

Rowland kicked a stone—one that had apparently settled at its angle of repose, since it was not rolling or sliding anywhere—and it skittered into the thick grass at the edge of the creek bed. "Thank you, Admiral Kirk," he said. "It's good to know that."

"You're welcome. And Rowland? It might not fly at headquarters, but for the duration of this mission, you're welcome to call me Jim."

Rowland broke into the first smile Kirk had seen on him in days. "Well, I appreciate that, Admiral Kirk. I truly do."

A scant few years earlier, Victory had been a sleepy village. Its architecture had reminded Kirk of pictures he'd seen of early California, during the days when Spanish missionaries, backed up by Spanish muskets, had built settlements that resembled, at least in the broad strokes, those they had left behind on another continent.

Now, Victory was well on its way to being an actual city, and an industrial one at that. The buildings were still crude, mostly constructed of stone and timbers and mortar. But they were numerous, and sprawling far beyond the original village's footprint. They were arrayed on roads paved with stones, the hard edges of which had not yet been worn down by the passage of feet and weather and time. They were gray, but whether by natural coloration or from caked-on soot deposited by the billows of smoke from the smelter stacks, Kirk couldn't say. Some of the houses had glass windows. Most had chimneys, but the day was warm and those chimneys did not add to the haze overhead. Electric lights showed in some windows, but more were lit by candles or oil lamps.

There were no guards at the city's edge, no soldiers or fortifications of any kind. There was only the valley and the open, grassy plain, and then a bare, rocky stretch where the grass had given up, and then a low stone wall surrounding the first of the buildings. These were not homes, but places with obvious functions: storehouses, a slaughterhouse surrounded by animals Kirk had never seen gathered in fenced pens, a couple of factories, one with wooden furniture piled high in an open doorway and another one churning out what looked like rifle barrels, though he only got a glimpse inside. He and Rowland walked past quickly, aware that their clothing was all wrong, that if they were spotted they'd be immediately apprehended or killed.

When they saw someone coming their way, they ducked into an alley between a pair of large, two-story buildings of indeterminate nature. On the other side of the alley, they spotted the first structure that was recognizably a residence. It was much smaller, a single story, encircled by a waist-high adobe wall. Behind it, a fenced yard contained a couple of animals like the ones they'd seen back at the slaughterhouse, about the size of sheep but with leathery skin, pushed-in faces, and six legs.

"Those are sure some ugly beasts, sir," Rowland said.

Kirk couldn't argue. He simply nodded. "I don't want to terrorize anyone," he said. "But if an adult male lives there, we might be able to find some more suitable attire."

"We show up looking like we do, we'll terrorize somebody for sure," Rowland replied. "I'm guessin' they don't have any guards posted because they don't expect anybody'd be stupid enough to come into town on purpose."

"That's how I read it, too. The Freeholders stay far away. Anyone else who's been victimized or enslaved by them would do the same. Unless they could band together in a considerably larger force, the Victors don't need to worry about an attack from outside. They've probably got their resources marshaled around the mine, to make sure the laborers don't escape."

"You think we should go for it?"

"Maybe no one's home," Kirk said. "That'd make it easier."

"We can hope," Rowland said.

When they were sure the roadway was clear, they darted out of the alley and across to the house. Vaulting over the wall, they reached the front door simultaneously. Kirk stepped back and let Rowland go first, raising his weapon to cover the younger man. Rowland worked the latch on the door, and it opened easily. He went inside. Kirk followed, closing the door behind him. In a front room they both froze, listening. After a few moments, they heard a voice.

"Who's out there?" it called. It sounded like a man, and his tone was challenging, angry, maybe a little scared but not very. The voice was followed by heavy footfalls from farther back in the house.

"Hello, sir," Kirk said. "We are not here to hurt you, or anybody. We are armed, but only for our own protection."

"Who are you?" the voice demanded. The footsteps came closer, and then a man heaved into view in the room's far doorway. He was enormous, filling the space and then some, a good head taller than Kirk, at least, and probably weighing in at more than three hundred pounds.

Kirk leveled his rifle at the man, though he appeared to be unarmed. He caught Rowland's eye briefly, then returned his full attention to the big man. "This is your home?" he asked.

"It is. Again, who are you? What do you want? You look like Hill People."

"We are dressed like them, that's true. But we are not from . . . anywhere around here. Actually, that's why we've come, and I have to apologize for barging in, and for the weapons. I'm sure you understand, dressed as we are, why we have to take certain precautions."

"I understand that if you did not have those weapons, I would be heaving your carcasses out my door right now."

"That may well be true," Kirk said, trying to maintain an even tone. "But we do. So tell me . . . is there, perhaps, an adult male smaller than you living here? We're in need of clothing, but I doubt that yours would work."

The man barked a surprised laugh. "You little men? You could wear my wife's clothing, perhaps. Or my son's."

"How big is your son?"

The man held his hands about eighteen inches apart. "He is a baby." He started laughing, then wheezing, red-faced, tears rolling down his cheeks.

"Admiral, I don't think we're gettin' anywhere here," Rowland said.

Kirk couldn't disagree. "Sir, we don't mean any harm. To you or your city. I know you have only my word on that, but it's true. I don't want to hurt you, but I can't have you alerting anyone about our presence here. And we still need a change of clothes. Do you have any suggestions?"

The man wiped his eyes with his massive fingers and struggled to bring his laughter under control. Kirk didn't think he remembered anyone facing two armed strangers ever having such a response. The man waved a hand toward the side of the house. "There," he said. "That house. Two men live there.

Small ones, like you. They are never home during the day. You will find clothing inside."

"Thank you," Kirk said. He eyeballed the big man. He had watched Spock render people unconscious with a Vulcan nerve pinch, dozens of times. But he had never been able to fully master it himself, despite Spock's lessons, and he wasn't sure he could get the right angle on this guy. And even if he could, whether he could get through the man's protective layers to reach his nerves. "When will your wife be home?"

"Three hours. Four, maybe."

"Tie him up, Mister Rowland. Make it tight, but not painfully so. I'll go next door and see about finding us something to wear."

Soon, dressed in baggy clothes with a texture resembling that of burlap bags and about as comfortable, Kirk and Rowland made their way toward the center of the city. They still carried the rifles, but as many of the Victors they saw were armed as not, so that didn't make them stand out. Their Freehold clothing was stuffed in a leather pouch draped across Rowland's chest. They had left the big man in his house, where his wife would find him when she came home. That gave them a few hours to get a look at Victory—more if, as he'd promised, he didn't raise an alarm. Kirk didn't trust that, however. The man had apparently not seen them as threats, but that didn't mean he would stake his city's safety on that impression.

"I sure hope we learn somethin' here, sir," Rowland said. "Because I got a feelin' there's gonna be some bad chafing before the day's out."

"I know what you mean," Kirk agreed. "If I had to wear these all the time, I'd be grumpy too."

After they crossed a bridge—the river seemed to be a dividing line between neighborhoods primarily comprising single-family dwellings and a more high-density residential-commercial mix—the more crowded the city became. Here, buildings were crammed close together, lining crowded roads. They passed a knot of people standing in the street, arguing with a vendor about the high prices for his meats. Steam rose from covered bins on his cart, wafting the aroma of his wares into the road and making Kirk's mouth water. Others sold produce that looked inferior in every way to that cultivated by the Freeholders; knives and other hand tools and weapons; and various decorative items, including forehead ornaments like those worn by just about every male on Neural, cheek decorations like the women wore, and multicolored metal bracelets that Kirk mostly saw adorning the wrists of small children. Others carried merchandise on their bodies, around their necks, or pinned to long sashes that draped over their shoulders. Shopkeepers stood in open doorways, enticing customers inside with well-rehearsed sales pitches.

"Commercial enterprise seems alive and well here," Kirk observed.

"People are buyin', too," Rowland said. "Guess not every worker is slave labor."

"They might be employed in support of the mines," Kirk said. "Or in trades like construction and retail that boom when the city grows. It's even possible that the Klingons are pumping currency into the economy."

"Why would they do that?"

"We don't know what they want here," Kirk reminded him. "When we do, maybe we'll know why."

Brilliant-hued, rainbow-colored birds lined rooftops and perched on chimneys and windowsills, like pigeons in cities back home. Doglike animals, with white or bright red or forest green fur and small, sharp tusks sprouting from their snouts, wandered the roads, sniffing and relieving themselves wherever they felt the need, scrounging dropped food or clustering around butcher shops and food carts. The smells from those carts and storefronts had to compete with the omnipresent stink of the smelter. The air felt almost gritty from the layer of smoke overhanging the city. And despite the bustle of the city streets, Kirk heard a constant rumble, punctuated by booming sounds that he felt in his teeth. A function of the mining or smelting operation, he supposed.

Past the city's center, the roads became wider, with buildings a little more spread out. This side of town was closer to the mine. As they strolled, trying to appear casual, in that direction, Rowland grabbed Kirk's arm.

"What is it?" Kirk asked.

"It took me a while to figure it out," Rowland said. "But, well, look at those men." He nodded toward a couple of men headed toward them, on the other side of the road. Their clothing looked, at first glance, like what everybody else was wearing—baggy, off-white shirts and pants of some rough, woven material. But as he eyed them, Kirk realized that the embroidered designs on both men were identical. They both wore long knives tucked into their wide leather belts and had rifles slung on their backs, straps cutting diagonals across their chests.

"They're law enforcement," Kirk said. "Or military."

"That's what I'm thinkin'."

Kirk and Rowland made a right turn at the nearest corner, which took them away from the two men. But on this road, there were four more people, wearing the same uniforms, and similarly armed. A couple of these were women. They stood in a casual circle, chatting. A couple of them glanced up at Kirk and Rowland.

Having deliberately turned the corner, the men couldn't change course again without raising suspicions. That understanding passed between them with a quick look, and they kept going, heads down, not staring.

"City guard, I guess," Kirk said softly. "Tyree said they don't have a standing army, as such, but most adults take part in hunting and slaving parties from time to time. They're watching us."

"I know."

"They're curious, but I don't think they have any grounds to approach us. We don't look like criminals, do we?"

"No, sir. Spies, maybe."

Kirk risked a quick peek to make sure there was a smile on Rowland's face.

Nearing the four uniformed guards, they let the conversation cease, so nothing in their accents or tones would reveal them as outsiders. Kirk looked over at the guards once, trying to appear natural, and tossed them a friendly smile. One of the men swiveled and took a step in their direction. Kirk's muscles tensed, ready to fight or run. But before the man moved again, one of his friends caught his shoulder and said something. The man turned back to his colleagues. After a few more words, they all broke into raucous laughter.

"Something's funny," Kirk said.

"Well, I'm just glad it's not us."

They walked to the end of the block without further incident and turned at the next corner, once again headed toward the mine. Along the way, they saw fewer and fewer civilians, and more and more uniformed guards. "There's something in this neighborhood that the Victors want well protected," Kirk said.

"Only thing I see of any value is the mine," Rowland said.

"But is the reason for all the uniforms the mine's commercial value?" Kirk asked. "Or the fact that it's the only thing the Klingons are interested in?"

"You said this used to be a quiet little village."

"That's right."

"Could it have turned into such a developed city so quickly through any natural progression you can imagine?"

"No. It's not just unlikely, it's impossible."

"Then the only logical explanation is that the Klingons helped. We don't know how yet—financially, helped with infrastructure, with planning. It's easy enough to see why—they've subjugated other villages, maybe even other towns and cities bigger than they were to begin with—through the use of the arms the Klingons supplied them but no one else. In order to work the mine that provides the Klingons whatever it is they need, they had to have places to house all the newcomers. They need ways to feed 'em. They need clothes and supplies. You get large, sudden population growth, you gotta have expanded goods and services to support that growth. Without help, it would have been hard, if not impossible, for the Villagers to take over all those other populations, much less grow the city to handle that influx. But with an advanced civilization showin' them how and providin' support, it happened. The city we're in is the proof."

"Circumstantial evidence," Kirk said. "It makes perfect sense, but it's not something the Federation Council can take to the Organians as confirmation of a broken treaty. We need something more concrete."

Rowland pointed toward the high fence cutting across the end of the road. "Well, we're almost at the mine," he said. "Maybe we'll find somethin' there."

The road they traveled dead-ended at the mine. Before the fence was another road, running alongside the fence. It was wide, and appeared little used. Weeds had sprouted between some of the stones. Kirk thought that odd, until they actually reached it and began to cross it. When they did, armed and uniformed guards came toward them from both directions, four from their left and three from their right. They had obviously been stationed at the fence. Along the fence line, Kirk saw more small clutches of them, staggered at irregular distances but never too far apart. No fewer than two in a group, sometimes as many as five or six. They appeared relaxed, as if this was a regular duty station but rarely one requiring any serious effort. Even the ones approaching them were sauntering, not running or marching, and their hands were at their sides instead of clutching their weapons.

"I guess maybe we're not supposed to approach the fence," Kirk said.

"Looks that way."

The mine was tantalizingly close. Kirk could look through the fence and see a wide empty swath of cobblestones between it and the pit itself, like the stretch of dirt on the other side. Across that were the terraced walls he had seen earlier. What he wanted was to get right up to the edge, to look down toward the bottom, and ideally to get a better view of the offices, the supporting infrastructure around the mine, which were off to his right, visible but not in any detail. That's where Klingons would be, if they were here at all. If they were loading ships with processed ore, there would some other kind of haulers, and facilities for the landing and maintenance of spacecraft. Those would be near the mine, but not necessarily adjacent, depending on how secretive the Klingons were about their presence and their capability.

But the guards weren't having it. "Here now!" one of them called. He gestured Kirk and Rowland back toward the far side of the road, and when they didn't immediately comply, he reached for his gun. "Get back! You know you're not to approach the mine."

"Unless you'd like to be put to work in it," another one added.

"We just wanted a quick look," Kirk said, trying to keep his face a mask of innocence. "It's such an impressive sight."

"If we wanted you to see, we'd toss you in."

"Admiral Kirk," Rowland whispered.

"I know," Kirk said softly. "Sorry, didn't mean to cause any trouble," he told the guards. He stopped, raised his hands and shrugged his shoulders to show he'd meant no harm, and started backing up. Rowland followed suit.

"As long as you're here," the man said, "you've got your documents on you, right?"

Kirk and Rowland exchanged glances.

*Documents?*

# Sixteen

"It is a bold plan," Enjara said. "Of course, that is no surprise. Kirk is a bold man. A natural leader."

"You only say that because he saved your life," Kenomo said, laughing.

"Which I appreciate a great deal, since you stood there and did nothing," Enjara shot back.

"It's a stupid plan," Keran said. Nyran was appalled to see that thug sitting with Tyree and other influential citizens of Freehold. The informal gathering was being held in the central plaza, and anyone who was interested could attend. But Keran was from Rocky Bluff, and Nyran's ribs still ached from the last time their paths had crossed. At least the bruises had faded from his face, depriving Keran of a chance to see his handiwork in the flesh.

"Why is it stupid?" Tyree asked.

"Because it *is*. Walking right into the middle of Victory? What can two men hope to accomplish by that?"

"They are unknown there," Meena said. "They seek only information. A larger party would attract attention, and most Hill People would be recognized."

"They hardly know their way around Freehold, much less Victory. They do not know our customs. How hard will it be for someone in Victory to unmask them as spies?"

"Kirk is aware of that possibility," Meena replied. "Yet he chose to go anyway, to risk his own life in hopes of saving ours. We should be appreciative, rather than scornful."

"If he can stop the slavers from preying on our people, I will honor him. If he can make it so we can return to Rocky Bluff, where we belong, I will celebrate him. My fear is that both of them will be caught, and the Victors will hold us all responsible."

Yutan rose suddenly from the log bench he had occupied. "What could they do to us worse than what they already do?" he demanded. "Kill us? They do that with depressing regularity. Enslave us? Even more common. No, my fear is not for what the Victors might do to us, but what they might do to Kirk and Rowland."

"Their fates are no concern to me," Keran said. "Except as they may affect our own."

Nyran wasn't sure what to think. From all he had seen and heard, Kirk and Rowland were good men, courageous and strong. But Keran might have a point—if they were taken prisoner, the Victors might react by increasing the pressure on Freehold.

Yutan was right, too—how much worse could things become? Already the settlement in which he'd grown up had been walled off from the world. The life of freedom he had known as a child was gone, walled off. Elders told the young ones tales about Selanee, the hero from ancient times who had led the people out of confining valleys and into the hills where he could touch the sky, how he sprouted wings and flew like a bird. Birds on the wing, the elders instructed, were the freest of all creatures, not bound to the earth or trapped behind walls. Second to birds were the Hill People, descended directly from Selanee. Sometimes, when a Hill Person saw a bird with a light cap on its head, dark wings, and a ruddy tail, he would point it out to any children nearby and shout, "Selanee watches over us!"

He had been surprised to learn that Joslen didn't know any stories of Selanee. The people of Rocky Bluff told different stories, of different heroes, but none of her tales made any sense to him.

By taking flight, Selanee had been able to soar above enemies, to know their every movement. In that way he had protected the Hill People, allowed them to prosper, to plant crops and hunt animals and live the free life they so coveted.

Remembering that—the example of Selanee, the message implicit in every story told about him—made Nyran realize what he had to do. The adults could argue all day and night about Kirk and Rowland, and their words would make no difference.

They would not help the men who had come here—some said, like Selanee, from the sky—to aid the Hill People.

It would take a hero.

Nyran slipped away from the plaza, and nobody even saw him go.

Tyree had long known that the weight of leadership was enough to make a man's shoulders slump. When it was just his people, it had been trouble enough. Rank had certain privileges, but he was not sure that they were enough to make up for the pains. When two people quarreled, if they could not settle things between themselves, they brought their troubles to him. When the crops failed or the hunt was unsuccessful, the people looked to him for answers. When the people were threatened, they looked to him to keep them safe.

After the Victors had acquired advanced weapons and become ever more warlike, resulting in the various hill and mountain peoples banding together for safety, the new, larger population had continued to turn to him. He had thought that perhaps he could throw off that mantle, or share the burden. Instead, the newcomers, all those who now called themselves Freeholders, expected him to continue in his leadership role. He had seen no choice but to agree, though the rewards of leadership were fewer and the demands ever greater.

Leadership was particularly hard when it required

a clear head. Ever since Nona had been killed, he had grown progressively angrier, vengeful. All he wanted to do was kill Victors. There were times when he was consumed by a red rage that blinded him to all else. He had to tamp it down, had to rein in his emotions for the benefit of others.

Today, the public meeting dragged on and on, seemingly endless. There was much to discuss; the attack on the fields in Providence Valley, the presence of James and Rowland, and the usual, routine issues of everyday life in the overcrowded settlement. Tyree was weary, and hungry, ready for a meal and a drink. Or to forget all else and go to Victory himself, to kill as many as he could.

He had lost the thread of the conversation—some ridiculous complaint about a child throwing his ball against the wall of a neighbor's home—when the Rocky Bluff girl, Joslen, burst into their midst. Her eyes were red; tears slicked her cheeks.

"What is it, girl?" Tyree asked. He was concerned that she'd been weeping, but secretly glad for the interruption. He could ask the complainant to start over, once Joslen's problem had been addressed, and this time he could try to pay attention.

"He's gone!" Joslen said.

"Who?" Meena asked. "Not Nyran?"

"Of course Nyran!" Joslen cried out.

"The boy who fetched your pot?" someone else asked.

"Yes, him."

"Gone where?"

"To Victory," she replied. She wiped her tears with the back of her hand, sniffled once. "He thinks Kirk and Rowland are in danger there. He believes he can keep them safe. I tried to stop him."

"He went by himself?" Tyree asked.

"Yes, by himself. All alone through the forests. All alone, to Victory itself."

"He's a fool," someone else said. "He has always been a headstrong whelp."

"Mind your tongue!" Elanna snapped. "That's my son."

"He went alone to Rocky Bluff, and came back none the worse for it," Kenomo pointed out.

"Why are you sitting here talking about it?" Joslen asked. The tears filled her eyes again, rolling down her cheeks. "Someone needs to go after him!"

Meena rose from her bench and went to the girl. She wrapped her arms around Joslen and drew her close. "Shh," she said. "I know how you feel, Joslen. Believe me, I know the worry that gnaws at your heart."

"Nyran is brave," Joslen said. "More brave, I fear, than he is wise. When he returned with the pot—the pot that cured my father—I called him a hero. He survived the wilderness, and the *mugato*. I fear he now believes himself indestructible. He as much as told me so, when he told me he was going."

"Joslen speaks truth," Elanna said. "Nyran has never feared for his own safety. Even as an infant, he would face danger with a smile. But going alone, into Victory, might be more than even he can withstand."

Tyree pushed himself to his feet, weariness and hunger forgotten. Let someone else deal with the petty squabbles between neighbors. He had promised James that he would not interfere, but he'd made no such pledge regarding Nyran. "We haven't much time if we're to catch the boy before he reaches the lowlands. Who's with me?"

"Me," Enjara said. He rose and stood beside Tyree.

"I'll go," Keran said. "The boy has guts, I'll give him that."

"And me," Meena said. She took a step toward Tyree, but Joslen grabbed her arm.

"No, Meena!" Joslen pleaded. "Stay with me. I need someone. I had thought that I had no friends in Freehold, but now I know that isn't true. I can't bear the thought of losing them all, though."

"He's my son," Elanna said. "I'm going."

After Elanna, a groundswell of volunteers spoke up. Tyree wanted to keep the party small, so it could move fast without drawing attention to itself. With luck, they could catch up to Nyran before he reached Victory. He tapped Gayan and Renaya on the shoulders. They were brother and sister, neither wedded or with children, their parents dead. They were strong, swift of foot, and deadly with rifles or bows. "We six," Tyree said. "We will catch Nyran and bring him safely home."

"Thank you," Joslen said, still clutching Meena's arm. "I do have friends here, I know that now. And I appreciate every one of you."

"We will find him, Joslen," Elanna said to her. "And I will make sure he understands how lucky he is to have a friend like you."

"We are not making wery good time, are we?" Chekov asked. He and Uhura and Scott were gathered in the quarters provided to Uhura for the voyage to Neural.

The ship was the *Potemkin,* a *Constitution*-class starship that had already undergone refitting after she had taken some significant damage. Scott had haunted engineering, making a nuisance of himself, until McCollough, the chief engineer, had told him, in no uncertain terms, that if he didn't stay out of her engine room, he'd be thrown in the brig.

"We're at warp eight, man," Scott replied. "To push her any harder would risk tearin' her apart."

"I'm sure Chekov understands that," Uhura said. She sat on the edge of her bunk. Chekov was slouched in a chair, and Scott leaned against the bulkhead. "He's just frustrated."

"It's a ways to go," Scott reminded them. "You know the reality."

"You are right, Scotty," Chekov said. "And so is

Nyota. The galaxy is wast, and I am frustrated by our progress. Or the lack of it."

"I knew McCollough in the Academy," Scott said. "Not well, but we came up together. She's good, and she's askin' everything she can from the engines. If I had time and tools, I could tweak her a wee bit—"

"It's not your ship, Scotty," Uhura reminded him. "I spoke to Kaysing, the communications officer." Uhura's face was devoid of expression, which told Scott all he needed to know. She was a woman for whom smiling was as natural as breathing. She was worried. "There's still been no communication from Admiral Kirk."

Scott had done all the reassuring he could. He shared their fears. The mission had been so secret that only a handful of people knew about it. Although Kirk was only a rear admiral, he had enough juice that he'd been able to pressure Command not to get in his way.

Now, Command had started to have second thoughts. According to Admiral Kucera, what had sent Kirk back to Neural was an uptick in Klingon activity in the area. He had wanted to check it out, personally. Admiral Kucera had bowed to his request, but the more time passed without any word, the more she worried about the possibility of a Starfleet admiral falling into Klingon hands.

"James Kirk can take care of himself," Scott told Uhura and Chekov. He had used the same words with Admiral Kucera. "Plenty of folks have made the mistake of underestimating him. They rarely do it twice."

"I know that, Scotty," Uhura said. "That doesn't stop me from being anxious."

Scott nodded. "We'll get there," he said again. He only hoped they would get there in time.

# Seventeen

"Documents?" Kirk asked. He patted where his pockets would be, if this outfit had any. He smiled, gave an uneasy chuckle. "Must have left them in my other pants."

The guard stalked toward them. Kirk could feel Rowland tense beside him, coiled, ready to react. The uniformed man glared at them as he advanced, a stern look Kirk could remember seeing on his own father's face a few times.

Those memories weren't happy ones.

The man reached out his right hand—and then burst into laughter. The others with him joined in, all but falling on the ground at the success of the prank.

Kirk forced a laugh and glanced at Rowland to make sure he was doing the same.

"D-doc-documents!" the guard roared. "You are not from here, are you?"

"No," Kirk said. "We're fairly new in town."

The guard stood, hunched over, hands above his knees, trying to catch his breath. His face was flushed. "From where?"

Kirk waved a hand, generally toward the south. He wasn't sure what he was indicating, but he made sure it wasn't Freehold. "That way," he said. "You wouldn't know it."

"New Hope?"

"Past there," Kirk said. "But nearby, yes."

"Lovely country."

"If you like that kind of place, yes."

The guard straightened his spine, and the mirth left his eyes. "Well, newcomers, the mine is off-limits. Unless you'd like to work it. That, I could arrange. Otherwise, keep away."

"Yes, sir," Kirk said. He turned away, trying hard to appear casual. Rowland joined him, and they headed back up the same road they had taken.

Behind them, they heard the laughter start up again. One of the guards said, "Documents!"

When they were out of earshot, Rowland said, "That was . . ."

"I know."

"You don't know what I was going to say."

"It doesn't matter. I agree. It was a lot of things, none of them good."

"But we got away with it."

"Keep walking," Kirk said. "And don't count your chickens . . ."

"Before they hatch," Rowland finished. "We used to say that at home, too."

"I think everybody did."

They covered a couple more blocks, and when they were able to blend in with the city's populace again, Kirk started to relax.

"What now?" Rowland asked. "Doesn't look like we're going to see inside that mine."

"I'm sure the smelter is guarded just as diligently," Kirk said.

"So where do we find Klingons?"

Kirk glanced at the sky. He wanted to get back to Freehold by dark. "I'm not sure we do," he said. "Today, anyway."

"We're runnin' out of time, Admiral."

Kirk cut him off. "Rowland, we have a job to do here, and we're staying until it's finished."

"Aye, aye, sir."

"Come on, let's get out of here. I'd like to get to Freehold before the *mugatos* come out to play."

Having changed back into their Freeholder garb, they started out under a sky piling up with dark clouds. They had just reached the foothills when they heard the *crack* of rifles, followed by a scream.

Kirk froze, listening. "That wasn't far away," he said after a quiet moment.

"Not at all."

"We need to check it out."

"I thought you wanted to get back."

"I do. But there are only two sides to this conflict. If somebody's getting shot at, it's likely that the Freeholders are involved."

"Sir," Rowland said, "it's not our fight. We came here to find out what the Klingons are up to."

"Mister Rowland." Kirk was unexpectedly angry, and he let it show in his tone. "The other reason we came was to find out if giving the Hill People flintlocks was a mistake. We know the Klingons are arming the Victors, and that makes the Freeholders' fight our fight." The admiral started toward where the sounds had come from, at a run. He didn't look back to see if Rowland followed.

As he got closer, Kirk could hear voices. The words were indistinct, but the tone was one of command. Working his way nearer still, he could see people just thirty meters or so downhill from his position.

Slavers.

They had killed someone—a body lay facedown in the grass, and Kirk could see enough of the head to know multiple gunshot wounds distorted it. Six other people stood around the body, their weapons on the ground, encircled by twenty or more Victors, all of them bearing lever-action rifles.

Kirk recognized the five captives.

The crunch of dry grass alerted Kirk to Rowland's presence. His aide crouched beside him, looking at the tableaux.

"That's Tyree," Rowland whispered.

"Tyree, Nyran, Elanna. I don't know the names of the others, and I can't tell who the dead one is."

"They'll be put to work in the mine," Rowland said.

"Unless someone recognizes Tyree," Kirk replied. "He's a symbol to those who love freedom. He'd be more valuable as a hostage. They could parade him through the streets, make a spectacle of him. His capture would be a blow to all of Freehold, and beyond. It would be dispiriting, to say the least."

"What do we do? We can't fight that many of them."

"We could have if we'd been with them. Nine of us against twenty? I'd take those odds. But the Freeholders have already disarmed. That leaves us without a lot of options."

"Do we have *any* options? Go back to Freehold and raise an attack party?"

"No time for that," Kirk said. "Whatever we do, it's got to be now."

"Orders, sir?"

Kirk contemplated the question for a moment. A couple of the slavers handed over their guns to their comrades and moved toward the captives with lengths of rope. They tied each captive's hands behind his or her back, then looped the rope around his or her throat a couple of times, then moved to the next captive and did the same, linking them in a chain. If any of them tried to balk, the ropes would tighten on the necks of those around them.

They didn't have much time. Shooting wouldn't help—the captives would be sitting ducks, and two against twenty was poor odds. They could just let the

Victors take the Freeholders. But they might never see any of them alive again, and Tyree would be a particularly valuable prize.

"We're going to be captured, too," Kirk said.

"We're *what*?"

"I want to be able to keep an eye on Tyree, try to protect his identity if I can. And we need to see what goes on in the mine, right? So we let ourselves be taken."

"Admiral, that could be suicide."

"Or it could accomplish what we came here to do."

"Well, I just don't see how gettin' us killed will—"

"Mister Rowland," Kirk interrupted. "You said you'd been studying my record. You must have an idea of how many times someone's tried to kill me."

"Lots."

"Do I look dead to you?"

"No, sir."

"That's right."

"Still . . ."

"Still, nothing. We've got to move or we'll miss our chance."

"Our chance to become slave labor?"

"Our chance to succeed at our mission."

"We could follow 'em, sir, wait for a chance to take 'em by surprise."

"They outnumber us. And they're not far from Victory; we wouldn't get much of a chance."

"Do you always have an answer for everything?"

"Not always," Kirk admitted. "But usually, yes."

Rowland blew out an exasperated sigh.

Kirk didn't blame him. If it hadn't been his idea, he would have hated it, too. As it was, he wasn't all that fond of it.

As the Victor slavers tightened the bonds on the Freeholders, Kirk stepped out from the cover of the trees. He held his rifle loosely in his hands. "There must be some mistake," he called. "Those are friends of ours."

He heard Rowland coming behind him, going along with the plan after all.

The Victors spun around, leveling their weapons at the newcomers. "Stop where you are!" one demanded.

Kirk recognized the danger of his situation. Some of the slavers were tense, fingers on their triggers. It wouldn't take much to start them shooting, and if they did, he and Rowland were dead. His hope was that having secured their prisoners, they'd be relaxed, their guards lowered, and he'd be able to give himself up without any trouble.

He watched their eyes, knowing that if one was going to shoot, he'd telegraph it there first. But as he and Rowland stood there, he moved his hands away from his body and held his rifle by the barrel, fingers well away from the trigger. A couple of the slavers approached, and Kirk offered the gun to the nearest one. Another one took Rowland's weapon. At that point, the rest of the group shifted their gun barrels away, placing their fingers outside their trigger guards, and it was clear there would be no more shooting. Kirk doubted that the dead one had been threatening them—it was probably standard practice to take out one victim when they first moved in, to show the rest they meant business. To slavers, the dead were worthless. They wanted their prey healthy, whole, and able to work.

The Victor who had taken Kirk's gun handed it off to another man. He carried himself like the man in charge, expecting others to simply know what he wanted done, and to do it. He was dressed in clothing similar to what Kirk and Rowland had worn in the city, and he had a thick, black beard and a flyaway shock of dark hair. "You are dressed like them," he said, indicating the captive Freeholders. "You are from Freehold?"

"Not . . . originally," Kirk said. "But we've been staying there."

"These are your friends?"

"Yes, they are."

He grabbed Kirk's vest with the hand not holding his rifle and hauled him down the slope. Kirk could easily have broken his grip, but only at the possible cost of bringing guns back into play. He let the man drag him toward the other captives. When they were close, the man released Kirk, shifted his grip on his rifle, and swung the stock into the brow of one of the Freeholders Kirk didn't know.

The man's forehead split open under the blow, and blood spurted from the gash. The other Freeholders shouted in alarm, and the knees of the injured man buckled. As he sagged, the lines around the throats of the others drew taut. They caught him, hoisted him back to his feet. He groaned and blinked at the blood flowing into his right eye, unable to raise his bound hands to wipe it away. But he shook his head and regained his balance. He would have a bad bruise for a few days, but he'd live.

"Do you know why I did that?" the Victor asked Kirk.

"I have . . . no idea," Kirk said.

"To show you—and them—that I am capable of anything. I can be kind, and I can be crueler than you could imagine. If you cooperate, if you please me, I will be your friend. Your best friend, perhaps, at a time when you feel like you have no friends at all. Or I can be your worst enemy, your nightmares made flesh. And most important? It is all up to you. You can choose which side of me you want to see. The kind side, or the cruel one. You do not even have to tell me—I will know, by your actions, which you want to see. So . . . do you feel cooperative?"

Kirk wasn't sure how he could be any more cooperative. He and Rowland had come out of hiding and given up without a struggle. But he didn't want to point out to the man how easy their capture had been, lest he find it as suspicious as it really was. "I don't see that we have much choice."

"You truly do not," the man said. He turned to one of those who obeyed him without question. "Add them to the string!"

Kirk and Rowland allowed the Victors to tie their wrists. As they had done with the others, they encircled the men's necks with the rope and knotted it to Tyree, who was the last Freeholder in line. But because a separate rope had been used, what happened to Tyree and the others would not risk strangling the Starfleet officers, and vice versa.

Tyree turned his head as far as his bonds would allow. "James," he said. "Why have you given yourselves up?"

"We need to get inside that mine," Kirk replied. "This was the only way to do it."

"But, as prisoners?"

"Nobody's going to let me take the tour."

"I do not understand."

"Bad joke, Tyree. Never mind." He didn't want to tell the man that a bigger part of the reason was that he wanted to keep an eye on Tyree himself, to try to make sure the Victors didn't realize what a prize they had stumbled across. "Who did they kill?"

Tyree craned his neck around even farther. The ropes bit into his flesh, and there were tears in his eyes. “Enjara,” he said. “They fired from the trees, killing him, then swooped in and took the rest of us.”

“Enjara? The man I . . .”

“Yes. You saved him one day, only for him to die on another.”

“I am sorry.”

“As am I. These people are vicious. Brutal.”

“I’m trying to find a way to put an end to it all, Tyree. To the taking of slave labor, to the fighting. To the dying.”

“By being captured yourself?”

“I recognize that it’s a little unorthodox.”

“It is more than that. That man, with the beard? He is called Carella. He is the leader of the Victor slavers, and notoriously ruthless.”

“Tell him the rest,” Elanna added. She was in front of Tyree in the chain.

“What’s the rest?”

“Carella was raised with the Hill People.”

“He was one of you?”

“His mother was. His father was a Villager. But he died when Carella was an infant. She came back to us and raised him among us. He left when he was in his fourteenth year and found his father’s people in the Village. He stayed there.”

“Did he recognize you?”

“I do not believe so. I was but a boy when he left.”

“But you recognized him.”

“His reputation is well known to all the Hill

People. To all Freeholders. We know him, and we fear him."

"You know how dangerous it would be if they realized who you are?"

"I am just one man, the same as any other."

"You're more than just a man, you represent the very freedom the Victors would take away. They'd use you to try to win concessions from the other Freeholders, at the very least. And the Freeholders love you—they would do almost anything to keep you safe, or if they believed that you might be freed."

"My people would not be so foolish."

"You'd be surprised, Tyree. The smartest people will do not-so-smart things if they think it will help somebody they respect and admire."

"But—I am just a man, James. Nobody special."

"Tyree, that," Kirk said, "is where you are very wrong indeed."

# Eighteen

Carella might have had the reputation, but he wasn't necessarily the worst of them.

Along the way, Tyree introduced Kirk and Rowland to those of their fellow captives they didn't already know: Keran, Gayan, whose head was still bleeding after being struck by Carella's rifle, and Renaya. He explained that Nyran had gone looking for Kirk and Rowland, to keep them out of trouble in Victory, and then the others went after Nyran. Kirk thanked Nyran for his concern and his courage.

While they were talking, one of the slavers, a hulking man with a jutting brow and almost no chin, clubbed Keran with a massive fist. "Silence, all of you!" he demanded. "I am sick of your mewling!" Keran's head snapped back, and blood ran from his nose and mouth, but he stayed upright thanks to those around him.

"We won't be much good to you, if you insist on beating us all," Kirk pointed out. "Strong laborers can get more work done than damaged ones."

The big man spun on Kirk and drove one of those

big fists into his midsection. Kirk had just enough time to brace for the punch, but the preparation did little to lessen the impact. He doubled over around the fist, the wind blowing out of him. As he tried to straighten, a wave of nausea passed through him and the world tilted crazily for a second.

"Are you all right, Ad—Jim?" Rowland asked.

Kirk couldn't respond for several moments, while he struggled for breath. The big man stood nearby, hands balled into fists, as if waiting for Kirk to say something.

When he had enough breath to spit it out, he said, "You're pretty tough when you're up against someone who can't fight back."

The big man punched him again. This time, the blow landed in the middle of Kirk's chest. He was sure his heart stopped for an instant. Again, the wind left him, and he slumped back, only Rowland's arms keeping him on his feet.

"Belo!" Carella shouted. "Stop!"

The big man had his fist back, shoulder cocked and ready to throw another punch. Carella clapped a hand on him and yanked him backward a couple of steps. "Stop!" he said again. "Don't damage the workers!"

Belo pointed at Kirk. "He . . . he said—"

"I heard what he said. Ignore him." Carella turned to Kirk and pressed his fingers against the spot on his chest where Belo's last blow had fallen, pushing hard enough to cause new pain. "You, don't taunt your betters. Belo's got a temper, and you look like you could put in some good hours in the mine if you're not too badly hurt before you get there."

"Take these ropes off me and we'll see who comes out the worst," Kirk said.

"You really do not want me to do that."

"I really do."

"He would tear you pieces so small you wouldn't feed them to a child."

"He could try. Untie me and let's find out."

Carella took Kirk's face in his hand, squeezing his cheeks hard between powerful fingers. "I can see that I will have to keep a close eye on you. What did he call you? Adjim?"

"That's right, I'm Adjim," Kirk said.

"Strange name." Carella gave a last hard squeeze and released him. "I have never heard it. I think I have never seen one such as you. You might be trouble, Adjim. I think not—I think we will break that reckless spirit of yours. And more quickly than you imagine. I almost admire you." He laughed and turned his back on Kirk. "But only almost. You would have to survive to be truly admirable, and I have a feeling that recklessness will get you in trouble. The kind of trouble that will ensure that you do not last long." He glanced over his shoulder before walking away. "Pity. You could be a hard worker, I think, if not for that mouth."

Belo glared at Kirk for another moment, then he

followed Carella toward the front of the pack. The other slavers kept their distance as the group started forward again.

"Admiral, pardon my language," Rowland said quietly. "But what the hell was that?"

"That," Kirk replied, "is called attracting attention. After that little display of testosterone, do you think anybody's going to look twice at Tyree?"

When they reached Victory, instead of being taken directly to the mine, they were paraded through the city streets. Kirk recognized some places he had seen earlier that day: individual shops he remembered passing, a building with a distinctive turret jutting into the air, an alley where men and women who looked like they hadn't bathed in months were congregated, whether by choice or official decree he couldn't tell.

If the transit of the city served any purpose, it seemed to be humiliation. People emerged from upstairs windows and lined the streets, jeering and spitting and throwing plump, overripe fruits at the prisoners. An ancient woman, her spine bent like a twig, shouted obscenities at them while waving a bony finger, like a mother scolding her toddler. Even the tusked doglike creatures got into the act, snarling and yapping at the captives. When Nyran complained, Belo clubbed the boy's ear with his heavy fist.

The intensity of the vitriol surprised Kirk. He

might have expected it had Freehold ever been antagonistic toward Victory, but to his knowledge, the Victors had initiated the war and the Hill People—the Freeholders—had defended themselves. They were being brought into the city to do work the Victors didn't care to do themselves, and they were being treated like plague-carriers, or worse.

"Are they always like this toward captives?" he asked.

"I do not know," Tyree answered. "Most who are captured never return. None of us have lived through this before."

"Let's hope we do this time," Rowland grumbled. Kirk turned and saw spittle on Rowland's forehead. The man tried to wipe it off with his shoulder, but he couldn't reach it. Kirk was sorry, and not for the first time, that he had involved him, Burch, and Hay in his mission.

He had always tried to consider all options carefully before making decisions that might have far-reaching implications. The pace of duty did not always allow for as thorough an examination as he would have preferred, though. Sometimes he'd had to make snap judgments, or decide, as he had on Neural, when he was exhausted, physically, mentally, and emotionally. Kirk resolved that if he ever occupied a captain's chair again, he would try even harder. In most cases, better a short delay than a snap decision that made things worse.

A particularly juicy piece of fruit struck him in the cheek and sprayed across his nose and lips, distracting him. He tasted it. Sweet, vaguely reminiscent of peaches back home, but with an unexpected hint of something else—not quite chocolate, but in that general neighborhood. Whatever it was, he wouldn't mind more of it, though he would rather eat it with his mouth and not his entire face.

Finally, they had wended their way to the less populous side of town, closer to the mine. Uniformed guards were all they saw now, and when Kirk spotted the same ones he and Rowland had encountered earlier, he turned his head away from them and whispered for Rowland to do the same. He didn't think they'd be recognized, having changed clothes and circumstances in such dramatic fashion, but it wouldn't do to take chances.

Immediately ahead was the tall fence that surrounded the mine, and a large gate flanked by guard towers. As they approached, someone at the front of the group shouted, "Coming through!"

The gate split down the middle and swung open. Guards in the towers trained their rifles on the prisoners—an unnecessary precaution, Kirk thought, since they had obviously been traipsed through the city. Would anybody really submit to that and then break away here?

Then the captives started through the gate, and he had to amend his initial assessment. A chill caught him by the back of the neck like icy fingers. He tried to determine the reason, and he decided that it was because he was not simply a prisoner.

They were slaves. More than just their freedom had been taken away; so had their dignity and their ability to decide for themselves what they would do and to whom they would answer.

Kirk had been taken captive many times. There had been times he didn't know how, or if, he would escape, but he always had.

This time was different. This time he was in the grip of an inherently inhuman system, and almost alone, without the force of a mighty starship to back him up. If he couldn't get to the buried communicators, he had no way to reach the *Captain Cook,* and there was no certainty that the civilian ship would alert Starfleet. As the gate scraped against the stones and clanged shut behind them, it occurred to Kirk that there was a good chance that he would die on Neural, and not as a free man.

The constant, bone-jarring thundering noises he'd heard earlier were louder here, nearer the mine and smelter. They were joined by other sounds: the ghostly music of voices from unseen throats, singing what he assumed was a kind of work song; the brittle *chunk-chunk* of tools striking stone; and occasional shouted, rage-filled demands that must have come from the Victor supervisors.

The sun was low in the sky, and instead of being

put directly to work, the captives were taken to where, Carella informed them, they would live out the rest of their miserable lives, except when they were lucky enough to contribute to the glory that was Victory by toiling in the mine. When they saw it, the Freeholders in the front of the line groaned. Kirk and Rowland shifted to the side, to get a view past those who preceded them.

Kirk stifled a groan of his own, but barely. "That's our quarters?" he asked. "You expect us to *live* there?"

"I expect you to be grateful you live at all, Adjim," Carella said. "And I warn you, I will not tolerate complaining or resistance from you. Belo would love to snap your neck, and I am tempted to let him."

"But—you want us to work, right? For people to work, they need food, shelter, care when they're sick or injured."

"You will work or you will die. The choice is simple."

"James," Tyree said quietly. "Do not make more trouble. Things are bad enough as it is."

"I can't just accept it," Kirk replied. "They can't treat us like sub-humans and expect us to do hard labor."

"They have the weapons and the numbers. They can treat us however they like."

Kirk had no answer to that. Instead of speaking, as the prisoners were goaded along down a narrow path that led into the deep, gaping hole carved from the earth by backbreaking labor with primitive tools, he regarded the quarters in which they were expected to live.

They weren't structures at all, but depressions scraped from the side of the pit walls. Some were barely four or five feet deep, others went back farther and appeared to have been inhabited for quite some time, with fire rings at their openings, lamps cutting the darkness within, and entrances worn smooth by the passing of feet over the years. Workers, most dressed in rags, many emaciated, with hair and teeth falling out from poor nutrition and possibly, Kirk suspected, some sort of mineral poisoning from the mine, sat inside their holes, or at the openings, watching the newcomers with little curiosity or interest. They were caked with brown earth: hair, limbs, bodies, and clothing. From those monochrome vessels, eyes blinked at them, the only external sign that life was present. Even at that, the gazes Kirk saw were largely vacant, beaten-down, and the story they told was one of surrender.

"It's like the life has been sucked out of them," Kirk said.

"Are you surprised?" Rowland asked.

"Sheer disregard for humanity surprises me," Kirk said. "It always does."

"Yes, sir," Rowland said.

"Tyree, my people once did something like this to others. But not for many, many years. Centuries.

We understand that labor has a value, and it's better to have workers who are willing and able to do what needs doing."

"That sounds like a remarkable place, James," Tyree said.

"No more chatter!" Belo cried.

"We like it," Kirk said. Belo responded by smashing his fist into Kirk's jaw, almost knocking him down. Kirk tasted blood, but when he checked his teeth with his tongue, all were intact. *Small favors,* he thought.

Finally, the party was stopped before a stretch of blank wall, where there were no carved-out niches. An assortment of crude tools resembling wooden-handled shovels and pickaxes leaned against it. Carella made sure he had everyone's attention, then he made a mark on the wall with his rifle, stalked down the path about twenty feet, and made another mark. "You will have this much space," he said. "Those are your tools. If I were you, I should get to work immediately on your new living quarters." He looked at the sky, almost dark now, with the sun nearly set and clouds blocking what little light it still provided. "If it rains tonight, you'll wish you had dug faster."

"We have to live like animals, in holes in the ground, and we have to dig our own holes?" Kirk asked.

Carella strode over to Kirk and stood close, his

face inches away, the stink of his sour breath feeling, as it washed over Kirk, like a spiderweb he had walked through in the dark. "You, Adjim, do not have to live at all. Belo, a reminder, please, for our honored guest."

# Nineteen

The other slavers knew what was expected of them. With no communication beyond a couple of head nods and the meeting of eyes, they cut Kirk loose from Rowland and Tyree. When Rowland objected, one of them butted him in the gut with a rifle stock. Kirk took a step in the direction of the Victor who had done that, but four others grabbed him and held him back.

"Leave him out of this," Kirk demanded. "He hasn't done anything."

"That is not your decision to make," Carella said. "But I leave you now in the capable hands of Belo, who will teach you your manners."

Three slavers held Rowland. The rest were either holding Kirk or standing between him and the remaining captives, still tied one to the next in a human chain. Belo came forward, a wide grin splitting his broad face.

"He does not like you," Belo said. "Carella."

"I'm not so fond of him, either."

"He can see you would like to make trouble."

"I just might."

"No. You won't."

"You keep thinking that, Belo. If it doesn't hurt too much to think."

The grin never left the big man's face. "Hurt? You will learn about hurt, Adjim."

"Leave him alone!" Rowland called. "I'm the one you should be worried about!"

Belo spared him a brief, dismissive glance, showed some teeth, and turned back to Kirk. Kirk struggled, but between his bonds and the men holding him, he couldn't break away. Belo moved fast for a man his size, drawing his fist back and then slamming it into Kirk's gut. The pain from the last beating hadn't gone away, but that triggered it again. Kirk doubled over as far as those holding him would allow and tried to brace for the next blow.

Belo hit him again, and again, and by the fourth time Kirk had stopped bracing. It was all he could do to breathe. Pain spread from his midsection throughout the rest of his body; nausea flooded him in waves, and the world darkened at the edges. He no longer felt the hands of the men gripping his arms and shoulders, couldn't have sworn that they were even there. His entire being was centered on the place that Belo was pounding. Kirk had enough presence of mind to hope that his assailant wasn't causing major organ damage. Distantly, as if from the far shore of a wide lake, he heard voices that he thought were imploring

Belo to stop, *stop!* But the words were meaningless, because there was no stopping. Belo was a machine, programmed to hurt, and Kirk was his target.

The rain woke him.

It splashed against his face, puddled on his chest. His hand rested in a slight indentation in the ground and he became aware of that, and then consciousness came to him in a single, wrenching moment.

Every molecule of his being hurt.

Sickness welled up inside him and he had to turn his head and let it out, and that motion was enough to ignite the agony, like matches held to a thousand fuses implanted in nerve endings everywhere, but centered most of all in the abdominal area.

He forced himself to lie still, to take stock.

A hard rain was falling. His clothing was soaked, and as consciousness grew, he began to shiver, genuinely cold for the first time since arriving on Neural. Shivering was painful, as was breathing. And not breathing. His abdomen had taken the worst of the beating, and although he was certain that it was bruised, even cut in places, he thought Belo had stopped short of damaging his vital organs. There might be internal bleeding, but he didn't think so.

Close around him were the sounds of tools working earth and stone. A smell like wet clay filled his nose, but with undercurrents of blood that he thought was his own. Testing with his tongue, he found no missing teeth, but sore spots where his cheeks had been cut. When he opened his eyes, rain quickly filled them, so he risked the spikes of agony and turned his head again.

Moonlight filtering through clouds showed him Rowland and Tyree, hacking at the hillside, carving away an opening. It was not yet deep enough to shield anyone from the rain, but it soon would be. He looked as far up the path as he could and saw the others doing the same, working in teams.

He groaned, involuntarily, and instantly regretted it because it sent bolts of pain shooting through him. At the sound, Rowland turned toward him. "Admiral!" he said. "You're awake! Sorry we aren't done with this yet—we've been workin' as fast as we can, but it's like tryin' to carve through granite with a dull spoon." He looked at Kirk as if expecting an answer, then apparently came to his senses. "Sorry. How bad are you hurt?" Another pause. He knelt beside Kirk. He, too, was soaked, dripping water onto Kirk's chest. "Can you talk?"

"C . . . an," Kirk managed. "Don't . . . want to. Hurts."

"We'll get you under shelter in just a little while, Admiral. If it's okay to move you."

"Don't . . . suppose there's a . . . doctor . . . in the house?"

"Tyree thinks there's a *Kahn-ut-tu* somewhere, but he doesn't know how to find her. Once we get shelter dug, he'll try and track her down, okay?"

She wouldn't have the medicinal herbs and roots she'd need to treat him, Kirk suspected. But some of them had other abilities, according to the stories he'd been told. Abilities that were so unknown to him, to the science he understood, that they might as well be magic. If Tyree could find her, she might be able to help.

At any rate, nothing she could do would make him hurt any more than he already did. This was a level of pain, core-deep, that he had never experienced. He hoped he never would again.

Rowland turned back to his work with renewed vigor. A bolt of lightning created a strobe effect, showing the lanky aide's arms moving in herky-jerky fashion as he attacked the shallow opening with a pickax.

Nausea gripped Kirk again, pulsing inside him like electricity through a closed circuit. It passed quickly, for which he was grateful. He knew better than to think it meant he was already healing, though. A beating like that would have consequences that would linger for days if he were lucky, and forever if he were not.

He woke again when Tyree and Rowland hoisted him off the wet ground and carried him into the shelter they had hewn from the wall of the pit. Being carried felt like he was being stabbed with hundred of knives. Being set down on the hard floor felt like those knives were on fire.

His eyelids fluttered. He tried to speak, but no sound emerged. Then, mercifully, he was unconscious again.

When Kirk next woke, sunlight streamed into the recess in the side of the pit. He heard the sounds of labor from below, of hundreds of steel tools clanking against rock. He heard voices raised in shouts, in song. He heard the steady, monotonous pulsing of the smelter.

He was dry, and although the pain was still omnipresent, it had lessened slightly, dialed back a notch or two on the scale of unbearable agony.

The smell, he would learn, would never change to any significant degree. It was the dull, chalky smell of hard-packed dirt and rock being turned to the air, mixed with the smell of hundreds of laborers sweating and the bitter sparks of their tools striking stone, overlaid with the sharp tang of ash from their cookfires and lanterns.

Kirk sat up. His head swam and his vision blurred. He almost sank down again, unwilling to risk yet more misery. But he forced himself not to. Once the first waves of nausea passed, he felt a little stronger, and he edged himself out of the alcove and onto the path. He moved a little farther, to the path's edge, and looked over.

The path he was on spiraled down and down and down, or others just like it did, terracing the walls of the pit in ever-declining layers. At the top, the hole in the earth was hundreds of yards wide—maybe a mile across, he judged. The pit was essentially conical in shape, though, so it got smaller as it descended, until at the bottom, it was probably less than a hundred yards across.

An army of workers was positioned all along the walkway, all of the workers the same brown color, covered in the dust and muck of the dirt they worked. At the top, they looked more or less human, while in the depths they were tiny, ant-sized.

Kirk shifted his gaze, looking up toward the top of the pit. Across from him was a tangle of stone buildings, some with what appeared to be observation decks reaching out over the pit's edge, as if daring anyone to trust the constructions of man over the ineluctable pull of gravity.

Someone stood there, hands on the rail, looking in.

Kirk rubbed his eyes. His vision was still a little bleary, his eyes gummy.

But he knew what he saw.

Klingons.

"They're gonna make you work, Admiral," Rowland said. Night had fallen and the laborers had climbed out of the pit. Rowland and the other Freeholders captured together were cooking their meager rations in a dented pot, over open flame. Rowland crouched beside Kirk, offering him water out of a canteen made from the internal organs of some local creature. Kirk drank from it, greedily, until he felt his stomach flip. Then he pulled it away from his mouth, spilling some down his chest.

"I'm not sure how much good I'll be."

"Don't matter. I heard Carella sayin' that tomorrow you'd use a shovel or he'd have Belo finish the job he started."

"He did a number on me, all right," Kirk said. He had looked at his torso, which was black and yellow and red and blue and, in some places, magenta and green. Colorful tissue damage, he decided, was no better for being visually dramatic.

"He did at that, Admiral Kirk. Woulda killed a lot of folks. I had to turn away—I couldn't stand to watch anymore, and not be able to do anything. I'm really sorry—I tried to break loose, we all did, but they had us too tight and wouldn't let go. We had to just stand there while that bastard worked you over. I looked away, but I could still hear the sound, like . . . like someone hitting a side of beef with a baseball bat, over and over. Made me sick. Still does—I heard it last night when I closed my eyes and tried to sleep. If I coulda done anything—"

"Don't worry about it, Rowland," Kirk said.

"It was just killin' me to listen to. You sure you're okay now?"

Kirk looked into the fire that Renaya tended. "I

wouldn't go that far. I'll live. I don't think he did any permanent damage. In fact, I think he's very good at his job. He knew just how much he could punish me without doing real harm. If he'd been less skilled, I'd be in considerably worse shape right now."

Rowland broke into a broad smile. "Well, I guess we can thank our lucky stars that he's a professional goon, then." He started to walk toward the fire, and then stopped, turned around. "Oh, hey, I almost forgot, I found out what we're minin' here."

"Oh?" Between seeing a Klingon for himself and this news, Kirk was starting to think they'd done the right thing by letting themselves be captured—beating to the contrary.

"Leutrinium," Rowland said. "Whatever that is."

"Klingons use it for power generation in big plants on Qo'noS and in the smaller power plants on their starships. If they're going to all this trouble here, their supply at home must be dwindling fast."

"That'd be my guess, too."

"That's good to know, Rowland. Thanks."

"Figured I might as well keep my ears open while I was at it."

"You figured right," Kirk said. "Good job."

# Twenty

The next morning, Kirk was handed a shovel and told to descend into the pit with the rest of the workers. Every step was agony, but he didn't show that to the Victors overseeing the work detail.

The Victors stood around or squatted in the shade or sprawled with their backs against the pit walls, rifles always at the ready. Their manner was casual, as if they had done the same thing for so long that they expected each day to be like the one before. They swapped jokes and stories, chatted about the weather, made fun of the laborers working in the hot sun, scratched themselves and spat, and sometimes relieved themselves, unconcerned with who else was around.

Kirk was positioned well into the pit, far from anybody he knew. He worked with four others, three men and a woman. The woman was from Tyree's Hill People group, but she was someone Kirk had never met before. He made a point not to mention that Tyree had been captured, because he didn't want the news to spread. They were assigned a particular section of the pit wall and were told to start digging.

"What are we looking for?" Kirk asked, wanting to delay work as long as he could.

"You need not worry about that," one of the Victors said. "If you find anything, we're right here."

"I just thought I could keep an eye out."

"You are not here for your eyes, Freeholder, but for your back. Dig!"

Kirk shrugged, which hurt, and then he set to digging, which hurt more. Every motion—shoving the blade into the earth, pushing it deeper with his foot, drawing it out mounded with dirt, turning and tossing that to the area the overseers told them to use, then repeating the whole process—sent lances of pain slicing through him. He tried to disguise it from his fellow laborers and the Victors, but every now and then he winced, and before long he was sweating even more profusely than the heat and the effort would account for.

"Are you ill?" the Hill woman asked.

"I'm . . . fine," Kirk said.

"No. You are far from fine."

Kirk lowered his voice. "I took a beating, when we were caught," he said. "I don't want to give those guys the satisfaction of knowing they hurt me."

"You are a foolish man. Brave, but foolish."

"I've been called that. And worse."

"I would expect nothing else. What is your name, brave fool?"

"James. James Kirk."

"James Kirk, I am called Alta."

"It's a pleasure to meet you, Alta. Although the circumstances could be better."

"Indeed."

"How long have you been here?"

She looked at the sky, as if the answer were floating in the sunlight or written on the scatter of clouds. "A year," she said. "A little more."

"I'm sorry," Kirk said. "Maybe we can get you out of here soon."

Alta laughed. "Out? How? Are you a magician? We are here now, and here is where we'll die."

Kirk realized, too late, that he shouldn't have broached that subject. He didn't intend to die in this pit, but he didn't have an actual escape plan yet. If and when he came up with one, he couldn't guarantee that everybody else would be released at the same time. His goal was to free the planet from Klingon interference, but that wouldn't necessarily translate into a lessening of the Victors' power.

"Let's just say I'm an eternal optimist," he said after a time. "And—"

"You two!" one of their guards shouted. "Less talking, more digging!"

Kirk glanced over his shoulder. The Victor had his rifle leveled at their backs. Talking to Alta had distracted him from the pain, but now it was back. He tried to ignore it, and he set to digging again.

* * *

During the day, he was too deep in the pit to see the buildings he believed housed the mine offices, supply depot, and other administrative functions. Making the arduous climb at day's end, shovel across his shoulders, feeling more drained than he'd ever been, he caught a glimpse of them and saw three Klingons standing by the railing, conferring about something. One of them looked into the pit, as if alerted by the intensity of Kirk's gaze. The admiral felt like they locked eyes, but he knew that from this distance that was an illusion—he could barely make out the Klingon's face, and the Klingon could not have seen him any better.

Still, three Klingons indicated that their presence in Victory was ongoing and that the one he had spotted the day before wasn't a fluke. Over the next several days, he saw more. Other Klingons showed up on the deck overlooking the pit. Once he spotted a Klingon freighter, green-skinned and stocky, not sleek like the Klingon ships he'd encountered before, landing near the smelter. The ship took off again before sundown, but it was confirmation that the mineral was being processed for the benefit of the Klingon Empire.

Now, Kirk knew what before he had only suspected. The question that remained: how to get that proof to the Federation Council, who could make a case that the Organian Treaty had been violated?

Trapped in a pit mine, sleeping in a shallow

depression hewn from the mine wall, Kirk had no way to contact the outside world, much less anyone beyond Neural itself. If he could get to his communicator . . . but at the moment, that was no more feasible than standing on the pathway into the pit, cupping his hands around his mouth, screaming to the heavens and expecting to be heard on Earth.

Joslen wandered Freehold like a ghost.

Her father was getting better, and there was little she could do for him except run for water when he wanted it or find whatever scraps of food he felt able to eat. Nyran was missing, along with Elanna and Tyree and Keran, plus the stranger named James and his friend, and the others.

The roads were full of familiar faces, people who were no longer strangers but not yet friends. Although people spoke to her as she passed—and there were those from Rocky Bluff, as well, who had known her since birth—Joslen felt removed from them all. Her heart was somewhere beyond the walls, with Nyran, and she didn't know where, and without it she was lost.

"Joslen!" someone called to her. The anxiety in it made her turn to look. Meena ran toward her. The severity of her gaze and the tightness of her jaw made Joslen wonder if she was angry.

"Meena?"

When the woman reached her, her arms flew

open and she wrapped them around Joslen in a hug so tight the girl began to fear for her ribs. "Joslen, thank goodness I found you. Have you heard?"

"Heard what?"

"Scouts have reported that they saw Nyran taken by slavers. Nyran, Tyree, Elanna, and the rest. The scouts were at a distance, too far to interfere, and then there was so much Victor activity they had to stay hidden for days. Now they're finally back in Freehold and spreading the news."

Joslen felt as if the very earth beneath her feet had given way and she was tumbling into an unending abyss. "No!" she cried, tears welling in her eyes. "They must be mistaken."

"Girl, they haven't returned. Don't you think they would have, if they were able? We knew something had happened to them. At least we know they're alive, not dead in some canyon."

"Dead might be better," Joslen said. "Nyran cannot be a slave. He's too sensitive. It would be torture."

"That boy is stronger than you think. Didn't he go to Rocky Bluff for you, alone? Escape from two *mugatos*? Then go off alone again, worried about James and Rowland? He has shown his courage and his strength."

"You know why he did all that?"

"Why?"

"To impress me. Some of the boys from Rocky Bluff beat him, in front of me. He could not bear that, so he was determined to show me that he had courage. It's my fault he left."

Meena was shaking her head, her long brown hair, escaped from its tie, flipping across her face. "No," she said. "He did what he did. His decision. The fact that he did it to impress you—at least, in part—does not make it your fault."

"But if I hadn't—"

"Did you beg him to go?"

"Of course not. I begged him to stay."

"But he decided not to."

"Yes, but—"

"His decision. Only Nyran is responsible for what he chooses to do."

Joslen had been blaming herself, but Meena's words rang true. Perhaps it was not her fault. Nyran was his own person, after all. Her control over him was limited, and she wouldn't have wanted it any other way. If he loved her, it was because he chose to. If he wanted to do things for her, or to impress her, that was certainly not because she needed impressing. She already loved him, and she would no matter what.

"We have to save him," Joslen said.

"Do what, now?"

"Save him. If he went after James and the other man to impress me, I cannot stay in Freehold while he rots in captivity. I am not responsible for his leaving. But if I do nothing, then I am responsible for his continued absence."

Meena studied her with a steady gaze. Joslen felt she was being measured, although for a dress or a shroud wasn't clear. "Joslen, you are a just a girl. What can you—"

"Nyran and I are the same age!" she said. "If he can do brave things, whatever the risk, then so can I."

"I suppose that is true," Meena said. "One thing I've learned about you, Joslen: You ought not be underestimated. You or Nyran, either one."

"Will you help me?"

"Help you? If I can. Help you do what?"

Joslen didn't have to consider the question for long. "If they're captives of the Victors, working in the pit, then there's only one thing to do," she said. "We need to raise an army."

# Twenty-One

When Kirk reached for his shovel in the morning, a pair of Victor overseers stepped between him and it. One put a hand protectively on the shovel. "You don't need that," he said.

The other one, a woman with a stocky build and a low center of gravity, gave him an unpleasant grimace. "The way I hear it, you might just be the most useless digger we've had here."

"May as well let me go, then." He didn't bother to point out that if Belo hadn't used him as a punching bag, he'd have been a lot more functional.

"Ha! Everybody has a purpose."

"True, but some of us object to being told what ours is by a thug holding a gun."

Her shoulders bunched and she started to raise her weapon, as if to club him with it. At a look from the other one, she lowered it again. "Come with me," she said, ignoring his remark. "We'll find something you're good at."

Kirk followed her up the winding path instead of down. At the top, she led him along a trail that skirted the decked building where he'd seen Klingons. They cut between buildings that were made from local stone, gray but shot through with veins of red and gold. The structures were functional, with little artistry put into their design, but lovely in an understated way; the stone caught the morning light and shone with its own radiance. The constant booming noise grew louder, and he realized they were heading for the smelter.

He could feel the heat intensify as they neared the massive stone structure. Chimneys sprouted from a slanted roof, dozens of them, each one spewing smoke into the sky. The booming noise was louder than ever, but he could hear other sounds now, clanging and hammering and more that he couldn't distinguish from the overall din.

At a huge doorway, another pair of armed Victors, both men, met them. "Here's one more," the woman escorting Kirk said. "He's damned useless, but maybe you can do something with him."

"Looks strong enough," one of the men said. He was tall and lean, with a red mustache that drooped over a cruel mouth and an appraising glint in his eyes. "We'll find a place for him."

"If not," the second added, "we always need fuel for the fires." This one was shorter and broader through the chest and shoulders, with a wide stance and a neck like a bull. He chuckled at his own joke, but the dryness of that laugh made Kirk wonder if it was really a joke at all.

The woman left him. The two men looked him up and down, as if making sure he'd fit in the furnace. "Hauler?" the thin one asked.

"I think so," the other replied.

The thin one grabbed Kirk's arm, squeezing hard. "Let's go, you."

The interior of the building was one vast space, broken into multiple functions. Kirk didn't know much about the smelting process, particularly as it had been practiced centuries ago on Earth—or, probably more applicable here, as it was practiced on Qo'noS. He doubted the Klingons had provided current technology. Although they had been breaking the treaty, presumably for years, they still wanted to maintain some deniability. Their contributions to Neural's level of technology were almost primitive enough that they could be denied. At least unless somebody examined them closely.

As he was marched through the place, sweat pouring from him in rivers, Kirk saw other slaves, most of them shirtless and similarly glistening. Some tended a massive furnace connected to a gigantic bellows. The booming noise Kirk had been hearing was the machinery that drove the bellows: water from a diverted section of river drove a pair of gargantuan paddlewheels that in turn operated metal levers, and the levers opened and closed valves that sent great puffs of air into the biggest furnace Kirk had ever seen. The furnace supplied the heat that had already caused him to soak his clothing in sweat, and the valves slammed closed with thunderous impact. The levers groaned and creaked as they moved, creating the cacophony that Kirk feared was deafening him more with every moment he spent inside the building.

Laborers, some so muscular that Kirk assumed they had been at this for years, shoveled piles of the mined ore into vats. The vats were moved over grates through which the furnace's heat was directed, and then other workers tipped the melted slag into long steel channels. Kirk couldn't follow the entire process from where he was, but he knew the basics—the ore was heated to separate the desired metal from the minerals surrounding it, then some other metal was blended in to give it the desired properties. Leutrinium needed to be hard but flexible, with a high melting point, to serve its purpose in the Klingon power plants. Whatever was pulled from the mine was too pure and had to be cut with something else—Kirk couldn't tell what—to strengthen it.

He felt stronger today than he had before, the beating a day further in the past, but his ribs were not yet healed. He didn't know what it meant to be a hauler, but it sounded like hard, demanding work—as, no doubt, every job in the mine was, except the ones performed by armed Victors.

He soon found out.

Once the metals were combined, they were

poured into rod-shaped molds and cooled. Then workers took the rods, rolled them on long tables, and inspected them for imperfections such as air bubbles that might result in cracking or popping under the conditions in which they would be employed; they then piled the ones that passed onto carts with small, heavy metal wheels. As a hauler, Kirk found, his job was to lug those carts—loaded with hundreds of two-meter leutrinium rods—by their T-shaped handles across the floor and outside and down a pathway, which eventually led to a flat surface that was paved with stones scorched by incredible heat, on which a Klingon freighter waited with its loading bay doors open.

The first cart that he took by himself, after assisting another worker with one for training purposes, almost got away from him. After the doorway to the smelter building, the path had the slightest decline. The other laborer had known about it and compensated, so Kirk had barely noticed it. But when he was hauling one by himself, with its half a metric ton of leutrinium rods, momentum took over on the down slope and the thing started to roll of its own accord. There was a wide turn before the landing pad, and if the cart didn't make that turn, it would go off the paved path and out into a stretch of open dirt and scattered weeds. If even one wheel hit that dirt, the cart's weight would make it sink, and even if it didn't tip, he would have to unload it to get it back on the path, then reload it and start it rolling again.

As the cart gathered speed, Kirk alternated between pushing against the handle in an attempt to slow it and trying to wrench it to the right to keep it on the path. His ribs screamed at the effort. He thought he would double over with the pain, but he kept pushing and pulling, hoping to slow and steady it. His shoulders had never had such a workout.

He backed up, ever faster, leaning into the handle as he did, understanding with every passing moment the futility of one man trying to control a great weight if it didn't want to be controlled.

He was James T. Kirk, and he would not be defeated by an enemy as simple as a rolling cart.

He changed his approach slightly. He couldn't bring enough force to bear to keep it from rolling, so instead of pushing back against it, Kirk switched to turning the handle, and therefore the front wheels, this way and that, back and forth. When it threatened to tip over, he lessened the angle of the turn but kept up the motion, and after a few frightening minutes, the pathway leveled out.

By then the cart was well over to the left, and that wide right turn was coming up. The cart was still rolling too fast. It hadn't crushed him or left the path, but he wasn't out of the woods yet. He wiped his hands, one at a time, on clothes so soaked with sweat that it hardly dried them, and gave a final yank to the right.

Every muscle in his body objected; he thought his ribs would snap under the strain.

But the cart shifted, and he was able to use its momentum to wheel it around the turn and toward the pad.

When he reached it, fighting for breath, sweat plastering his clothes to his skin, using every ounce of strength he possessed to muscle the cart the last four meters, the ship's Klingon crew stood there, laughing at him. He didn't get the joke until they informed him that he—and he alone—would have to unload the cart and carry the rods into the bay. The first time, some of the crew had helped him and the laborer showing him the ropes. This time, no one offered. He wouldn't be able to take his cart back for another load until this one was emptied.

One of the Victor overseers stood with the Klingons, as amused as they were by his struggle with the cart. As Kirk started unloading it, carrying rods three at a time into the freighter, he said, "What happens if I take the rest of the day to get this load taken care of?"

The Victor shrugged. "How long it takes is up to you," he said. "But every hauler has to move ten carts a day. You don't sleep until you finish, so if you take all day, you may never sleep again."

"Ten carts?"

"Since this is your first day, we will count the one you helped with as your first. That leaves you only eight to go."

"Thanks a lot," Kirk said, fearing as he did that sarcasm was lost on this guy.

"But when we tell the man you helped that it counts as yours, you will have made an enemy, because he will have lost one. Let it be your choice, then—an enemy among your own kind, or one more cartload to contend with."

Kirk considered for only a moment. He was already exhausted, his muscles laced with pain. But he would need every ally he could get, if he was to make a difference here. "Never mind," he said, hoisting up five rods with a grunt. "Nine carts to go."

Long after the sun had set, Kirk walked back toward the pit, exhausted and starving. He hoped there was food saved for him, but the meager rations provided by the Victors didn't go far. A single Victor guard, with her ever-present rifle, accompanied him. She'd had a meal, and grease still glistened around her mouth.

A door to the building nearest the pit, the one on the decks of which Kirk had seen Klingons, opened as they approached. A trio of Klingons emerged, accompanied by a Victor with a thick mass of dark hair and a heavy mustache. He wasn't a big man, but he carried himself with an air of command—or, more accurately, Kirk reflected, an air of wished-for command. His manner was subservient toward the Klingons, but Kirk doubted that it would be with his own people. He'd met enough petty tyrants to recognize the type at a glance.

". . . if we could only have some more advanced technology, we could increase production," the Victor was saying. "Since you have ships that can travel through the skies, surely there are wagons more advanced than those that we use in the mine. Dragging those ore cars from the depths of the pit to the smelter costs us time and kills more workers than anything else. If you saw—"

A Klingon with a short stub of a beard and a haughty manner interrupted him, his tone as stern as that of a mother disciplining a consistently wayward son. "Will it always be thus with you, Apella? I want, I want. Workers are cheap, and we are satisfied with the mine's output. Why must you always seek to 'improve' that which needs no improvement?"

"I only wish to be of service to the empire," Apella said. Kirk remembered that name—Tyree had told him that Apella was the governor here, and he had heard the name once, before that. "You know, honored Krell, that I serve the empire's interests in all things."

"I know you think the empire's interests mirror your own," Krell said. "You think more, more, *more* will please me, and you will be rewarded in kind, with more power, more influence. What pleases me is consistency. I want to know that what I have promised will be delivered. Our production capacity meets the empire's needs. Your laborers are of no concern to me. I have provided the resources you need and will entertain no additional pleas for more. Need I remind you that there are plenty more like you who would love the opportunity to serve us?"

"Others, Krell? None as faithful as I have been, none so loyal to you and to the great cause of Qo'noS."

"If you would continue serving that cause, then give me what I demand, not what you think I want."

The Victor didn't quite throw himself to the ground at the Klingon's feet, but Kirk gathered he wasn't far from it. "Of course, Krell. As I always have." The Klingons were already walking away from him, but still Apella pleaded his case. "And as I always will! I have never failed you. You know that. I never will, Krell."

*Give it up,* Kirk thought. *You can't win.*

The Klingons strode away without a glance back at Apella. Kirk and his escort reached him at that moment, and the Victor, surprised to hear footsteps approaching him, whirled around. His gaze took in a laborer and a guard, and his expression turned to one of dismissal.

But then he focused on Kirk. His eyes went wide with shock and then something Kirk took as recognition. At the same instant, Kirk recognized Apella, and the whole scene rushed back to him.

He had told Rowland about going into the Village on his last trip to Neural, on a reconnaissance mission. He and McCoy had found a forge and were nearly discovered there by a Villager and a Klingon. They'd had to knock them both down to escape.

The voices he'd heard tonight had sounded familiar, but it wasn't until Apella had looked at him so intently that he knew why. Apella had been the Villager, and Krell the Klingon, on that occasion. Krell had promised Apella riches beyond imagining, promised him that he would be the leader of a whole world.

Apella didn't say anything to him now, but as Kirk passed him and continued toward the pit, he could feel the man's gaze boring into his back. Kirk knew he had been recognized—he just didn't know how. Apella hadn't seen him that first time, or if he had, it had only been a glimpse. He and Bones had charged the men and escaped. They'd collected Tyree and left the Village before any significant alarm could be raised.

Kirk knew why he recognized Apella—and Krell—but why did Apella recognize him?

# Twenty-Two

Kirk collapsed in the shallow recess he shared with Rowland and Tyree, certain that he could close his eyes and sleep until the end of time. But Rowland brought him a bowl of food, a few scraps of meat and some vegetables past their prime, cooked up in a weak stew. "Here, Admiral."

Kirk mumbled. "Just spoon it into my mouth."

"Really . . . ?"

Kirk opened his eyes. "No. I'm tired, not dead. Thanks for saving me some."

"Where were you today?"

"Hauling leutrinium rods at the smelter. Believe me, digging's a better job. Keep it if you can."

"It's that bad?"

Kirk scooped the stew into his mouth, using the meat in lieu of utensils. "You have no idea."

"Diggin' was the same." Rowland flexed his hands. "I've got blisters on my blisters."

"They'll callous over eventually."

"I know. Until then, though, it feels like the shovel's made of fire every time I touch it."

"We'll get out of here."

"How, sir?"

"I haven't figured that out yet."

"Our deadline's comin' soon."

The day the *Captain Cook* came back into communicator range. The communicators might as well have been in orbit, too, for all the good they did Kirk. But if their captors had searched them on that first day, if they'd carried the communicators or phasers, the Victors would have them now.

"I'm aware of that. If we don't report in, Captain Grumm will report our absence to Starfleet."

"We hope."

"We can't not hope."

"When that happens, Starfleet will send a starship. At least. Maybe more than one. And if they come in and engage the Klingons . . ."

"There could be trouble."

"There could be war. The Klingons have blatantly violated the Organian Peace Treaty. There'll be consequences. But I'd rather not have Neural caught in the crossfire."

"Can that be avoided, Admiral?"

"I hope so. I have to try."

Giancarlo slumped against the wall. "Hopin' again. Hopin's not much of a plan."

"Do you know what sets us off from lesser animals, Mister Rowland?"

"Opposable thumbs?"

"The ability to wonder about tomorrow. About all our tomorrows. And the corresponding ability to hope that they'll be better than today. More than that, we have the ability to extend that hope, to apply it, not just to ourselves, but also to other people. Strangers, even. I'd like to see Neural's tomorrows be better than today. If they're stuck in the middle of interstellar war, they might not get that chance."

"But what can you do about it? Or we, rather. We're stuck here."

"For the moment. And I haven't figured out precisely what to do about it, any more than I've figured out how we get out. What I'm thinking"—Kirk stifled a yawn, but he knew there were more coming, and soon—"is that if I can get the Victors and the Freeholders on the same side—"

"Sir?"

"Okay, I know it's a reach, but stay with me. If we can get them both to declare the Klingons unwelcome here—and while I'm not certain, I believe that since both groups now encompass many more tribes than they used to, they make up the lion's share of the world's population—then the Klingons will have to leave."

"Do you really think so?"

"Under the terms of the treaty, they'll have to. If they don't, the Organians can force them to. With the Federation's full support."

"They're already in violation of the Treaty."

"You and I know that. But they're keeping a light footprint here. In a day, I expect, they could vanish and leave behind no trace of their presence here, unless someone analyzed the technology they've left behind. And that's primitive enough not to be proof. Not at first glance. The Freeholders could complain, and we could back them up. But the Victors could deny everything. They'd make it hard for anyone from the Federation to inspect their facilities, and they'd do everything they could to cover up for the Klingons. By the time substantial evidence was found, the Klingons would be long gone. But if the Victors and the Freeholders both protest the Klingon presence, they will either leave or be forced out."

"Which could still involve Neural in a war."

"It could. But with the two local powers on the same side instead of at each other's throats."

"True."

"Neural could become a Federation protectorate, which would keep the Klingons away. At worst, it'd go back to hands-off status." Kirk had finished his stew as they talked. He shifted positions and closed his eyes. "Anyway, that's not really a plan, just the outline of something that could become a plan. Not tonight, though. I've got to get some shut-eye, Rowland."

"Good night, Admiral."

Rowland might have said something else, but if he did, Kirk missed it. In moments, he was sound asleep.

* * *

Nyran, his mother, and Keran had been forced to dig their sleeping niche together. Since then they had worked each night on deepening it. Although the day's work left them aching and weary, through an unspoken agreement they shared the goal of creating enough room that they wouldn't bump into each other during the night. Nyran thought the day would come—soon, he hoped—that Keran could find a new place to sleep. If he and Keran were not quite mortal enemies, they would never be close, and he would rather not spend every night wondering if he would get his throat slit as he slept.

At the same time, he didn't like the way Keran looked at his mother these days. Keran was older than he, but not by a lot, and still far too young to pair with her. But he seemed to think that, given the circumstances, the ordinary rules of society had changed. For all Nyran knew—although he thought Joslen would have told him if they had been dramatically different—in Rocky Bluff, a man barely out of his youth could pair with a woman old enough to be his mother, and no one would think anything of it. But Rocky Bluff's ways didn't apply to the Hill People, and if Elanna ever settled with another mate, it would be someone established and mature. Certainly not Keran.

When morning dawned, Nyran swallowed the few

bites of dried-out fruit he had saved from the night before. The overseers came out with the sun, marching down the pit-side path, handing out work assignments. As had happened on every day so far, Nyran and Keran were both given pickaxes to loosen the hard rock and to clear space around veins of leutrinium so the shovel-wielders could get in and free the ore.

Nyran couldn't have said why he finally asked the question that had been nagging at him for days. Exhaustion? Maybe that was it; perhaps days of back-breaking work, nights of sleeping on a stone floor, with never enough in his stomach, had lessened his ability to control his tongue. At any rate, as they trudged solemnly down to their duty station, picks slung over their shoulders, he turned to Keran. "I've been meaning to ask you," he said. "Why?"

"Why what?"

"When Tyree and Enjara and the others went out to look for me, why did you go along? We aren't friends. The last time we were together, you beat me bloody."

Keran shrugged. "You didn't tell anyone about that, though you could have. You showed courage, going to Rocky Bluff, and then going off to try to help Kirk and Rowland. And I don't like you, but Joslen does, so I figure you've something going for you."

"Still, you knew it could be dangerous."

"If I'd known this might happen," Keran said with a chuckle, "believe me, I'd never have gone."

Apparently his laughter caught the attention of one of their guards. "Enough jabber, you two!" she said. Her tone of voice made it seem as if their conversation was a personal affront, or perhaps an insult to deceased and beloved relatives.

"What's the harm in us talking?" Nyran asked. A reasonable enough question, he believed.

"I don't like it."

"I don't like being forced to work. But here I am."

"You have a choice," the overseer said.

"I do?"

She hefted her rifle. "Try something. Attack me. Run. You'll have worked your last."

"What's your name?" Keran asked her.

"Never you mind."

"Really, what is it? I might have a useful piece of information for you one of these days. But I'll only give it to someone I think will make proper use of it. I thought we might get acquainted. If you don't want to . . ."

"Whatever it is, I'm not interested," she said. "I do my work, I collect my wages, and I go home. Then I come back and start over. Making friends with the likes of you is nothing I care to do."

"Suit yourself."

As they walked away from her, Nyran turned to him. "Why would you offer them anything?"

Keran's eyes flashed with anger, and for an instant, the face Nyran found so dull was animated with something that looked like fierce intelligence. "*You* might be content to live as a slave and to die in this hole," Keran snapped. "Not me."

"I'm not either," Nyran said.

"Make your own deal, then," Keran said. He showed Nyran his back and started swinging his pick against the wall, signaling that the discussion was over.

As they worked, Nyran tried to puzzle out what it was Keran could tell the Victors that would be of any interest to them. He thought of a few things—the nature of Freehold's defenses, the frequency of their trips to the fields in Providence Valley—but one seemed likelier than all the rest.

So far, no one in the pit had betrayed Tyree's identity. James had warned them of the possible consequences. Nyran understood; Joslen said she had heard of Tyree long before there was any talk of the people of Rocky Bluff moving to Freehold. From what she said, people in Rocky Bluff told tales of him in the same way Hill People spoke of the legendary hero Selanee. Until she had met Tyree for herself, Joslen hadn't been entirely convinced he was real. When Nyran said that he'd known the chief his whole life—that Tyree had been one of the first to welcome him into the world and had himself daubed the spot of dye on Nyran's forehead that marked where his gem would go once he reached manhood—she had gaped in disbelief.

Nyran worked hard that day, putting his back and shoulders into his efforts, slamming the pick into rock over and over again, prying it free, breaking the stone so the shovelers could come in behind. And as he did, he thought about what Keran might do. Would he really betray Tyree? And for what—better treatment at the hands of their captors? Extra food rations? Lighter duty? The more he pondered, the angrier he got, and the angrier he became, the harder he drove the point of his pickax into the wall.

If he asked Keran, straight out, he would probably deny it. And then Nyran would really have to worry about his throat at night, because Keran would want his scheme kept secret. And if he warned Tyree, he might be upsetting the chief for no reason, because he might have misunderstood Keran's intentions.

One other alternative occurred to him, and he thought it might be the best of all.

Before Keran slit his throat, he could slit Keran's. That, more than anything, would ensure his silence.

But what would the Victors do to a slave who killed another slave? Anything at all? He didn't want to throw away his life for no reason, if his guess was wrong.

He would try to ask around of those who had been here longer, if he could do so in a way that wouldn't expose his plans. At the same time, he would try to gently prod Keran into revealing what information he had to offer. He'd have to do it all fast, because who knew when Keran might make his move?

And failing all else, he would just slit Keran's throat and hope for the best. It seemed unlikely that he would ever see Joslen again, anyway. And at this point, that was all he lived for—the hope that he would one day hold her in his arms again, smell her fresh scent as she nuzzled against him, feel the press of her lips on his.

Without Joslen, the rest of it didn't matter at all.

# Twenty-Three

"This man you call Kirk," Apella said. "What is he to you, honored one?"

Krell's nostrils flared, and contempt etched itself across his face. "Kirk is an enemy to all Klingons," he said.

"But why?"

"Too many times has he disrupted our plans. Were it not for Kirk, the Klingon Empire would be even more widespread, more powerful than it is today. Officially, we are at peace with Kirk's masters because of a treaty none of us wanted but were forced to accept. Honor demands that I adhere to this treaty, but circumstance demands that other considerations take precedence."

From what Apella had been able to gather, the circumstance in question was the need for leutrinium in large quantities. He knew honor was important to the Klingons, and he had seen signs that Krell was torn between faithfulness to his code and his duties here on Neural. He had also gathered that the Klingon presence here was a violation of some sort of agreement; otherwise, they would have brought in a larger force than the fifty or so warriors barracked near the landing pad. Given their technological advantages, complete conquest of the relatively backward Neural would have been easy. The fact that they worked through Apella, and the people of Victory, indicated that they wanted to disguise their presence here. Apella had never known before from whom they were hiding it.

That part was beginning to come into focus. Kirk—and whatever he represented—was their enemy. Krell obviously hated him, but Apella believed he also feared Kirk, or he at least feared the force that stood behind him.

"Why do you ask about him? Is there news?"

"News? Oh, no," Apella lied. "We have not stopped searching, though, and will not until he is in our hands. I only thought that perhaps you could offer some insight that would help locate him."

"Look wherever insects hide."

Apella's first thought had been to tell Krell immediately that he had Kirk, right here in the mine. Now, suspecting that Krell was afraid of Kirk, he changed his mind. He would keep Kirk's presence a secret and save it until just the right moment. He didn't know when that moment would be, but it would come. Sometime, when Krell was berating him in front of his fellow Klingons, perhaps. There would come a time when he wanted to gain favor with Krell's superiors, even to put Krell in his place for the dismissive way he'd been treated all this time.

He had been patient this long, and he could bide his time a while longer. All that really mattered was the end result.

And with this prize in his pocket, he would get the result he wanted.

Kirk pulled another cartload of processed leutrinium out toward a waiting freighter. The day was overcast, the sky pewter and thick with clouds, and already a few cooling raindrops had fallen. Kirk didn't care for the nighttime storms that had flooded their sleeping area for the last few nights, but he had no objection to rains that lessened the heat of the day, especially when he had to work near the smelter's furnace or do the sweaty, backbreaking labor of hauling the carts.

He negotiated the turn with only minor issues despite the rain-slick pavement, but when he started down the last straight section, toward the landing area, he saw Apella standing before him. A broad smile lifted the ends of the man's thick mustache, but there was no mirth showing in his eyes. His hands rested lightly on his hips, and his feet were spread apart, as if he was braced to dodge out of the cart's way if need be.

"This is . . . hard to stop once it's going," Kirk warned. "You'd better move."

"I'll give you a push," Apella said.

Kirk briefly contemplated letting the cart run him over, but the presence of armed guards watching from twenty feet away made him reconsider. He muscled the thing to a reluctant halt on the slippery path.

"Do you know who I am?" Apella asked.

Since he didn't know what the man's intent was, Kirk thought playing dumb was his best choice. "Someone who's in my way?"

"My name is Apella. I am the governor of all Victory."

Kirk was breathing heavily from his exertion, but he managed to say, "Congratulations."

"And you," Apella continued, "your name is not Adjim, as you have convinced some of my people."

"It's not?"

"No. Your name is Kirk."

Kirk tried not to show his surprise. "It is?"

"Yes." Now Apella smiled for real, baring teeth and tightening the skin of his cheeks. It was not, Kirk thought, a pleasant sight. "And you are not of Neural, but have come here from somewhere else. I should like to know why. Are you a spy? A saboteur?"

"I'm just a simple slave," Kirk said. "Like any other."

"Do not take me for some kind of fool, Kirk. Victory is a sophisticated city, technologically far ahead of the rest of our world. It takes a smart man to govern it well."

"About that technology . . ." Kirk began.

"Yes?"

"What price do the Klingons demand when they provide it? Do they just want your obedience, or do they insist on your dignity as well?"

Kirk watched Apella struggle to control his face, his body language, and fail miserably at both. "I have no idea what you're talking about."

"Yes, you do. I saw you with the Klingons the other night. I'm loading leutrinium rods for them right now. They're not a secret, Apella. Not here. So you might as well come clean. What do they want from you, in exchange for their technology? Besides, of course, all the leutrinium they'll ever need."

Apella chewed on his lower lip but didn't answer, so Kirk continued. "Except, of course, you can't promise that. Their empire is constantly growing. More worlds to conquer means more ships, which means ever more demand for leutrinium. Maybe you're meeting that demand now, but you won't always. There will come a time when you'll run low, as Qo'noS has, and probably other worlds as well. While they're happy with you, collaborating with them is probably fine. But what happens when you can't serve their needs anymore? Do you think they'll just hand you some kind of reward for past service and walk away? Don't count on it. That's not how Klingons operate.

"Let me give you a little advice," Kirk went on.

"When the time comes—and it will—that you have to let Krell know you're out of leutrinium for him, you don't want to be the one who tells him. That won't be a pleasant conversation."

At the mention of Krell's name, Apella blanched. Kirk shrugged, as nonchalant as he could be. "If you don't mind," he said, "I've got to get this cart unloaded. Six more to go before I can knock off for the day."

He got the heavy contraption rolling again—without the push Apella had promised—and pulled it past the seemingly paralyzed governor. He didn't know how Apella had found out who he was, or who else might know. But there was no denying the impact his words had made on Apella. If nothing else, the knowledge that Apella had a Starfleet rear admiral in his hands would probably keep the pressure off Tyree.

But it also increased the urgency of finding a way out of this mess. Kirk doubted that the Klingons were aware of his presence—yet. They would not have let him simply walk away, as Apella had.

That meant that Apella had not yet told them, and there had to be a reason for that. If Kirk could figure out what it was, maybe he could use it. He would use whatever tools were put in front of him.

The clock was ticking, and he was almost out of time.

# Twenty-Four

When Kirk made his way back to the carved-out sleeping nooks that evening, Rowland and Elanna were bent over a small cook-fire, warming up the scant rations provided to the laborers. The sour aroma of some kind of legumes mixed with shreds of old meat might once have turned his stomach, but now it rumbled when he caught a whiff, and saliva filled his mouth.

". . . miss her like crazy," Rowland was saying as he approached.

"Tell me about her," Elanna urged.

They both noticed Kirk then, greeting him only with their eyes because Rowland spoke in a heated rush. "Shonna's beautiful," he said. He straightened up, as if he couldn't discuss his fiancée at anything other than a standing position. "She makes me laugh, so much. And cry sometimes, I guess. She plays piano, and when she does, sometimes she closes her eyes and her head moves ever so slightly with the music, and you can see on her face that she feels it, that every keystroke carries the full emotion of the piece. She can play a sad song that'll rip out your heart, or a fast, lively one that just makes you have to dance."

"She sounds lovely, and skilled. I know how music touches the heart."

Kirk lowered himself gently to the ground, back against the wall. They were engaged in an ongoing conversation, and he had no interest in intruding. He just wanted to sit for a while, to rest, and then to eat.

Rowland touched a point midway down his torso. "She's got long, straight black hair, down to here. When her head's movin' as she plays, her hair sways, just back and forth a little, but it's hypnotic."

Elanna stirred the pot, looking up at Rowland and smiling.

"You remind me of her, a little. She's taller, but strong like you are. And funny. When she starts tellin' stories about her family, it just cracks me up. And—oh, listen to me ramblin' on, blah, blah, blah. I'm sorry, Elanna."

"There is no need," she said. "You miss her."

"I do. Terribly."

"She must be a good woman." Leaving the spoon in the pot, Elanna rose. "Because you love her, and I believe you are a good man."

She took a step toward Rowland, and he put his arms out, and she came into them. It was a friendly embrace, nothing more. Just then, Nyran and Keran came around the bend, just as the two broke away, and although Nyran smiled at the sight, Keran's face darkened, his brow furrowing. It was only momentary, before he seemed to notice his reaction and smooth out his features, but it lasted long enough for Kirk to see it and wonder at the cause. Did he have feelings for Elanna? She was old enough to be his mother, or nearly so. He knew that didn't mean anything; nobody could know what was in another person's heart, and age, like other factors beyond anyone's control, was often ignored. Elanna was a striking woman, outgoing and kind, and Kirk would not be shocked at anyone falling for her.

But the fire in Keran's eyes had been, for that brief moment, frightening.

After they had eaten, Kirk took a brief stroll to the upper edge of the pit, as high as the guards would allow. He scanned the buildings for signs of activity, for evidence of Klingons, as he always did. When he turned back, he met Nyran on the path and quickly discovered that it was no coincidence.

Nyran peered through the gloom in every direction. His hands clenched and unclenched, and as he cleared his throat for the third time, Kirk realized he was nervous. "What is it, Nyran?" he asked.

"I must . . . may I speak my true mind?"

"Yes, of course. Always."

Nyran cleared his throat again, then the words spilled out in a flood. "James, you must not trust Keran."

"Why do you say that?"

Nyran looked all around again, as if to see who might be listening. "He means to betray Tyree," he said.

"Betray how?"

"He told one of the guards this morning that he had information for her. Information he said might be useful. She didn't care. But he might find another who will pay attention to him. And I don't know what information he could have that would be useful to the Victors, except Tyree's true name."

Kirk ran through his own interactions with the young man and satisfied himself that Keran didn't know anything about his origins. Anyway, Apella was already aware of his identity.

Which meant Nyran was probably correct. Tyree would be his best bargaining chip. "What did he want in exchange?" Kirk asked.

"He didn't say, but he told me he does not intend to die as a slave in this pit. I gathered he meant to trade information for his own freedom."

"And you're sure about this?"

"If you mean, am I only saying this because Keran is from Rocky Bluff and because I believe he once wanted Joslen and now might lust for my mother . . . the answer is no. Those would be reasons enough, perhaps. But Tyree is my chief, and the Hill People are my people, and it is with them that my loyalties lie."

"I appreciate the warning, Nyran. I'll keep an eye on him."

"Good," Nyran said. "I can ask no more."

He headed back down the path, leaving Kirk alone with his thoughts. He didn't know either young man well, though he admired the courage Nyran had demonstrated on more than one occasion. But he remembered Keran's face, when he had rounded the curve and seen Rowland and Elanna locked in an embrace. If Nyran had actually heard Keran offering to trade information, that was significant. But he couldn't discount the idea that Keran did, in fact, have a thing for Elanna. And that could easily rile a young man who had lost his father.

Kirk would watch for signs of betrayal, but he had to keep an open mind to any possibility, including that Nyran might be trying to set Keran up. Every starship captain had to deal with tension in the ranks. He had to get the situation here settled, had to get out of this pit and in touch with the *Captain Cook,* and he had to convince the Klingons to abandon Neural before full-scale war broke out.

That would be challenging enough, without trouble between two of his supposed allies and the looming threat of betrayal.

Later that night, Kirk sat with Rowland and Tyree in their sleeping area. The fires had died to smoldering embers and the night was cool; winter was coming to

Neural, the Freeholder chief had said, and Kirk was beginning to believe him.

Kirk took a position nearest the pathway, so he could see if Keran came within earshot as they spoke. The conversation began with casual chatter about their workdays—Kirk hauling, Tyree shoveling, and Rowland carting containers of raw ore up to the smelter from the recesses of the pit. It shifted quickly to more pressing concerns.

"If we can't do something in a hurry, Tyree," Kirk said, "there's going to be war."

"We are already at war. Freeholders and Victors are constantly at one another's throats."

Kirk nodded. "I'm talking about something of greater proportions—and much greater destructive capability. The Klingons—the aliens working with the Victors, taking the leutrinium processed here—are a vicious, aggressive race bent on expanding their empire." He indicated himself and Rowland. "Our people are not warlike, but we are powerful."

"This war?" Tyree said. "It will ravage our homes, our villages?"

"It might," Kirk said. "Or it might take place entirely among the stars, where you won't see it. But it would affect you just the same."

"What would be the reason for this war?"

Kirk considered how to phrase his answer without giving away too much. "The Klingons made a promise," he said after a while. "They would leave worlds like yours alone. We agreed to the same thing." He paused, took a drink of water. "I came back here because I wondered if I had made a mistake when I gave you those flintlocks."

"We needed them! I did not want to admit it. You know, James, that I never wanted to fight, to kill. But the Villagers would have killed us all, or enslaved us. The weapons you gave us kept us alive long enough to join with other bands, to build defenses. They were our only chance for survival."

"I know that now. I no longer think providing them was a mistake. The Klingons would have made sure that the Victors were better armed than you, no matter what. Knowing that, if by giving you those weapons I helped you defend yourselves, then it was the right thing to do. If I made a mistake, it was in expecting my people to adequately investigate the Klingon presence here. They had a light footprint at the time. They still do, but heavier than it was. Chances are whoever was tasked with checking out my report simply asked the Klingons—and, to be fair, the agreement was very new then, and everybody was walking on eggshells—"

"Why?" Tyree interrupted.

"Why what?"

"Why would they walk on eggshells?"

Kirk and Rowland chuckled. "It's just an expression," Kirk explained. "They were very cautious about how they dealt with the Klingons, so as not to upset the apple ca—never mind. Not to make any trouble. I believe that the Klingons lied, and my people believed them." He couldn't explain that he had been busy exploring the galaxy, attending to crises on dozens of other worlds, even facing down Klingons over different matters. Heading up diplomatic efforts with the Klingons, over Neural or anything else, hadn't been one of his responsibilities. Still, he could have followed up, had a conversation with somebody at Command. The Klingons had taken advantage of perceived Federation disinterest, and the situation here—entire populations put to work as slaves to feed the hungry maw of the Klingon Empire—was the result.

Tyree, squatting on the ground, dug a finger into the dirt. "You said war will come if we do not do something. If through this war we could kill every last Victor, then I would beg you to let it happen. But what can we do? We are prisoners. Slaves. How can we affect anything?"

"I'm not sure we can, Tyree. But we might have a chance."

"What are you thinkin', Admiral?" Rowland asked.

"The Klingons can now claim that they are invited guests of the Victors and that the Victors are the dominant society on Neural. That may be true. But to invite the kind of presence the Klingons have here, the invitation would need to be universal, or nearly so. One aggressively dominant group can't decide, on its own, to hand their world over to an occupying force. Still, the Klingons would use that defense, and the more vigorously they're told to leave, the more they'd resist. Klingons are nothing if not contrary."

"Commanding them to leave would make them want to stay?" Tyree asked.

"Exactly. But if we could remove their excuse—their justification—they might be more willing."

Rowland shifted his position on the hard ground, so he was sitting with his legs crossed, knees outspread. He looked like a student awaiting words of wisdom from a great scholar. "How do you mean, sir?"

"Victory and Freehold together don't account for everyone on the planet, but they make up the vast majority. Certainly they're the ones with the greatest level of civilization. The remaining tribes are scattered across the planet, and essentially powerless. That doesn't mean their opinion has no value. If the Victor . . . sponsorship, for lack of a better word . . . were taken away, the Klingons would have a much harder time making the case that they were wanted here. If the two largest groups on the planet were united in opposition to a Klingon presence, then the—" Kirk didn't want to name the Organians in front of Tyree. "—those who created the agreement in the first place would be driven to enforce it. And they have means to do so that even my people don't."

"You believe that the Victors would join with us in opposing these Klingons?" Tyree asked.

"It's a stretch, I know," Kirk said. "But it might be our best shot."

"How? The Klingons give them weapons. Power."

"That," Kirk replied, "is something I haven't figured out yet."

# Twenty-Five

For the next several days, Kirk hauled leutrinium rods to Klingon freighters, through rain that fell from morning until well after nightfall. Each day was cooler than the last, and after the sun's minimal warmth had faded, the damp nights grew bitterly cold. Kirk and Rowland had spent what spare moments they had looking for a way out of the pit, testing defenses, sometimes taking beatings for their efforts. At every possible opportunity, Kirk passed by the mine headquarters buildings, looking for Apella.

This morning, he knew, was more momentous than most. Kirk was aware that this was the day the *Captain Cook* would come back and would only reach communicators buried next to a tree. Kirk was heading up toward the smelter in the morning, and he saw Apella talking to a couple of other Victors. He looked like he was issuing orders for the day. When he saw Kirk, he made eye contact, and Kirk started toward Apella.

The guard accompanying Kirk and a few other laborers to the smelter shouted after him, but Apella dismissed the man's concerns. "Let him be," he said. "I'll personally have him delivered to his duty station."

The guard grumbled, as did a few of the other workers, Kirk noted. He wasn't surprised—when everybody was oppressed, anything that smacked of preferential treatment for one was regarded with suspicion and resentment. Ordinarily Kirk would have refused any special privileges. But these were not ordinary times, and the task ahead of him was a crucial one.

"Good morning, Kirk," Apella said as the admiral neared him. "Are you enjoying our weather?"

Kirk glanced skyward. The clouds were thick and dark, and a steady drizzle had been falling since before dawn. "I've seen better."

"You are nonetheless comfortable, I take it?"

"I'm sure our comfort is far down your list of priorities, Apella."

The man's thick brush of a mustache twitched. It might have been a smile. "True, Kirk. Productivity is my top priority."

"Got to get that ore processed for your Klingon masters, right?"

"That is not the word I would use. But yes, getting the ore processed is why you are all here."

"Master is the word I'd use, Apella. We may be your slaves, but you're slaves to the Klingons."

Apella laughed, but Kirk didn't hear any humor in it. "I have wealth, I have power."

“Power over what, exactly? Us? Are you free to walk away from your responsibilities, if you want to? Are you free to refuse the Klingons their ore? To refuse them anything?”

“Why would I want to?”

“To demonstrate that you’re a free man. What have they promised you, Apella? Why do you do their bidding?”

A scowl came over the Victor’s face, and Kirk knew he had touched a nerve. “What, Apella? Did they promise that you would rule over Victory? Maybe you do, but Victory is devoted to one end—satisfying their need for leutrinium. That still makes you their servant.”

“Not just Victory, Kirk. My fist—”

“Your fist does what? Rules over the rest of Neural? It doesn’t reach Freehold. There are other peoples, other tribes, that you don’t have dominion over.” There was a faraway look in Apella’s eyes, and Kirk made an intuitive leap. “Is that what you were promised? That you’d rule not just this city, but the entire planet? Is that why you’re letting them have everything they want?”

Apella’s jaw worked, but no sound issued from his mouth. Kirk laughed. “And you fell for it. That’s the oldest one in the book, Apella. I guess there really is always a sucker born every minute.”

“I do not like your implication, Kirk.”

“I’m not implying anything, Apella. I’m coming

right out and saying it. You're a sucker. With your help, the Klingons are stripping your world of a resource that is valuable to them—and therefore, presumably, to other races, other planets, or even right here on Neural. With a resource like that, you could trade for whatever you might need. Instead, you're just handing it over to the Klingons, and in return, they're telling you what to do and how to do it. Promising you power that they're not delivering. When they've taken everything they can get, they'll move on to someplace else, leaving you with nothing but perpetual war and hatred. Doesn't seem like a very good deal to me. Maybe it's time to renegotiate."

As Kirk spoke, Apella's face darkened, and a vein on his forehead started to pulse like a big, dark worm. "You have work to do, Kirk. Better you pay attention to that than to the affairs of your betters."

"If I run across any betters, I'll keep that in mind," Kirk said. "In the meantime, you might want to give some serious thought to what I said. You could do much better than you're doing now."

Apella summoned a guard and told him to escort Kirk to the smelter. "Just because he reports there late does not mean his quota is any less. Tell his supervisors there that it is my wish that his quota be increased by two loads."

"Yes, Apella," the guard said. He nudged Kirk in the ribs with the barrel of his rifle. It was all Kirk could do to not snatch the weapon away from him, which he easily could have. But a small act of rebellion now might make a more significant one later more complicated. For the sake of his mission, Kirk swallowed his pride and let himself be herded to the smelter.

Apella was still pondering Kirk's words when Krell stormed into his office. "You need to step up production," the Klingon said, without preamble.

"You told me just days ago that you were happy with our output," Apella replied. "I told you we could produce more, if you supplied better weapons and tools. We could take Freehold itself and put everyone there to work."

"You will get what you want, perhaps, if you increase production," Krell said. "Increase first, reward later."

"But . . . how are we to—"

"*How* is your concern, not mine, Apella. I have told you what I require. I will not answer any more questions."

"But, honored Krell, to do that I need more workers."

"Then find them. Or work the ones you have harder. Or both. The empire needs leutrinium. You supply it, or we find someone who will."

Apella was at a loss. He had not given any thought to increasing production, since Krell had so recently—and forcefully—turned down his offer to do just that. Instead, he had called back the slaver parties, intending to let the population of potential workers grow unimpeded while he maintained current levels. "May I at least ask—"

"You may ask nothing," Krell insisted. "You may only do."

With that, he stormed out of the office, leaving Apella sitting at his desk with a dumbfounded look on his face. *What could have prompted that?* he wondered. *Was there something going on with the Klingon Empire that had increased their demand for leutrinium? Or was Krell simply changing his mind for no reason other than to torment him?*

*Or was Kirk right, and Krell was just using him to get his leutrinium without ever meaning to elevate his status beyond governor of Victory?* Which was, he thought, not worthless in itself. But he had been promised so much more.

If he refused Krell's demand, the Klingon could easily kill him and appoint someone more agreeable in his place. Which meant Apella was stuck. He had no choice but to increase production—somehow—or face Klingon wrath.

He heard footsteps outside, and then a quick rapping at his door. Not Krell, then—he had stopped knocking long ago. "Enter!" he called, relieved that it wasn't Krell with some other impossible demand.

A pair of guards came through the door holding between them a Freeholder Apella didn't know. He was a young man, although not so young he didn't have a forehead gem. "Yes?" Apella asked. "I am very busy today."

"Our apologies, Governor," one of the guards said. "This man claims he has important information for you. About one of the slaves."

Apella took a closer look at the Freeholder. He had broad shoulders and strong arms and was likely a good hand with a shovel or pick. His face was plain and did not hint at guile or trickery. "What is it?" Apella demanded, aware that he was taking the same tone Krell had with him, just minutes before. "I'm a busy man."

"May we speak in private?" the slave asked, indicating his keepers with the slightest shifting of his eyes, back and forth.

"No, we may not. Whatever you have to say, say it now."

The young man let out a sigh. "Very well. One of the slaves, captured with me, is Tyree. Chief of all—"

"I know who Tyree is!" Apella cried. He turned his gaze to the senior of the guards. "You had Tyree in the pit and didn't tell me?"

"I knew nothing of it!" the older one said. "He would speak only to you."

"I trust I will be compensated for this information," the Freeholder said.

"Compensated in what way?"

"My freedom?"

"How about your life?"

"My—"

"The Freeholders would kill you for betraying their chief. I could kill you now, for any reason or none at all. But because you pleased me, I will spare you."

"But . . . I could be of great service to you, Governor."

Apella barked laughter. "I would never *trust* you, Freeholder. You have already shown yourself to be a traitor. Are you also a fool?"

"I . . ."

"Take him out of my sight!" Apella ordered. "And bring Tyree to me. Now!"

"No answer, J. D.," Makin said.

J. D. Grumm swiveled in his chair and fixed his navigator with a steady gaze. "Try again."

"I've been trying," Makin replied. She worked the controls at her console. "Twenty times. Nothing."

Grumm muttered a curse. The *Captain Cook* had been in Neural's orbit for almost an hour already. Admiral Kirk had been explicit in his instructions. He had not wanted the Klingons to know the ship was in the vicinity, and he had definitely not wanted them to know that a Starfleet admiral was on the planet. That meant communications had to be brief, limited to specific times, and the ship couldn't stay in orbit for long.

"What do you wanna do, Cap?" Makin asked.

"I want Kirk to answer our hails."

"I'll keep trying."

"J. D.," LaMotte said from his position at the helm. "You're going to have to make the call."

"When I'm ready."

"I'm just saying. Kirk said if we couldn't raise him on this run, we were to let Starfleet Command know."

The helmsman wasn't telling him anything he didn't already know. Grumm had left Starfleet because he didn't like taking orders. He wasn't cut out for bureaucracy, and despite all the freedom a starship captain had—and he'd been a long way from achieving that rank—Starfleet was still a bureaucracy.

The idea of giving up on Kirk and reporting him as missing grated on him. Not just because he would, no doubt, have to deal with layers upon layers of bureaucracy, although that was a driving consideration. But he had met Kirk, and he'd admired him. Subspace communication with Starfleet, from this distance, would eat up precious time. They couldn't even begin it until they had left Neural's system, so as not to tip off the Klingons.

For the first time since he had resigned his commission, Grumm wished he had a Starfleet ship under his command, with all its weapons and defenses. But his decommissioned Starfleet vessel had only the barest defensive capabilities. He couldn't attack the Klingons, couldn't show himself.

He had to retreat, to leave Kirk down there, and to call in Starfleet.

He hated to do it. But he had no choice.

"Take us out, Mister LaMotte," Grumm said at last. "I have a call to make."

# Twenty-Six

Kirk dragged himself back into the pit at the end of his workday, more exhausted than usual thanks to the increase in his quota, and frustrated that he had not yet found a way out of captivity and back to the buried communicators. He had failed Neural once before; this mission was supposed to set that right. Instead, he had failed again, or so it appeared. The *Captain Cook* had, by now, entered the planet's orbit and left it again. Starfleet would have to dispatch ships to Neural, and when they came they would encounter Klingon vessels. War, at that point, would be hard to avoid.

The sun had set, the evening was cool, and fires had already been lit. The flames warmed him as he passed them, but Kirk barely noticed. He had almost reached his cutaway—he wanted nothing more than to lie down and sleep, even food held no appeal at the moment—when he saw Nyran bolt upright, from a sitting position, and charge up the path toward him. Vengeful fire burned in the boy's eyes.

Kirk braced for attack, although he didn't know

why. Then he realized that Nyran's gaze was directed *past* him, not at him. He spun around and saw Keran coming behind, escorted by two guards. Kirk's own escort had left him at the top of the path, as usual.

"Nyran!" Kirk called. "Why . . ."

Nyran rocketed past him. The guards, caught as unaware as Kirk was, reacted too slowly, and in an instant Nyran sprang, fingers hooked into claws, at Keran. The two of them fell in a heap, barely missing somebody's fire. They rolled the other way—toward the edge of the path and the drop-off into the pit.

"Stop them!" Kirk shouted.

The guards stood by, watching but not interfering. Kirk brushed past them and waded into the melee. He reached down and snared a limb; a forearm, he thought, though he couldn't tell whose. The wrestling pair's momentum threatened to drag him to the edge, but he planted his feet and held on to the writhing arm with both hands. Then somebody—Rowland—got a grip on him. Kirk was sliding toward the precipice, and he scrambled for purchase. But Rowland's weight held him back, and together they kept the Freeholders from plummeting over the side.

When their momentum had been broken, Kirk grabbed Nyran and pulled him away from Keran. Nyran wriggled and tried to break free, throwing ineffectual punches toward Keran and trying to kick Kirk's legs out from under him. "Nyran, calm down," Kirk said. "What's this all about?"

Rowland, meanwhile, was holding Keran back. Kirk noted that Keran wasn't trying nearly as hard as Nyran to continue the brawl.

"He—he—he betrayed Tyree!" Nyran managed. His face was filthy, the dirt streaked through with tears.

"He what?"

"He went to talk to someone, one of the Victors. A short while later, guards came for Tyree!"

"Where is he now?" Kirk asked. "Where's Tyree?"

"I don't know!" Nyran cried. "They took him!"

Kirk turned to the guards who had accompanied Keran. They had stood back and watched the ruckus without doing anything about it. "Where is he? The man who was taken from here?"

"I know nothing of any man," one of the guards answered. The other stared silently.

"Take me to Apella!" Kirk demanded.

"You are to stay in the pit at night."

Kirk grabbed the guard's shirt and shook the man, perilously close to the edge. "Take me to him! Now!"

The guards locked eyes for a moment. "Very well," the one Kirk was hanging on to said. "We'll take you. Whether he will see you, I cannot say."

"He'll see *me*," Kirk said.

Despite the hour, lights were burning inside the mine office building. One of the guards entered, and Kirk heard muffled conversation. The guard reappeared a moment later, held the door open, and said, "He'll see you."

Flanked by the guards, Kirk entered a long, high-ceilinged room, illuminated only by the light spilling from a doorway at its other end. The walls were lined with storage for mining equipment, medical supplies, weapons and ammunition, and more. A vaguely musty odor hung in the air. Another pair of guards stood to either side of that far doorway, eyeing Kirk with suspicion. Kirk kept his gaze forward, his head high, and strode quickly toward the open door. His escorts had to hustle to keep up.

The guards at the doorway moved as if to block his way, but then, perhaps in response to a signal from behind that Kirk couldn't see, they shifted aside again and allowed him to pass into an inner office.

Tyree stood, bound and bloodied, against a wall. His head was down, chin on his chest, until Kirk spoke his name. Then he lifted it, blinked a couple of times. "James."

"I'll get you out of here, Tyree," Kirk said. He turned to Apella, who sat at what looked like a poorly made wooden desk. The office was plain, its walls bare, with only the desk and a couple of chairs as furnishings. A single lightbulb dangled from an exposed cord, flickering as it swayed slightly from side to side. A set of windows provided a view of the pit, dark now but for whatever fires were burning, and a door opened onto the deck that Kirk had seen from below. Apella didn't seem to have a computer, which didn't surprise Kirk, but neither did he apparently put much stock in paperwork.

Two other uniformed men were in the room, and one of them was lightly rubbing skinned knuckles with his other hand. He was the first bald man Kirk had seen here on Neural, where a thick head of hair was almost *de rigeur*. This guy's head was like a pale cannonball perched atop a massive torso, with no neck in between.

"Why . . . ?" Kirk began.

"Simply a demonstration," Apella said. "Tyree had to be shown who is in control of his life now."

"If you've hurt him, Apella, I'll—"

"You are in no position to make threats," Apella said. He put his elbows on the desk and folded his hands together. Kirk half-expected him to twirl the tips of his mustache, like the villain in a silent movie from early twentieth-century Earth. "Or promises, for that matter."

Kirk glanced once more at the guards, letting his gaze rest slightly longer on the one with the damaged hand, then silently dismissed them by sitting and turning his full attention to the Victor governor. "We have a problem here, Apella."

"We?"

"Okay, more to the point, *you* have a problem."

"And that would be . . . ?"

"You might want some privacy for this part."

Apella regarded him for a long moment, then waved his hand toward the door. "Leave us," he instructed. "Wait just outside, though. If there is any commotion, kill him first, then his friend."

One of the guards started to protest, but Apella quieted him with a glance. They filed dutifully outside, and Kirk waited until the door had closed. When they were gone, Kirk carried another chair over to Tyree and helped him sit.

"Your problem is me," Kirk said, returning to his own seat. "And I'll tell you why." He was winging it, and he knew he had to tread carefully around the Prime Directive, although the Victors in general and Apella in particular had already been exposed to greatly advanced technology, through their contact with Klingons. "Your friends the Klingons are a technologically sophisticated race. They're aggressive and imperialistic and have no doubt made you a lot of promises, some of them backed up by action. They've no doubt made a lot of threats, too. And they're capable of following through on those.

"But the people I represent are not a single race. They're a confederation of many races, from many planets. As such, our technology is more advanced than the Klingons'. We are more numerous than they. We have more ships, with more powerful weapons.

"As of today, I am officially considered missing. Which means my people will be sending ships to look for me. Lots of them. I'm a pretty important guy."

Kirk paused a moment to let his tale sink in. Some of it he was making up on the fly—he didn't really know how numerous the Klingons were, though he doubted there were more of them than of all the member races of the Federation. And they had developed some technology, like cloaking devices, ahead of the Federation. They were not a force to be taken lightly.

Then again, neither was Starfleet.

"So, what you are saying is—" Apella began.

Kirk cut him off. "I'm saying that soon there's going to be a massive armada knocking on your door, wondering where I am. They're almost here, in ships outfitted with weapons you can't even conceive of. I'm not at liberty to describe them in any detail, but you should know that what the Klingons have given you are primitive—not much more advanced than arrows and spears—in comparison.

"Now, your Klingon friends might try to protect you—well, no, they wouldn't do that. But they'd want to protect their vital interests here. If they did, it could mean war against my people. A war my people would win. But the cost to you, in blood and in treasure, would be incalculable. I can't guarantee that any of you would survive."

He was laying it on thick, but he had to be persuasive while still not providing much in the way of actual detail. His hope was that he could make Apella believe he was better off not knowing the facts of the situation.

Apella's face had started to go pale, and he was picking nervously at a hangnail, so Kirk thought he was succeeding.

"They've been using you for a long time, Apella. Making promises. Keeping just enough of them to string you along. But I doubt that whatever you're getting back is worth dying for. You were promised a whole world, once. Do you have it yet?"

Apella's bushy eyebrows rose and his mouth dropped open. "How do you know that?"

"It's enough that I do," Kirk said.

The governor brought himself under control again. "Many have died already. On both sides," Apella said.

"And yet, the first time I came here, Villagers and Hill People lived in peace. Villagers started the war. You changed what had been an idyllic paradise into a bloody battlefield, and for what? So you could be used, taken advantage of, by the Klingons."

"James is right, Apella," Tyree said. His voice was thick, and Kirk saw bruising on his throat. When he opened his mouth again, he revealed a gap where two teeth had been. "Your people and mine had lived in harmony for all time, until those aliens gave you fire sticks. Only then did the killing begin. And the dying."

"It's not too late to set things right," Kirk said. "And to prevent much more bloodshed—maybe even the total eradication of your people, the destruction of this planet."

"But how?" Apella asked. "Your ships are already on the way, you said."

"I can still call them off. If they arrive and don't find Klingons here, there'll be no need for war."

Apella swallowed, and his eyes were liquid with terror and pain. "The Klingons do not listen to me," he admitted. "You are right, Kirk. The one called Krell has promised much and delivered little."

"They'll listen to all of us together," Kirk said. "You can speak for all the Victors, and Tyree for all the Freeholders—that makes up the vast majority of Neural's people. By being here and arming you, the Klingons have broken an agreement they made with another race, which they fear—and rightly so—even more than they do my people. They won't want to face us, but they especially won't want to face us and those others combined." He was again stretching the truth; the Organians had the capability to enforce the treaty they had imposed, but he doubted they'd join with the Federation. They had proven themselves to be officially neutral, interested only in peace.

Still, Kirk's goal was to frighten Apella, and it looked like he might be succeeding. The sides of the man's shirt were plastered to him, drenched in sweat. More trickled from beneath his thick mop of hair.

"You believe if we just tell the Klingons to leave here, they will?"

"If we phrase it the right way," Kirk replied. "Yes, I think they will."

"Why should we not have the Freeholders join us in inviting them to stay? Would that not satisfy the treaty?"

"It might," Kirk admitted. "But at what cost? Working together, cooperatively, you could run the mine for the benefit of all Neural. The leutrinium will always have value. As it is, all Neural is enslaved by the Klingons—even those of you who believe yourselves unshackled. That won't last. In the end, everybody wants to live free."

"And if I refuse?"

"Then I'm not sure that war can be avoided. *Real* war, with devastating effects."

"Apella," Tyree said. "I would sooner see you dead than take another breath. But I am a chief, and I must think of tomorrow. The lives of our children, and our children's children, may depend on the next thing you say."

Apella hesitated. Kirk filled the silence. "It's never easy to change course, or to admit a mistake. Believe me, I know that. But the choice here is simple, Apella. You go along with me, and everybody lives. Or you stick with the Klingons, and there's no telling who lives. If anybody."

Apella was breathing through his mouth, taking

short, rasping inhalations and blowing them out quickly. He looked, Kirk thought, like he was on the verge of a panic attack. His gaze darted back and forth, to Kirk, then Tyree, then some indeterminate space between them before starting the circuit again. Kirk almost felt bad for putting him in this position.

Almost, but not quite.

Finally, the governor seemed to make up his mind. His fists clenched on the desk, his jaw became set, and he nodded once. "I will do it," he said. "I will tell the Klingons to leave Neural."

"*We* will," Tyree corrected.

Kirk was about to say something else when he became aware of a noise from outside, a swelling rumble, as if from many voices speaking at once. Apella heard it, too, and rose from his chair. He was almost to a window when the front door burst open. One of the guards came in. "Apella!" he cried. "We're under attack!"

# Twenty-Seven

"Is it your people, then?" Apella asked Kirk.

Kirk tried to make out details from the dull roar outside. "I don't think so."

Apella rose from his seat and hurried to the door, flinging it wide and stepping out onto the deck. Kirk followed, and Tyree, moving more slowly, joined them moments later.

Across the pit, a throng had gathered outside the fence. Uniformed guards and armed Victors were racing toward them, on the broad, flat plain around the pit. Rifles cracked in the night on both sides, their muzzle flashes bright, and acrid smoke already filled the air.

A couple of guards crowded into the doorway behind them. "What's going on down there?" Apella asked.

"Freeholders, sir," one replied. "Lots of them."

"Freeholders?" Apella whirled on Tyree. "*Your* people!"

"You have had me in custody all afternoon," Tyree said. "I had nothing to do with this."

As Kirk watched, helpless to interfere, the Freeholders on the far side of the fence tore at it, while others tried to climb over. Victors fired on them, and Freeholders dropped like stones. Still, more came. Hundreds of them, it seemed. They would get through the fence, Kirk was certain.

But it would be a bloodbath.

"You've got to stop it!" Kirk said.

"How?" Apella asked. "I am here, and they are down there."

"Tell your people not to fire. Tell them that the Victors and the Freeholders are on the same side. Tell them we're united against the Klingon threat—and once we inform the Klingons of that, they'll leave."

Apella stood clutching the railing, seemingly transfixed by the scene before him. "Apella!" Kirk snapped. "Do something! Only you can put an end to this!"

"Those are my people, James," Tyree said. "I must go to them!"

Before Kirk could stop him, Tyree dashed past the guards and back into the office, then through the door into the big front room. Kirk hesitated only a moment. He had said his piece to Apella, and what the man did or didn't do was up to him.

But Tyree was already injured, brutalized by Apella's thugs. Now he was about to wade, unarmed, into a full-blown battle.

One of the guards tried to catch Kirk as he passed,

but he shot an elbow to the man's jaw and he folded. Kirk snatched the rifle from his suddenly limp hands and darted past the remaining guards.

Kirk hoped he wouldn't have to use the weapon. He would, though, if forced to. A bad situation had just become blood-drenched chaos, and there was no telling when, or how, it would end.

The captives flowed in every direction at once, without order or apparent logic. With the guards having abandoned their posts at the pit gates, laborers flooded out, bearing shovels, picks, burning logs, or whatever else they could lay hands on as weapons. A steady stream of Victors headed from the city toward the fence, rifles in hand.

Where the two rivers of humanity came together, blood was spilled.

Searching for Tyree in the crowd, Kirk heard a drawn-out, full-throated scream off to his right, toward the pit entrance. A man raced toward him, bent over almost double, arms thrown wide. The noise that tore from his throat sounded barely human.

Kirk braced for impact. At the last instant, the man altered his course slightly and crashed into someone behind Kirk, a Victor toting one of the old flintlock rifles. Both men went down, a flailing arm striking Kirk in the back of the thigh as they did.

The flintlock fell from the Victor's hands as the enslaved Freeholder pummeled and clawed at him.

Kirk grabbed for it, holding his own stolen weapon under his arm, and snapped off the cock. It would still serve as a club, but it wouldn't fire.

One gun down, out of how many? Was it worth the time it took?

Kirk thought he caught a glimpse of Tyree through the mob. One platinum-blond head looked much like another, especially in flickering firelight, and there were plenty in evidence. But he knew Tyree's gait, the width of his shoulders, the way he carried himself. He started after the man.

He'd made it four steps before somebody slammed into him from the left. Kirk tried to brush past the man—an unarmed, uniformed Victor guard—but a pair of hands grabbed onto his vest. He was bringing his free right hand up to break the hold when the guard drove his head toward Kirk's mouth.

Kirk threw up a shoulder, taking the brunt of the impact. At the same moment, he swept out with one leg, knocking the man's feet from beneath him. Staggering, the man released Kirk's vest. When he had regained his balance and tried again, a blow to the solar plexus with the butt of Kirk's rifle dissuaded him.

With that out of the way, Kirk scanned for Tyree again—or the man he had thought was Tyree.

Gone, vanished into the darkness and the throng.

Tyree had been headed toward the fence. And Kirk knew that was his destination initially, because he'd been reacting to the presence of the Freeholders assaulting it. Kirk went that way, dodging and weaving through the crowd, trying to avoid the fights breaking out all around him.

The fence was bedlam. Gunshots rang out every few seconds, a fusillade that blended with the cacophony of voices into a deafening roar. The fence swayed so much that those trying to climb it were shaken off, like dying leaves in a gale. Then it collapsed, and the Freeholders scrambled over it, and the din grew even louder.

People were dying by the score. If Tyree had reached the thick of it, Kirk would never find him in time.

Using the rifle as a wedge, he shoved through the crowd. A knife's blade slashed his upper arm, but he ignored it and kept going. A body, thrown down by an opponent, crashed into his legs. Kirk stumbled but continued on. Watching, always, for any glimpse of his friend.

Nyran joined the crush of laborers charging up the winding pathway toward the pit's entrance. When he heard the commotion at the fence, he knew with utter certainty what it meant—Freeholders had banded together to rescue the captives. His heart leapt with the firm knowledge that Joslen was among them. He could have sworn that he heard her calling for him through the chaos, despite the fact that it was impossible to pick out a single word, a single voice.

Still, she was out there. He knew it to the core of his being. There were guns being fired, and screams piercing the darkness, and if anything happened to her he would . . . he would—

Well, he didn't know what. *Something,* though.

The walkway was packed. He squirmed and slithered and writhed through, sometimes grabbing a stranger's shoulder or arm and swinging wide, out over the drop-off, to gain ground. Everyone was in a hurry, but there were so many, and the way so narrow, that they had to move slowly.

Slowly didn't work for him. Even fast wasn't good enough. If there were only a way to just *be* there—to stand *here* one instant, and *there* the next—maybe that would do.

But that was lunacy. He needed to focus. Joslen might be in danger.

Nyran ducked under somebody's arm, took a knee to the ribs, grabbed an old woman for balance and almost spun her around, caromed off another woman, this one younger and stout enough to stand up to the impact, and then he was through the gate.

Free.

He'd only been a slave for a few days, far less time than many of the others. Still, there was something about breaking free, about being out of the pit and going where he wanted for a change, that felt so good, so right, so true, he thought his heart would burst. He was already panting slightly from the mad dash up the pathway, but now that there was more room to maneuver, he poured on the speed. Hands grasped at him but he eluded them, dodged a shovel being swung indiscriminately in the crowd, dropped into a skid when he saw a guard aiming a rifle right at him. The gun spat flame and noise, but the round shot over Nyran, and if it hit anyone behind him, he couldn't tell. He smashed into the legs of the woman who had fired it, and as she tumbled over, he snatched the rifle from her and kept going.

He was almost to the fence when it toppled. People who had been scrambling on it hung on, spiderlike, or fell screaming into the crowd. Shards of light from fires and guns revealed glimpses of people: shouting, crying, faces twisted with rage or broken from sorrow.

Then he saw her, swept forward in the crush of Freeholders surging through where the fence had been. "Joslen!" he cried, though he knew she couldn't hear. "Joslen!"

She looked up. Had she heard, after all? For an instant, it seemed that her gaze locked on his, and something like a smile brightened her face.

Then, just as suddenly, she was gone.

Apella stood on the deck, clutching the rail with trembling hands. He was afraid if he released it, he would fall. His legs would not support his weight. Though he had never before feared tumbling over the side—the railing was sturdy, secure—he was convinced that if he lost his balance now, rather than dropping to the plank floor, he would crash through or flip over the rail and plummet into the pit.

And if he, through some miracle, survived the fall, those he had imprisoned there would tear him to shreds.

So he stood on rubbery legs, hands locked on the rail, and watched his world fall apart.

He was not, he knew now, a brave man. He had thought before that he was. Brave, powerful, possessed of a killer instinct and knife-edge reflexes and tactical brilliance surpassing all his peers. He had ascended to the very pinnacle of society. He had *remade* society, through force of will and the partnership he had dared to create with the Klingons.

Those people down there, the ones rushing to defend Victory, were really defending *him*. They worshipped him. He had not chosen the name Victory by accident—it had been a statement of purpose, a vision of the future. Victory would prevail now, as it always had and always must.

But he was not down there with them, racing headlong into danger. Instead, he stood here, above the fray and afraid to budge.

And he didn't care.

Accepting one's own essential cowardice, Apella thought, was a form of liberation. Rid of illusions about himself, he could face the world with a truer sense of purpose. It was not, after all, his courage that had held Victory together. It was his cunning and his charm, his ability to persuade others to his point of view. He had—

"Apella!"

He spun around, releasing the rail without thinking about it, and almost fell. He had to reach back and catch it again to steady himself. "Honored Krell!"

"You have a disaster on your hands," Krell said. There were three other Klingons with him, ones Apella didn't know. Krell's hands were empty, but his disruptor pistol and his knife hung from his belt. The others all held disruptor pistols. From the crests on their sashes, they appeared to be of a different house than Krell. Apella wondered what was going on, but he didn't dare ask. "What steps are you taking to deal with it?"

"I—my forces are down there now, trying to rebuff the assault and restore order."

"They are clearly failing."

"It is early yet. The battle has just been begun."

"The fence is down," Krell pointed out. "And the pit is emptying."

"A little more time," Apella said. He didn't want to plead, but he was afraid that was how he sounded. "You'll see."

"Time? That may not be mine to give. It may be determined by how successful your guards are."

"The . . . the tide of battle already turns, honored Krell."

"Does it? I had not noticed." The other Klingons chuckled at this. Apella wondered how often they laughed about him, when he wasn't there to see. Constantly, he believed. Now this fresh self-knowledge felt like a curse. He was a coward and a laughingstock to the only ones who could grant him power. What other discoveries might he make about himself on this night? "Get this under control, Apella," Krell said, starting for the door. He stopped, just at the doorway, and added, "And quickly. Or I will take action myself, and you may not like the action I take."

"Yes, Krell. Of course." Apella's legs started shaking again, and he knew if he removed his hands from the railing, they would flop around like a fish on the banks of a stream. He didn't know what he could do, from here or down there in the thick of it.

He would have to do something, though, and he would have to do it soon.

# Twenty-Eight

The crush of bodies became even more pronounced when the wave of Freeholders coming over the downed fence met those already on the inside. Gunfire didn't stop, but it slowed, since it was hard to see individual targets, much less pick out enemy from friend. Kirk was bashed and buffeted from every side. Blood ran down his wounded arm in a steady stream.

He was beginning to despair of ever finding Tyree. There were hundreds of people around him, or more, and in the flickering half-light, telling one from another was almost impossible.

Someone's fist landed in Kirk's sternum. The breath went out of him in a whoosh. As he struggled to remain upright, thinking it had been a random act, he recognized Belo's grinning face. "We have unfinished business, Adjim," Belo said.

"I suppose we do, at that," Kirk agreed. He tried to take a step back, to give himself room to move, but the crowd blocked him. Belo was already in motion, his right arm drawing back for another punch. Kirk, still winded, raised his left shoulder to block it, while dropping to a crouch and swinging the rifle with his right hand on the barrel.

There was barely space for the weapon's arc, but it narrowly missed the surrounding mob and the butt crashed into Belo's left knee. The big man grunted and he listed to that side.

His fist shot out, but the blow to his knee skewed his aim slightly. Kirk was able to block it, though the impact made him reel backward.

Belo was bigger than Kirk, and stronger, and not bleeding from a bad gash in his arm. Kirk would have to finish this in a hurry, or he wouldn't finish it at all. He thought about turning the gun around and shooting the man, but at this range, the round would likely pass through him and endanger those behind him.

Anyway, Kirk wasn't sure Belo could be hurt with a bullet. Maybe with a cannonball, or a tank round, or a phaser bank.

But that knee . . .

He took a step back, swinging the gun to clear a space. Belo followed. Kirk took another step, and Belo kept coming. He was favoring that left knee. He was a huge man, and the weight he carried probably strained his knees at the best of times.

Kirk took one more step, watching Belo's face as he put weight on that leg. He was rewarded by a perceptible wince.

As Belo drew back for another swing, Kirk slammed the gun forward, butt first, into that left knee. Belo let out a wordless complaint, and his arm dropped to his side. Kirk brought the weapon back and jammed it again, at the same spot. Belo's pants showed blood there.

Before Kirk could pull the rifle away, Belo caught it and wrenched it from his hands. He hurled it into the crowd. Kirk tried to step away again, but the throng pushed back this time. Kirk was pressed toward Belo instead of moving away, and the big man got a huge hand on Kirk's throat. He squeezed, and Kirk knew he wouldn't last long under that pressure. His hands went to Belo's, to try to pry his fingers away. But with his free hand, Belo began punching: solid, powerful blows that Kirk couldn't dodge.

With the world turning black at the edges, Kirk had to do something fast. He brought his foot up and drove it into Belo's knee. Belo grunted, and Kirk felt him buckle a little. He kicked again and again. Belo's flesh gave way under the assault, but he kept his grip on Kirk's neck, squeezing tighter than ever. Kirk smashed his foot into the knee once more, until finally he felt something pop under his assault. When it did, Belo collapsed like a felled tree. His grip on Kirk's throat loosened and he was free.

He coughed, gasping for breath. Belo's fall had cleared a swath around them, and Kirk tried to use the space to recover. But Belo wasn't done.

He grabbed for Kirk's legs. The crowd surged, forcing Kirk back toward him. Belo caught his right ankle and yanked, and Kirk fell to the ground beside him. The big man drew himself up on one elbow, pain apparent in his expression, and started pummeling Kirk again.

Kirk took the blows as best he could, but he was weakening. Other Victors, realizing what was going on, joined in, kicking Kirk and hitting him with their fists and their rifles. One drew a knife and stabbed at him, but Kirk managed to squirm away and the blade only grazed his ribs.

He tried to tear his leg from Belo's grasp, but in spite of his injuries, the man still had incredible strength. Instead, Kirk lashed out with his free leg. His foot caught Belo's jaw and the big man slumped again. Kirk kicked twice more. Blood ran from Belo's nose and mouth, and when Kirk kicked again, he felt Belo's jaw give way. Belo's grasp relaxed, and Kirk was able to wrench his leg free and make it to his feet. He was still ringed by Victors, though, still taking blows and kicks, still threatened with knives and rifles.

"Finish him," someone said. The voice was familiar. Kirk peered through the flickering light and saw Carella, the slaver, standing at the edge of the circle. He spoke with casual authority, and Kirk didn't doubt that someone would obey. He heard rifles being cocked.

But Belo had other ideas. "No!" he cried. Kirk spun around and saw the big man rise unsteadily, hanging on to those around him for support. Belo said something else—Kirk thought it was "He's mine," but his mangled jaw made it hard to understand.

Kirk was stuck. If Belo didn't kill him, the Victors surrounding him would. He was unarmed and injured. He could take Belo, maybe, but that would only postpone the inevitable by seconds, if that. Carella looked on with a bloodthirsty grin. No help there.

Someone behind Kirk shoved him toward Belo. The big man caught Kirk's left arm, his grip weaker than before. Kirk didn't wait for a blow, but drove his fist into Belo's ruined face. Belo cried out, squeezing more tightly, and Kirk did it again. His third punch threatened to tear Belo's jaw completely off. Blood sprayed everywhere. Still, Belo hung on.

But he wouldn't for long, Kirk knew. And he knew, likewise, that the other Victors around him were already preparing for the kill. He saw knives and guns everywhere he looked. Carella watched, arms folded casually across his chest.

Belo punched. The blow landed weakly. Kirk fired one back, but Belo lurched forward and Kirk's fist landed against his temple. Belo swayed. Fell.

And the knives lanced toward Kirk.

Then another figure entered the fray, crashing through the mob, knocking down the two nearest knife-wielders. In the chaos, Kirk snatched a rifle from someone's hands and swung it like a bat, clearing away others. He spun around to find Carella, but the slaver had already fled.

Other Freeholders joined the brawl, and Kirk had a few seconds to collect his thoughts. The man who had broken up the circle turned to him with a grin. "You okay, Admiral?" he asked.

"I am now, Mister Rowland," Kirk said. "Thanks for the assist."

"Any time, sir."

"You know, you really can call me Jim."

"I'll think about it, sir."

Brawling with Belo, Kirk hadn't realized how close he was to the pit's edge. With the ring around him dispersed, he saw that there was only a narrow band of people between him and empty space. And in that band, slightly forward of his position, he spotted Tyree.

He nudged Rowland's shoulder and pointed. "It's Tyree!"

"Sure is," Rowland said.

Kirk risked shouting the chief's name once, but his call went unheard over the din. As he watched to see if Tyree reacted, he realized that Tyree and a few others were standing near an ore cart perched at the edge of the pit. When the ore cart tilted slightly, Kirk recognized what it meant.

"They're too close!" he cried.

"I'm on it!" Rowland answered. He was a few feet closer than Kirk to the edge. Both men took off sprinting toward Tyree and the others, but with his head start and long legs, Rowland got there first.

"Tyree!" Kirk called again. This time, the chief heard. He turned to seek out the source of the shout and took a couple of steps toward Kirk, away from the edge. But as he did, people around him shifted course to go behind him, taking them closer to it. The ore cart shifted again, swaying a little, and so did the people near it. Kirk raced toward them, crying, "Get away from the edge!"

Rowland, still out in front, herded some toward Kirk. At the last moment, out of time, he simply grabbed the last two people—a Freeholder and a Victor—and hurled them clear.

And then the ground gave way.

The ore cart slid into Rowland, and he went over the side.

Kirk rushed past Tyree. Maybe there was a pathway just below, a ledge. Something.

But no. He looked down until the pit wall disappeared in the darkness below. Over the cacophony of voices and footsteps, fighting and gunshots, shouting and tears, he couldn't even hear the impact when Rowland hit bottom.

# Twenty-Nine

Kirk stood at the edge, peering down into darkness that thickened with distance, from a flickering, shadowed gray into deepest, purest black as formless as the void. The battle swirled around him, forgotten. After a while, he was aware of Tyree at his side.

"I am sorry, James," Tyree said.

"I . . . thank you, Tyree."

"He was a brave man. He saved many lives."

"That was his calling. All of us in—in my organization. That's why we do what we do. To help others. To advance the cause of freedom, of knowledge. To save lives."

"That is a noble thing."

Despite his sorrow, Kirk offered a dry chuckle. "Noble? That's not why we do it. I think it's because that's what we *can* do. The contribution we can make. We aren't necessarily the smartest, the strongest, the most admirable. We're just human beings. But we feel obliged to give something back . . . to the world, to the galaxy . . . that created us. That gave us so much. We do what we can with the gifts we possess."

Tyree put a sympathetic hand on Kirk's shoulder. "No one could ask for more. Or expect more."

"Thanks," Kirk said again.

"James . . ."

Tyree was trying to draw his attention to something. Kirk had been lost in reflection, weighted with sorrow. He tried to focus on his surroundings.

"I fear this battle spells doom," Tyree said. "For my people."

"Why?"

"I am told that Apella's foreign masters have been roused."

"The Klingons?"

"They are coming to finish the fight. Freeholders still stream from the hills, but they have no chance against the Victors and the Klingons."

"Can we stop them? The Freeholders? Have them retreat, to fight another day?"

Even as he asked the question, Kirk knew the answer. The battle had been joined. It would be impossible, at this juncture, to separate the combatants. Maybe some Freeholders could be dissuaded, but most would see their friends, their kin, in danger and would rush into the fray.

When Klingon warriors sided with the Victors, a fight that was already lopsided would become, as Tyree suggested, a slaughter.

"Apella," Kirk said. "We have to get to him, make him understand that the Klingons are the real enemy."

"Do you think we can?"

"We won't know unless we try."

Kirk took off at a run, making his way through the melee. Tyree ran beside him. Together they dodged blades and bullets, fists and clubs, each sometimes helping the other weave through or around hot spots.

They soon reached the mine offices. The same Victor guards who had been there when Tyree and Kirk had fled were still clustered near the door. Apella remained on the deck, watching the conflagration below.

Kirk and his friend rushed past the guards, who made no move to stop them. Apella stood with his hands on the railing, but at the sound of Kirk and Tyree approaching, he slowly faced them.

"I did not think you would return," he said.

"This has got to end, Apella," Kirk said.

"What does?" The governor seemed barely present, as if his attention was still on the tableaux to which he had turned his back.

"This whole thing. The killing, the slave labor. You and Tyree aren't enemies, or you weren't a short while ago. The Klingons set you against each other for their own ends. They're using you as much as you're using the Freeholders. It's time you all threw off your yokes and claimed your planet for yourselves, instead of living in thrall to a more powerful race. You'll need the Freeholders for that—as allies, not servants."

"I . . . what can I do?" Apella asked. "I am only one man."

"The Victors look to you for leadership. A leader can't just be in charge when things are easy. It's when things get tough that you find out what you're made of. If you are truly their leader, you'll prove it now, when they really need you. You've got to stop the fighting. Once those Klingons get involved, it'll be a bloodbath."

"If I could, Kirk, I would. It's too late."

Kirk couldn't tell how much of Apella's refusal was simply acceptance of the fact that the Klingons were the true power here, and he little more than a convenient figurehead. Probably most of it.

And Kirk knew that he bore more than a little responsibility for the situation. If he had done more in the first place to keep the Klingons away from Neural, none of this might have happened. He believed he'd been right to supply the Hill People with weapons, although he had not foreseen all the consequences. With the Klingons arming the Victors, the balance of power the flintlocks provided had probably saved lives, kept the Freeholders safe until his return.

No, not safe. *Safer,* though.

What they needed now, the Freeholders and the Victors, was a reminder that they were natural allies, not enemies. But turning them—in the midst of a pitched battle—from foes to friends would be next to impossible. Diplomacy took months or years, and even then bad blood could remain in many hearts, for lifetimes or longer.

The admiral had to do it in minutes, or the Freeholders might be nothing more than a memory. Even if some survived, it would be generations before trust could be reestablished.

He needed to stop the fighting and convince both sides that only peace offered Neural a chance.

He needed a distraction. A big one. Something that would give Freeholders and Victors alike a common cause.

If he had a starship, he could create one.

He didn't.

But he might be able to get his hands on one.

"Apella, have you told the Klingons what we talked about? That you and the Freeholders are in agreement, that they need to leave?"

"No," Apella said. "I thought we should all discuss it together."

Kirk agreed, but there wasn't time for that.

The Klingons had a ship—a freighter, not a battle cruiser—but they'd never let Kirk borrow it.

Which just meant he wouldn't ask permission.

"Apella, listen," he said. "I've got an idea . . ."

"Joslen!" Nyran cried again.

He ducked under a fist aimed at his face, skidded briefly on the ground, but then his feet found purchase and he darted toward where he had last seen her.

When Nyran reached that spot, though, he couldn't find her. He saw two people he knew from Freehold, one a woman who had lived two houses away his whole life, the other a newcomer who might have been from Joslen's town, or one of the others, lying dead on the ground in pools of their own blood. Beyond them, a small clutch of Victor men headed toward the trees, rifles at the ready.

Nyran's heart pounded in his throat. For a terrible moment, he had thought that Joslen might be under one of the women, but then realized that the woman's arm was pinned beneath her and the hand sticking out from her side was her own. He didn't think Joslen could have gone past him—which meant she was back there, in the darkness of the trees.

The trees toward which the armed, murderous Victors trudged.

She'd had a couple of minutes. Perhaps she'd gotten away.

But what if she hadn't? What if she was there, hunkered down in the trees, unarmed?

Nyran was unarmed as well. But he had to do something, had to draw the attention of those men away from the tree line.

At the moment, he could only think of one way.

He reached down and scooped up the biggest rock he could find, then threw it at the Victors. In the dark he couldn't see where it hit, but one of them cried out. "What was that?" another one asked.

"It was me!" Nyran shouted. He ran to one side, snatched up another stone, hurled it, and kept running, away from the trees. The Victors gave chase. One of them fired his gun. Nyran heard the report and the bullet raking through dirt and grass, but well away from him. Just the same, he zigzagged a couple of times, then started to loop back around toward where he had first encountered them. He didn't know if they were all following—it was too dark to see for sure, and he didn't want to spend a lot of time trying. But if only some were, Nyran hoped to get them shooting at each other instead of him.

But that hadn't happened yet when he ran into someone in the darkness. It was a man, solid as a tree, and quick. Nyran crashed into him and fell back, surprised and stunned by the impact, but before he could right himself, the man got a hand on his shirt and reeled him in, then clamped another around the back of his neck. "Got him!" the man called out. Nyran recognized the voice. "Keran?"

"Hang on to him!" one of the pursuers shouted.

"Don't worry, I've got the little bastard!"

Nyran tried to wriggle out of Keran's grasp, but he shifted his grip and hung on. "Keran, why are you doing this? You're one of us!" Nyran complained.

"Let's just say I know the winning side when I see it."

Arguing was pointless, Nyran thought. He grabbed Keran's arm and pushed, trying to snap it, or if not that at least to make him let go. Instead, Keran held him all the tighter. Finally, with the others getting closer, Nyran threw a series of savage kicks at his legs and groin. Keran blocked as best he could, but finally his grip loosened enough for Nyran to break free.

Before Nyran had taken three steps, though, another pair of strong arms grabbed him, and then yet another. "He's ours!" one of his captors called.

"Watch out for the pup's feet!"

"He won't live long enough to use 'em!"

Again, Nyran tried to twist and writhe out of the hands that held him, and when that didn't work, he lashed out this way and that with fists and feet. But the men holding him—Keran and a Victor Nyran had never seen—were ready for that and stayed clear. Nyran saw the glint of steel in Keran's fist and redoubled his efforts. Still twisting, Nyran felt a blade slice through his shirt and graze his ribs. "Hey!" he cried.

"Hold still, you little runt bastard!" Keran stabbed at him again, but Nyran dodged the blade.

He wouldn't be able to do so for long.

His breath tore from his chest in ragged gasps. The men holding him huffed and struggled to hang on. The knife jabbed at him again, this time finding its target in the flesh of Nyran's waist, at the side, just above his right hip. It tore, and he cried out in pain and yanked away and it tore more going out. Nyran screamed.

He felt the hot gush of blood down his side. Another strike would surely kill him, even if he didn't bleed to death from this one.

Somewhere out there, in the night, was Joslen. If he had distracted the men with guns long enough for her to escape, he was glad of it. The fact that he would never see her again hurt, though, perhaps more than the blade itself had. His legs buckled beneath him, and only the men still hanging on to his arms kept him from falling.

Then he heard a sharp sound, but distantly, as though he were underwater. He recognized it as the sound of a rifle, but he couldn't determine how near, or from where.

But one of the men holding him suddenly made a small animal sound and let go. The other man swore, and the gun cracked again, three times, and Nyran saw the flashes. Then Keran also released him and crumpled to the ground.

Nyran was free. But he was weakening rapidly, and in the dark he couldn't tell who was shooting at them. He could be next, shot where he stood, but if he moved he might be walking into the path of the next bullet.

His legs settled things by collapsing underneath him. He hit the ground with his arms flung out, one of them landing across the fallen form of one of the men, whose breathing was uneven and who pawed at the earth, as if trying to dig his own grave.

Lying there, unable to rise, Nyran heard another shot ring out, another man drop. Then somebody approached—multiple somebodies, in fact. Nyran could see only vague outlines, dark against dark, but he could tell they carried rifles.

"Nyran?" a familiar voice asked the night. "Did I hear your voice?"

"Joslen!" he replied with as much strength as he could muster. "Joslen, I'm here!"

She broke from the others and ran to his side, crouching close. Her hands touched him and he winced. "You're hurt, Nyran!"

"But I'm better now," he said, managing to clutch her hand. He held it tight, not sure he would ever be able to let go. Or want to. He wanted to see the world—but he was afraid that however crowded it might be, it would always feel empty without Joslen beside him. "I'm so much better," he said, and he was.

# Thirty

At Kirk's urging, Apella went back onto his deck overlooking the pit. Chances were, no one would hear him over the fray.

But he tried. Kirk had to give him that. "People of Victory!" Apella shouted. "My people! My friends, please listen!"

No one paid any attention. On the broad, flat space around the pit, Victor fought Freeholder. A few Klingons stood back, watching from a safe distance, but more were joining them.

"May I?" Tyree asked.

Apella took a step back and Tyree came to the rail. "Hill People!" he called. His voice was naturally louder than Apella's, and he put everything he had into it. "Freeholders! Stop fighting! The Victors are not our enemies."

Kirk watched the Klingons, off to the side. They appeared intent on Tyree, and possibly concerned.

Apella joined Tyree at the railing and draped his arm over the other man's shoulders. "Victors! See us, standing together. Tyree of the Hill People, and me, your beloved governor! Remember how long we lived in peace! Remember how we cooperated in the hunt, in growing crops! Remember how Hill People and Villagers, as we were known then, married one another! They are not our enemies and we are not theirs! We have lost our way, but we can find it again!"

More people were listening, now. Gunfire hadn't entirely ceased, but it had slowed. Freeholders and Victors alike gazed up toward the deck. In the uneven light of the fires, it was hard to see many faces, but the ones Kirk could make out looked confused or thoughtful.

"Keep going," he urged. "You're getting through."

"My friends!" Tyree called. "We lived here as slaves, but no longer! Now we are free! The Victors, too, lived under the thumbs of others. They were turned against us by those called Klingons."

At that, Kirk noted, the Klingons looking on engaged one another in quick conversation.

"You know who the Klingons are!" Tyree went on. He pointed toward the group Kirk had been watching. "Them! They, not the Victors, are our enemies. Those are the ones who would make us work until we dropped. Not for the Victors, but for them, to fuel their own civilization!"

Even more were listening now. Most of the fighting had stopped. Anxiously, the Klingons looked back toward the spaceport, from which more of their numbers were coming all the time.

"Victors and Freeholders are once again brothers and sisters!" Apella cried. "Neural is our world, not theirs!"

At that, a roar went up from the crowd. "Our world!" people shouted. Freeholders and Victors alike joined in. "Ours, not theirs!"

Kirk was glad for the temporary truce. It might not last more than a few minutes. As soon as one Freeholder with a grudge spotted the Victor he hated, the fighting would resume. And the Klingons had weapons that could cut through Victors and Freeholders alike. If the mob turned on them, even though outnumbered, they would have the advantage.

In a bloodbath, there were no real winners. Only the losers and the dead.

"Let's go," he said. "We don't have much time."

Kirk, Apella, and Tyree hurried toward the smelter. On the way, Kirk told Tyree what he needed to do. When Tyree understood, he peeled off and strode confidently into the building while Kirk and Apella veered down the path Kirk knew well, from the smelter to the spaceport.

The unlikely allies slowed to a brisk walk as they neared it, and Apella took the lead position. Two Klingon guards stood at the spaceport's open gate. From where they stood, they couldn't see the fighting, but Kirk guessed they would rather be there than here.

"We need to see Krell," Apella told them as he approached. "He has summoned me to the ship."

The guards obviously knew Apella, and recognized Kirk, but nothing was normal about this night, and they spread out to block the way.

"Let us pass," Apella said. "Krell would not want to be kept waiting!"

"I will ask Krell," one of the guards said, looking in the ship's direction though it couldn't be seen from here. "With all the trouble tonight, I would not take—"

Kirk took advantage of the Klingon's distraction. He threw a powerful chop to the back of the guard's neck, and in the same instant, kicked the back of his left knee. The guard sagged and Kirk snatched the disruptor pistol from his hand and turned it on him. The weapon wailed, its beam caught the guard, and the Klingon lost consciousness and pitched forward onto his face.

Apella was trying to wrestle the disruptor pistol away from the other. Kirk fired the captured weapon again and the second Klingon dropped. Kirk snatched up his disruptor and handed it to Apella. For all his supposed influence, the governor had never been trusted with one. After Kirk offered a quick lesson, they set off toward the freighter, staying close to the buildings, using shadows for cover when they could. They wouldn't have much time. As soon as anyone found those guards, the alarm would be sounded and the place would be overrun. If, that was, there were enough Klingons around to mount an effective search. His mad idea would never work if the Klingons had more than a skeleton crew aboard the ship.

So far, their luck was holding. They hugged the last building before the open space of the launch pad. As they reached the corner, they saw just two Klingons outside the freighter.

One was Krell.

The Klingon was deep in conversation with a female, a little taller than he and broader through the shoulders. “Do you think you can shoot her?” Kirk asked.

“I have never fired this weapon,” Apella said. “If I had a rifle, yes.”

“Same principle,” Kirk said. “This won’t kick like a rifle does, but you’ll aim it and push that button like I showed you.”

“I will try, then.”

“Let me take care of Krell,” Kirk said.

Apella eyed Kirk with his chin thrust forward, his forehead wrinkled. He didn’t like taking orders. But the fire that blazed in his eyes for a moment faded quickly. He didn’t like it, but he was used to it. He’d taken orders from Krell for long enough, and now he was taking them from Kirk. He resented it, though, and that would make him potentially dangerous. “Yes,” he said flatly.

Kirk whispered a couple more quick instructions,

then counted down on his fingers. On one, they stepped around the corner. "Krell!" Kirk said.

Both Klingons whirled to face them. Apella fired while they were still reaching for their weapons, and the female keeled over backward. "Freeze, Krell," Kirk warned. He nodded toward Apella. "His was set to stun, but mine's not. Keep your hands away from your belt."

Krell looked like he wanted to argue, but he saw the expression on Apella's face and thought better of it. He had a disruptor pistol and a knife at his waist. "Take his weapons, Apella," Kirk said. "I've got you covered."

Apella stepped forward, still carrying his stolen disruptor. "You might want to put that weapon down, Apella," Kirk suggested.

Apella visibly cringed. Kirk figured he was probably blushing, too, but he couldn't see the man's face. Apella squatted and set the weapon gingerly on the ground, then straightened and continued to Krell. Apella had been ordered around by his former captive, and then embarrassed in front of Krell. Kirk guessed there was a fifty-fifty chance that Apella would turn one of Krell's weapons on his one-time master. And then perhaps on him.

"Make it quick, Apella," he said. They were within full view of the freighter here. If anyone came out, they were done.

Apella determinedly maintained a steady pace.

A small rebellion. Maybe it would ease some of the pressure building inside him, but it could also get them both killed. Kirk decided not to push the issue, and he remained quiet until Apella had the disruptor and the knife.

When he had returned to the weapon he'd laid down, picked it up, and put Krell's weapons in his waistband, Kirk spoke again. "Krell, we're boarding that ship. I only want it for a few minutes, to try to put a stop to that battle. It's to your advantage, too. Your soldiers have better weapons than the locals, but they're badly outnumbered."

"There is no dishonor in dying a warrior's death," Krell said.

"There's no dishonor in not dying, either. Let's go."

"You will have to kill me," Krell said.

"I can arrange that," Kirk replied. "But like I said, we're in a hurry, and it'll be easier with your cooperation."

"Do you know nothing of Klingon culture, Kirk?"

"Not much. You're warlike, imperialistic, and you don't mind pushing around people weaker than you. Is there more?"

"So much. I am surprised at your ignorance. And saddened. We are a great people."

Kirk knew more than he was letting on, but he didn't want to get into it. They might already be too late to prevent wholesale slaughter. Krell was right, there was more to Klingon culture, but he didn't like the Klingons he'd met so far, and he didn't trust this one.

"We can have a cultural awareness session later on, Krell," he said. "For now, let's get aboard this ship. And don't tell me again that I'll have to kill you, because if you do, I'll have to kill you."

A momentary smile flashed across Krell's face, and was gone as quickly. Kirk must have looked surprised, because Krell arched an eyebrow at him. "You didn't know Klingons had a sense of humor, Kirk? I see you truly are ignorant about us."

"Move, Krell," Kirk said. Impatience lent his voice an angry edge. "Now. While there's anybody left to save, on either side."

"Very well," Krell said. "But only because I have so often told Apella not to wipe out his best source of labor."

Kirk didn't bother to point out that Krell wouldn't need Neuralese laborers anymore. That conversation would come soon enough, and for the moment, he wanted Krell's cooperation. "We've got one chance to prevent that," Kirk replied. "But we're almost out of time."

Krell led them onto the ship and through a warren of narrow, smoky corridors to the dimly lit bridge. When they encountered Klingons on the way, Krell ordered them to leave the ship. Kirk knew that at some point, Krell would turn on him. The only question was when.

Krell spoke to the bridge crew in Klingon, and they responded in kind. Most of them left, as Kirk had instructed, but it made him uneasy. He had told Krell to tell the ship's crew that they were taking honored guests on a short victory flight, to let their appointed governor experience the sensation. But he had no way of knowing what was being said.

"Speak Neuralese," he said. "Or Federation Standard."

"I merely told them what you instructed me to," Krell said, returning to the language of Neural. "Only the bare minimum of crew necessary to operate the ship has remained onboard."

"And they'll cooperate?"

"They have given their word. We do not give that lightly. Prepare yourselves."

"Hang on to something," Kirk warned Apella. He spread his own feet out for balance. "This isn't like anything you've ever felt."

The heavy freighter rumbled and rocked as it lifted off the pad. Although Apella had grabbed a railing, he looked a little green.

"Now what, Kirk?" Krell asked.

Kirk knew that a Klingon bird-of-prey could take off vertically, and it could be maneuvered close to the ground. He hoped the same was true of freighters—he had seen them lift off from the pad, but he had never had occasion to find out how maneuverable they were at low altitude. "I want to come in low." He was about to add more when one of the bridge instruments began an insistent beeping. "What's that?"

"An alert," Krell replied casually. "Something I forgot to mention."

"An alert about what?"

"When I first learned that you were here on Neural, Kirk, I sent a message back to Qo'noS. A bird-of-prey, the *ChonnaQ*, was dispatched. By the time it got here, you were a guest of Apella's, so I suggested that it wait, just outside Neural's atmosphere. When we lifted off without the proper signal, it began its approach, in case it needs to blow this freighter from the sky."

"You'd sacrifice this ship? Its crew? The leutrinium?"

"I told you that I would cooperate with your plan, Kirk. And might I remind you, you have not told me yet what it is. But as far as the *ChonnaQ* is concerned, this is an unauthorized appropriation of a Klingon vessel, and that will be dealt with as such. One day—if you lived long enough—you might have come to understand us. It appears that day will never come."

"Thanks for the warning," Kirk said. "Now I need to take over your flight controls for a few minutes. Apella, if anybody has a problem with that, shoot them."

"I would be happy to," Apella said. He was starting to like this turning of the tables a little too much, Kirk thought. He couldn't worry about it now, though.

He climbed up into the raised command platform and sat down at the controls. This ship's systems were foreign to him, but he'd had some basic instruction in Klingon technology at the Academy, and refreshers since.

The displays were not so different from Starfleet standards that he couldn't make some sense of them, even though he couldn't read the Klingon text alongside the visuals. A triangle, flashing red, probably indicated the bird-of-prey coming toward them.

He checked his path through the viewscreen, and using the flight controls, he steered the ship over the outbuildings and toward the smelter. He recalled that Klingon birds-of-prey carried photon torpedoes. He doubted that freighters did, and that was too much firepower for his purposes anyway. He wanted a distraction, not a catastrophe.

When he had a clear view of the smelter building, he called Krell over. "Disruptor cannon?" he asked. "This control here?"

"Yes," Krell said.

"Good." Kirk stopped with his hand poised above the control and hoped this was the right decision.

# Thirty-One

Tyree ran to the smelter building. The usual racket had stopped, and when he burst through the door Tyree saw why. The place was almost deserted. Those working here must have gone to the pit when they heard the sounds of battle.

"Clear everyone out," James had said. "Freeholder, Victor, or Klingon, it doesn't matter. You need to empty that building."

"Get out!" Tyree shouted as he ran inside. His words echoed back to him. He had only been in the place once, but the quiet surprised him. The heat didn't—apparently even with no one tending it, the furnace still blazed. But whatever made the constant booming noises was still.

"Why should we?" a voice asked. Tyree peered into the gloom of the building's depths and saw a pair of Victors, armed with rifles, emerging from the shadows surrounding a bank of machinery. One was female, and she pointed her weapon at Tyree. "Why should we do anything a Freeholder dog says? Why should I not shoot you where you stand?"

"Is there anyone else here?" Tyree asked.

"Everyone else ran away. The cowardly Freeholders first, of course."

Tyree's emotions fought a war every bit as complex as the one at the pit. James's instruction had been specific. Everyone needed to leave. He had not explained why, because time had been short. But Tyree had the sense that nobody inside would live through whatever James had planned.

But these people were Victors. They threatened him for no reason except that they had guns and numbers; because of that, they considered themselves better than Freeholders. Guns and numbers had caused them to believe that.

Tyree had believed the opposite. He had descended to their level when he started to kill. He had set himself and his people above the Victors, in his own heart.

James had tried to point out that people were people, each as good as the other, though outside forces could lead them astray. For most of his life, Tyree had believed that. But then he had stopped, had started to think one group was better than others, simply by virtue of who they were, who their mothers and fathers had been.

He saw, now, where such thinking led.

"Please," Tyree said. "You do not have to trust me, but please believe me. You need to get away from this building, and quickly. Once you have, you can kill me if you still want to. But get out, now."

The Victors exchanged glances. The woman lowered her weapon. "You're not even worth a bullet," she said with a sneer. "Go. Run away, like the dog you are."

"You'll go?" Tyree asked, ignoring the insult.

"Yes, all right. We'll go."

"And there's no one else inside?"

"Don't press your luck," the male Victor said. "We're alone, and we're leaving."

"Thank you," Tyree said. He stood there a moment longer, until the woman gestured toward the door with her rifle. Tyree ran, half-expecting a bullet in his back. When he was well clear of the building, he looked over his shoulder and saw the Victors emerging. Then he heard a low rumble, coming closer, from the direction that James and Apella had gone.

A huge, floating *thing* came toward him. He had never seen its like. It was enormous, bigger than the grandest tent he had ever seen. Any of the buildings in Victory could fit inside it and leave room for more. It moved through the air—warping the space beneath it as heat did rising from a fire—like a slow, ungainly bird.

When they saw it, the pair of Victors broke into a run, putting as much distance between themselves and the smelter building as they could. Tyree thought that was a most excellent plan, and he did the same.

He was still running when a bolt of green

lightning arced from the floating thing and hit the smelter, wailing as if to mourn all the dead since the first Villager had used the first fire stick.

Instinctively, Tyree threw himself to the ground.

As he did, the smelter building exploded. The walls blew apart, sending debris in every direction. Tyree, flat on the ground, felt a wave of force, like a strong wind, wash over him, and then bits of wreckage sliced into his arms and legs and face. A ball of fire erupted from inside, brightening the night like daytime and rising toward the sky as it seared into his vision. A deafening thunder struck at the same time.

When those things passed, bits of the structure plummeted down from on high, a rain of stone and metal and he knew not what else. What was left of the building was aflame, and thick, oily black smoke billowed up until it disappeared against the blackness of the night, only the lack of visible stars defining its existence.

Although he could not see James, he assumed the floating thing was some kind of craft, perhaps the Klingon freighter James had spoken of, and he knew his friend was responsible for what had happened.

Tyree rose unsteadily to his feet, bleeding from a score of wounds. His ears rang, he was dizzy, and he couldn't blink away a pale green afterimage of the fireball. But he started toward the pit, and within moments Tyree saw people coming toward him, Freeholders and Victors. They weren't fighting, for the moment. They wore expressions of awe, terror, or confusion. But they came together, side by side, and no one was shooting or hitting or stabbing the other.

Was this what James had in mind? He couldn't say, for sure.

For the moment, though, it would do.

"Impressive, Kirk," Krell said. "But what did it get you?"

"I won't know that for a while yet," Kirk said. He jabbed a finger at the red triangle on the flight control panel. "Right now, we've got another problem to worry about."

"Ah, yes, the *ChonnaQ* grows closer."

"Will your crew do what I tell them to?"

"Within reason."

"Then get us into orbit. If that ship attacks us, I don't want casualties on the ground."

"You don't think your little display already did that?"

"If my instructions were followed, the building was empty, and the area around it clear," Kirk said.

"And if they were not?"

"I'm only one man. I can't do everything myself."

"A shortcoming we all share, I'm afraid." Krell turned toward the remaining two members of the bridge crew. "Do as he says."

One of them grunted assent and tapped at his controls, and the ship soared skyward. Kirk felt the familiar stomach-dropping sensation of a rapid ascent, in atmosphere. He looked to see how Apella was handling it, but the man simply looked morose. "My smelter," he said.

"It can be rebuilt," Kirk offered. He turned back to the control panel. Every ship, even a Klingon freighter, had a comm system. He doubted that Krell's cooperation would extend to showing him how to work it. But it was possible that the *Captain Cook* was still in range, and if it was, he needed to reach it.

If it wasn't . . . well, this ship's defenses would not hold off a Klingon bird-of-prey for long. "Does this vessel have shields?" he asked.

"Of course," Krell answered. "Low-level ones."

"Get them up," Kirk said. "How about cloaking?"

"No."

"Shields, then. And keep climbing."

"The faster we climb, the sooner we meet our end."

"That's a chance we'll have to take. Employ all possible defensive measures." He wasn't sure to what extent the Klingons could be trusted to obey that order. The fact that Krell talked so much about honor led Kirk to believe that the concept was genuinely one that mattered to him. He had always had a low opinion of Klingons, but he was willing to admit that he might have misjudged them. Their priorities were different than his, their goals and motivations alien to him. But Krell had said the crew would obey orders, within reason, and he had no basis on which to doubt him.

He turned back to the comm system, determined to figure it out.

# Thirty-Two

*"We're en route, Admiral,"* Captain Grumm said. *"Hang on as long as you can."*

One more volley from the Klingon bird-of-prey hit the freighter squarely. The ship rocked sickeningly. Sparks flew from an instrument panel as the punishing impact shorted out yet another circuit. The bridge was already thick with smoke; this simply exacerbated that and added a sharp, coppery tang to the air.

"Hanging on, Grumm," Kirk said into the comm panel. "But if you don't hurry, you won't be able to do anything for us but pick up the pieces." He turned toward his bridge crew, such as it was. "Shields?"

"Sixty-one percent," one of the Klingons said. His tone was casual, as if the outcome didn't matter to him one way or the other. "We will weather another direct hit. I cannot say if we can take two."

"Reinforcements are on the way, but I can't say when they'll get here."

"We don't have much time, Kirk!" Apella said.

"Complaining won't make them arrive any faster."

"Spoken like a true Klingon, Kirk," Krell said. "One must always face death with pride and dignity."

"If it's all the same to you," Kirk replied, "I'd rather put off that particular privilege a while longer." He tapped a control on the panel before him and the ship went into a sudden dive. The bird-of-prey was considerably more agile than the lumbering freighter, but he was pretty sure the other crew had never had to contend with an opponent who made so many unexpected moves. As the bird-of-prey shifted position to swoop down and fire again, Kirk maneuvered the freighter's nose up—glad the ship's artificial gravity lessened the sensation—and triggered the disruptor cannons.

"Direct hit!" the second crewmember shouted. The near-certainty of impending death had done nothing to quell his enjoyment of the battle itself. Nor had the fact that their opponents were his own kind.

"Full speed ahead," Kirk said, finessing the controls. Once he had the hang of it, the Klingon craft responded as well as a utilitarian craft made for hauling heavy cargo could. The ship darted past the bird-of-prey, even as that turned to keep it in sight. "Open the cargo bay."

"But the leutrinium—"

"If we lose the ship, we lose the cargo anyway," Kirk said. "Open the bay, now!"

One of the crewmembers complied. The freighter was just zipping past the bird-of-prey's nose, thrust forward like the bill of a bird in flight. Gravity wouldn't be a factor here, but Kirk hoped that nonetheless, the metric tons of leutrinium rods in the bay might do some damage. And lightening the freighter's load might help gain some speed.

Kirk wondered in passing what sorts of birds they had on Qo'noS. The silhouette of a bird-of-prey had always looked like a duck to him, though a Klingon battle cruiser had no direct corollary in the avian world on Earth, unless it was a goose that had suffered serious disfigurement, including having its neck stretched triple its normal length.

"Maintaining course and speed," Kirk reported. He was trying to move the fight closer to where the *Captain Cook* would be coming from. Every minute counted now, so if he could shave one or two, it might make all the difference.

On the viewscreen, he saw hundreds of leutrinium rods strike the bird-of-prey, though he couldn't tell if there was any effect. A moment later, the other ship powered through them and rocketed toward the freighter again.

And then he saw a new red triangle show up on the screen. He touched the comm controls. "Is that you, Grumm?"

*"If those other two are you and your dance partner, Jim."*

"That's us. If you hurry, you'll be in time for the next number."

*"Pushing it as fast as we can."*

"She's closing in," Krell said. Kirk glanced at the red triangles on the screen, then at the viewscreen. It showed him the bird-of-prey powering in their direction, wings down. "We will be in range in three, two—"

"Shields up," Kirk said. He pushed the freighter's nose down, hoping to skate under the incoming blast.

It almost worked. The freighter lurched and shook, and smoke poured out of one of the bridge consoles. "Apella, put out that fire," Kirk said.

"With what?"

Krell said something in Klingon—Kirk couldn't tell what, but it sounded rude—and snatched a tubular device off a grip on the wall. He thrust it into Apella's hands, and the governor got down on his knees and starting trying to open the console.

"Damage report," Kirk said.

"No vital systems affected," one of the Klingons reported. "Some minor structural damage to the underside of the hull and the cargo bay door. Shields at thirty-six percent."

The *ChonnaQ* still had its full complement of photon torpedoes. It was toying with them. One torpedo would obliterate the freighter. "Can we manage another shot with the disruptor cannon?"

"One, perhaps. That will be our last."

"We're taking it." Kirk eased the unwieldy vessel back into firing position and triggered the cannon.

The enthusiastic Klingon—now Kirk regretted not having learned their names—barked a laugh. "Another fine shot, Kirk," he said.

Kirk was already rolling the freighter out of the way of any return fire and then pushing it toward the *Captain Cook* with every ounce of power it had to give. "Grumm," he said into the comm unit, "are you ready to engage?"

*"We're not a fighting ship, Jim,"* Grumm reminded him. *"We've got some capabilities, but not a lot."*

"Use whatever you've got, Grumm. And thanks."

*"No problem, sir."*

"Are you in range?"

*"Not yet. Almost."*

"I'm just about out of tricks here, I'm afraid."

*"Closing in."*

"Be careful. We might have weakened her a little, but that bird-of-prey still has plenty of punch."

*"Careful's my middle name."*

"I thought that started with a D."

*"David, if you ask my folks. I'll stick with 'careful,' though."* The *Captain Cook* stopped transmitting for a moment, then came back. *"I'm going to shut up for a few minutes here, if that's okay. Got some things to do.* Cook *out."*

Kirk veered off to starboard and tried to open a space for the incoming ship to cover them. Grumm was risking his ship and his crew. When this was all over—if anybody survived—Kirk would make sure that Grumm got as many Federation contracts as he could handle.

The *Captain Cook* streaked toward the bird-of-prey. The Klingon captain seemed to understand that this newcomer was a threat now. Kirk wished he still had some offensive capabilities. Two-to-one, they might have had a chance against the Klingon fighter. As it was, short of ramming the thing, all he could do was watch.

It might come to ramming, at that.

"You have steady nerves, Kirk," Krell said. "Pity you were not born a Klingon."

"I never considered that a drawback," Kirk said. He watched on the viewscreen as the *Captain Cook* and the bird-of-prey exchanged fire. These were getting-acquainted volleys, each ship feeling out the other without fully committing.

That didn't last long. Soon enough, the *ChonnaQ* was pummeling the *Captain Cook* and ignoring the Klingon freighter.

Kirk took advantage of the opportunity to reposition the freighter, edging in ever closer to the bird-of-prey while trying to stay just far enough away not to attract undue attention. Apella had finished with the fire and stood over Kirk's shoulder. "What are you doing, Kirk? That's too close!"

"Getting us into ramming position," Kirk said.

"Ramming? We'll die!"

"No doubt. But if it looks bad for the *Cook*, then we're ramming that bird-of-prey."

"Are you *certain* there is no Klingon blood in you?" Krell asked.

"He is too ugly," one of the crewmembers said. "But he *is* bold."

Kirk held the freighter in place, keeping up as the bird-of-prey maneuvered to exchange shots with the *Captain Cook*. He checked in periodically with Makin, since Grumm was a little busy. The communication officer's last update was, *"I don't know how much more we can take, Admiral."*

"We're going in," Kirk said. He eased the freighter's nose down just a little and began to accelerate toward the bird-of-prey.

"But Kirk—" Apella began.

"I'm not letting those people die for us." He didn't bother to add that if the *Captain Cook* was lost, the freighter would be next, anyway.

The bird-of-prey seemed to know what he had in mind. It was turning toward the freighter, intent on vaporizing it before it could reach ramming speed. Those photon torpedoes had not yet come into play. Now it would be a race against time. Before the freighter had built up any speed, the comm system crackled and a familiar female voice sounded. *"Klingon freighter, if you're doing what I think you are, you might want to hold off and let us take a crack at it."*

Kirk glanced down at the screen. A new red triangle showed, moving fast toward the bird-of-prey.

Even so, Kirk couldn't quite believe his ears. "Uhura?"

# Thirty-Three

"The *ChonnaQ* readies torpedoes," one of the Klingon crewmembers said.

The bird-of-prey hadn't even reacted to the presence of the new ship, which was coming in so fast Kirk could already tell it was a *Constitution*-class starship. The *Enterprise*? Couldn't be, not yet. The Klingon ship would have to respond soon, but first it was intent on accomplishing its original goal—wiping the freighter from existence.

*"Kirk, were you expecting somebody else?"* the captain of the *Potemkin* said over the comm.

Kirk recognized the voice. "Tutakai, if you've got any tricks up your sleeve, now would be the time to play them."

*"Stand by, Klingon freighter . . ."* he said.

"Photon torpedoes launching," the Klingon said.

*". . . to beam out."*

"*Now,* Tutakai."

Even as he spoke the words, Kirk, Apella, Krell, and the other two Klingons were starting to shimmer. Their outlines became vague, indistinct, and Kirk felt the familiar sensation of insubstantiality.

"Impact in four," the Klingon was saying. "Three. Two."

As always, there was no time lag, not even time for thought between here and there.

"One," the Klingon said. But he was blinking into solidity on a transporter pad, on a Starfleet ship.

Apella stared about in stunned silence.

"Where are we?" Krell demanded.

Kirk looked across to the control podium and saw Montgomery Scott grinning at him, flanked by three armed security officers.

"Mister Scott," Kirk said. He stepped off the pad and joined Scotty at the controls. "Do you think you could put our guests down on the surface of that planet? Quickly."

"Aye, Admiral. I believe I can accommodate that request."

"Kirk . . ." Krell said. He started toward the edge of the pad, but the security officers moved to intercept him and he froze in place.

"You'll be put down someplace not far from Victory, but not in the middle of the fighting, if it's still going on. I'll join you soon. We're going to have a talk about how quickly the Klingon presence on Neural will be eliminated."

"But Kirk—"

Kirk glanced at the coordinates Scott had entered. "That'll work," he said, "Energize."

As the transporter began its process, Kirk added,

"When I say quickly, I mean immediately, Krell. We'll talk."

Then the Klingons were gone, along with Apella.

Kirk turned to Scott. "The bridge," he said. "Let's go."

On the turbolift, Scott explained that the *Potemkin*'s captain, Sukaru Tutakai, had allowed them to assist in his rescue. When they reached the bridge, Kirk nodded to Uhura and Chekov, then turned back to Scott. "The freighter?"

Uhura indicated the big viewscreen. The *Captain Cook* was there, as was the bird-of-prey. All that remained of the freighter were shards of debris floating in space.

"Uhura, tell the *Captain Cook* to get out of here," Kirk ordered. "We'll take over now."

"Aye, sir," she said.

Admiral Kirk stepped down into the command well. "I apologize, Captain Tutakai. I've overstepped."

"No need, sir," the *Potemkin*'s captain said. "Do you have something in mind?"

"I do."

"Then the vessel's yours, sir." Tutakai stood up, surrendering his seat. "As long as you need her."

"Thank you, Sukaru," Kirk said. He settled into the captain's chair. Back where he belonged. Not behind a desk, not in the hills and gardens of Neural. No other place had ever felt so much like home.

"Now, Uhura, get the *Captain Cook* out of there. We've got a bird to pluck."

# Thirty-Four

"They're gone?" Kirk asked.

"Every last one of them," Apella said. "I watched them leave myself. Krell assured me that they would not return."

"Do you believe him?"

"As much as I have ever believed a Klingon. More. He could not wait to leave."

"Krell knew the Organians would be checking in," Kirk said. "He knew that if the Klingons were still here, there would be trouble. The kind he couldn't talk his way out of."

They sat at a long table in Freehold's open plaza. Kirk, Tyree, and Apella were clustered at its head, where they'd been discussing Neural's future. Meena was next to Kirk, Elanna across from her, then Nyran, bandaged and pale, and Joslen. Then more, and still more; the plaza was full of Freeholders and Victors alike.

"Tomorrow," Tyree said, "we begin rebuilding the smelter."

"To operate for the benefit of us all," Apella added. "As you suggested."

"Cooperation builds worlds," Kirk said. "And it's better to be friends than enemies."

Apella launched into a discussion about plans for improving the smelter. Kirk was only half-listening, distracted by thoughts of Rowland, Burch, and Hay, whose bodies had been recovered and beamed to the *Potemkin*. He didn't even notice Meena leaning in until she touched his shoulder. "James," she said. "May we walk for a bit?"

Kirk looked back at Apella and Tyree. They were so engrossed in conversation, they wouldn't even notice he was gone. He rose from the bench and took Meena's hand as they left the plaza.

"I know you have to leave," she said when they were alone.

"Meena, I—"

She put a finger against his lips. "No, don't. I understand. You have other things to do. Things that are more important than the affairs of a lot of silly people on a backward planet. I'm impressed that you took as much time here as you did."

He could have told her that wasn't entirely by choice—he hadn't been able to contact his ride home anyway. But even if he had been able to, would he have left before the job was done? Probably not, he decided.

He hoped it was done now, and for good. Tyree and Apella were getting along, and peace seemed to have been established between the warring factions.

There would be trouble going forward, of course. Old grudges would flare up, people who had lost loved ones might not find forgiving as easy as they would like. But as long as most of the people were in agreement, those issues could be dealt with.

"Yes," he said at last. "I do have to go. I have . . . things to do. Responsibilities. And to tell you the truth, Meena, as much as I like it here, I belong . . ." He couldn't explain to her how it had felt to sit in a captain's chair again, on the bridge of a starship. He knew what it signified, though. "I belong somewhere else."

"You will think of me, from time to time, won't you?"

He put his hands on her arms and drew her close. "I'll think of you often, Meena."

She pressed herself against him. "Just . . . don't tell me you will come back, James. I would like it, if you did. But I do not want to wait for you. Especially if you never make it."

"I won't make any promises, then," he said. He knew he wanted to return. If nothing else, he wanted to make sure the peace held, and that the Klingons respected Neural's hands-off status.

"Good," she said. "It's better that way." She went up on her tiptoes and planted a kiss on his lips. "Surprise me if you can. And James?"

"Yes, Meena?"

"Thank you. For all you have done. For us, for Neural. For Tyree."

"It's . . ." He paused. He couldn't explain it any better than he already had. It was what a starship captain did. It was the job. And that job meant more to him than anything. "You're welcome," he said.

"We should get back to the celebration," Meena said. "You are already somewhere else. In your mind." She waved toward the sky. "Up there, among the stars."

"I suppose I am, Meena," Kirk said. "You're right. We should get back."

But he didn't make any moves in that direction. Instead he stood there, on Freehold's dark road, looking up. Looking at the stars blazing overhead, the constellations, and the black spaces between the stars. Those roads that only a starship could travel.

"We should get back," he said again.

Even he couldn't have said exactly what he meant by that. He didn't try. He took Meena's hand, and they walked together, back into the noise of celebration, the laughter and the song, the smells of meat cooked over open flame, of fresh vegetables and fruits arrayed on tables. Back to where people, liberated from fear, spoke about the futures they might have. Back into the light.

They waited for him, aboard the *Potemkin*, Uhura and Scotty and Chekov, and the ship's crew. They were no doubt eager to be on their way, to head for home. Scotty wanted to get back to work on the *Enterprise* refit. Even Kirk felt a new urgency, to begin the necessary steps that would lead him back to a captain's chair.

But they had waited this long. They could wait a little while longer.

Kirk took his seat at the table, next to Meena, and he lifted his glass. "This is something we do at home," he said. "A toast. To my friend Tyree . . ."

# Acknowledgments

Great thanks to Bud and Debby Hart, who raised a *Star Trek* fan and provided invaluable assistance with this book. Thanks also to Margaret Clark and Ed Schlesinger, Howard Morhaim, Beth Phelan, Marsheila Rockwell, Dianne Larson, and, as ever, Maryelizabeth Hart, Holly Mariotte, and David Mariotte.

# About the Author

Jeff Mariotte is the award-winning author of more than fifty novels, including the supernatural thrillers *Season of the Wolf, River Runs Red, Missing White Girl,* and *Cold Black Hearts*; thriller *The Devil's Bait*; horror epic *The Slab,* the *Dark Vengeance* teen horror quartet; and others, as well as dozens of comic books, notably *Desperadoes* and *Zombie Cop*. In addition to two previous *Star Trek* novels, he has written books, stories, and comics set in other beloved fictional universes, including those of *Buffy the Vampire Slayer, Angel, CSI: Crime Scene Investigation* and *CSI: Miami, The Shield, Criminal Minds, Conan, Superman, Spider-Man, Hellraiser,* and many more. He's a co-owner of specialty bookstore Mysterious Galaxy in San Diego and Redondo Beach, California, and he lives in southeastern Arizona on the Flying M Ranch. Please visit him at jeffmariotte.com or facebook.com/JeffreyJMariotte.